ANYTHING FOR ANNA

STELLA MACLEAN

Cataloguing and Publication information is available from The Canadian ISBN Service System, Library and Archives Canada.

Title: Anything for Anna/Stella MacLean

Identifiers:

ISBN: Print: 978-1-7381405-7-2

E-book: 978-1-7381405-6-5

Formatting Services: Sweet' N Spicy Designs

Cover Design: Sweet' N Spicy Designs

PROLOGUE

*H*i there. It's me, Helen Mason, again. You may wonder why I've taken on the job of introducing these stories about people from Spencer Island. And sometimes I wonder myself why I do it. But what it comes down to is this: I taught these young people in school and I admire their courage to live full lives, while facing issues they never imagined possible.

And this is definitely the case with Cathy Collins and Mark Wilson. If ever there were two people who didn't like one another, it is these two...in the beginning. Now, I don't know much about Mark, only that he is a psychologist in Spencer Island and a good one. He comes from away as we like to say. I hear that most of his professional work is with young people, a much-valued service in this day and age when young people face so many challenges. Oh, my, I don't know how I'd manage if I were still teaching these young people with so many distractions in their lives today.

But I digress, and I don't mean to. I've known Cathy Collins (nee Atwood) since she was a little girl. Her mother, Margaret, raised Cathy on her own, trying to balance her career as an artist with the responsibilities of being a mother. So many of us have been in that situation.

Cathy was always a sweet little girl at school, liked by all her teachers. She has always been a people pleaser. As a student she was at the top of her class, always volunteering for school activities. A wonderful young person. Then she met and married Scott Collins, and what a piece of work he turned out to be. You'll know what I mean when you read about him in this story.

But Cathy has done her best to raise her daughter, Anna; always the loving mother and so pleased with her daughter. But when she first met Mark...things didn't go well. But like so much in life, things change, and people change.

You're going to admire Cathy's devotion to Anna. And Mark, well, he's really special. They're both special. I'll let you read their story and I'm sure when you're done reading you'll know these two were meant to be together.

CHAPTER ONE

*C*athy Collins's SUV swerved as she swung the wheel, changed lanes then headed down the exit ramp toward Spencer Island. She was late for an appointment to show a house to a new client. She had loaded her smartphone with a tentative viewing schedule for other properties to discuss with the young couple when they met at this first house, which would be in a few minutes if all went as planned.

Because she'd grown up in Spencer Island, she had personal knowledge of this house, knew its interior features and its beauty. She'd love to own a house just like it someday. She was on track to be the top salesperson at her real estate firm if she made this sale. Reaching her sales goal would make her feel more a part of the real estate business, as an accomplished professional in her own right. The money would be a great bonus, as well. She wanted to take her daughter, Anna, on a nice vacation to California.

While waiting for the light at the bottom of the ramp, she glanced at her face in the rear-view mirror, touched up her lipstick and then checked her cell phone for messages. The client had said he'd call when he left his office to pick up his wife. He'd been so insistent that they look at this house today she'd arranged to have her real estate partner, Gina Dowd, take Anna to her hair appointment.

Cathy glanced again at her phone when she realized Anna hadn't responded to any of the messages she'd left. Knowing her daughter, she was probably talking to her friend Chloe about their sleepover. Anna, her sixteen-year-old daughter, was considerate and respectful—the best daughter any mother could ask for.

Cathy turned right into the gated subdivision just as her cell phone rang. It had to be either her daughter or her client. Relieved, she checked the caller ID.

Cambridge High School? She hit the answer button. "Cathy Collins speaking."

"Ms. Collins, this is Mrs. Barton, Anna's homeroom teacher. Your daughter has been taken to the hospital."

Panic pushed against her ribs. "Hospital? Why?" she asked, easing her foot off the gas pedal. A horn blasted behind her.

"She's been...injured."

Injured? Who would hurt Anna? It wasn't possible.

She pulled to the curb. "What do you mean?"

"You need to get to the hospital." Mrs. Barton hesitated. "I can meet you there if you'd like."

Cathy couldn't take in the woman's words. Anna couldn't be hurt. "Was she in an accident?"

"I'm not sure. Anna's in the emergency room," the teacher said. "They need you there now."

Emergency room?

"Thank you. I'm on my way." Stunned, Cathy ended the call, only to have her cell phone ring again.

"Is this Anna Collins's mother?" a very cool, professional voice asked.

"Yes. Who's this?"

"My name is Karen. I'm calling from the hospital. Anna has been injured."

Cathy held the phone closer to stop her hands from shaking. "Her teacher just called me. Please tell me what's going on."

"Your daughter was brought in with abrasions on her arms, face and knees from a fall onto the sidewalk. The doctor is doing a few tests and a chest X-ray for possible injury to her rib cage."

There had to be some mistake. "Are you sure?"

"Yes."

Cathy glanced at her watch. Anna should have been at the hairdresser an hour ago. She would never change her plans without calling first. "Who is there with her?" she asked, her mind fumbling for an explanation.

"Kyle Donahue. A classmate, I believe."

Kyle was Anna's math tutor. He was always polite and kind when he came to the house. Cathy liked him mostly because Anna was always happy to have him around. Anna never discussed the boys in her class other than Kyle, leading Cathy to wonder if they were more than friends. "I'm on my way," she said, her heart racing as she tried to remain calm. She turned the wheel sharply and did a U-turn in the middle of the street.

She drove quickly as she dialed Gina's number. When it went to voice mail, she left a message asking Gina to call her immediately. Her friend would be able to fill her in.

Cathy called her client, explained the situation and promised to set up another appointment as quickly as possible. She called her mother's house. Edna, her mother's housekeeper, picked up. "Is Mom there?" Cathy asked without preamble.

"Margaret is landing in Boston as we speak. Can I give her a message?"

"Tell her to call me as soon as she can."

"I will. Anything wrong? Anything I can do?"

Cathy hesitated. Edna had been her mother's housekeeper and a part of Cathy's life for as long as she could remember. "Anna's in Emergency. I don't know the details. I'm on the way to the hospital now."

"No! That can't be. I'll come right over."

She heard tears in Edna's voice and tried to hold her own at bay as she responded. "Please don't. I'm sorry to upset you, but I'm sure she's okay. Just give Mom the message."

Traffic was backed up on the exit that led to Bonar Medical Center. Cathy gripped the wheel, waiting. She forced herself to breathe deeply and slowly. Finally, the traffic eased forward. Cathy turned onto the street leading to the hospital then made her way into the parking area. In a matter of minutes, she'd be with her little girl.

She hurried to the reception desk in the emergency department. "I'm Cathy Collins. I'm here to see my daughter, Anna."

"There is a waiting room for family members. I'll let the staff know you're here. Please follow the red dots just beyond the door," the woman said.

With a click the doors slowly opened, and Cathy went in, making her way along the wide corridor leading into the brightly lit space.

Inside the waiting room there were groupings of chairs and a refreshment stand with a coffeepot and bottled water. Relieved to see the room empty, Cathy fought back the worry she'd been struggling with.

Moving toward a comfortable chair near the center of the room, she glanced around at the muted blue walls displaying paintings by local artists. The clock on the wall behind the sofa clunked at each passing minute. The coffeepot hissed. The muffled sounds emanating from the hospital corridor did nothing to soothe her anxiety. How long would she have to wait? They'd told her to get here as soon as possible. She was here. Where were they?

A woman wearing blue scrubs and a white lab coat appeared at the door. "Mrs. Collins?"

Cathy's heart felt as if it were going to leap out of her chest. "Yes."

"I'm Dr. Janet Everett. I've examined Anna. She has some cuts and a bruised knee, a welt on her forehead. We're running a few tests on her now."

"What happened? Why would a fall on the sidewalk result in my daughter being brought to the hospital?"

"An ambulance was called to the scene, so obviously someone was very concerned. As far as I know, she didn't lose consciousness. Your daughter has said very little other than that she fell. A young man came in with her but left about ten minutes ago."

"Kyle Donahue?" Why had Kyle left Anna alone instead of waiting for Cathy to arrive? Was he involved somehow in what happened? And how had Anna ended up being hurt when she was supposed to be at home?

"I believe that's the name, but your daughter should be able to tell you." The doctor's quizzical expression made Cathy feel inadequate, as if she should have known who was with her daughter. And she should have... Which was a problem she intended to fix as soon as she could see Anna.

Dr. Everett's glance swept over her. "Are you okay?"

Anna had never been in the hospital before. Not once. She must be so frightened by all this. "I—I think so. When can I see her?"

"In a few minutes." The doctor's weary smile didn't offer her much comfort.

Cathy tried to absorb it all, to calm her racing heart. She had more questions after speaking with the doctor. The ring of her phone sent a spike of adrenaline through her.

She checked the caller ID. *Scott Collins?*

Her ex-husband was the last person she wanted to speak

with, yet she couldn't ignore him. "Scott, why are you calling me?"

"Anna just phoned. Did you know she's in the hospital?"

Why would Anna call her father? The man only wanted contact with their daughter when he needed something. "Yes. I'm at the hospital now."

"Have you seen her yet?"

"I'm on my way to her room in a few minutes," Cathy said, the old feelings of inadequacy roiling her stomach.

"What are you doing to help her?" Scott demanded, his voice suddenly loud and angry. "You'd better be looking after her."

"That's not fair! Anna's safe with me. You know that," she said as she began to pace.

She listened to more angry words about her parenting skills from the man who had tried to take her daughter from her. This was not the time or place for his tirade. "I'll get back to you once I've talked to Anna." Cathy hung up before he could respond.

A woman walked into the waiting room. "I'm Karen, Anna's nurse. I can take you to see her now."

They walked toward the trauma area, through a set of swinging doors to an area behind a white curtain.

"Anna?" Cathy asked as she slipped behind the cotton drape.

"Mom? Mom, I'm so sorry. I never meant—"

"Oh, sweetie, you're okay. That's all that matters," she said, her voice shaking as she hugged her daughter. "I was so worried. Why didn't you call me?"

"Mom, please don't," Anna said, easing away, clutching her elbows as she stared at a spot over Cathy's shoulder.

She eased away and checked Anna's face for any sign of injury. Other than a small white bandage on her forehead and a reddened area on her cheek, there didn't seem to be any visible damage. "Where do you hurt?" she asked, smoothing the pillow behind Anna's head.

"I'm fine, Mom. You don't need to worry."

"Why didn't you call me after school?" It took surprising effort to keep the recriminations from spilling out. If Anna had answered her phone, perhaps this could have been avoided. At the very least, Cathy would have known what was going on with her daughter.

"I was busy and forgot."

How could her only child forget to call her? That wasn't how their relationship worked. They stayed in contact, always letting the other know when plans changed. When had Anna stopped telling Cathy everything? And why hadn't she noticed that her daughter seemed...different? What had gone wrong, and was Kyle the reason for Anna's odd behavior? "Was Kyle with you?"

"He was, but he had to get home. His mom was looking for him," Anna said, her anxious glance partially obscured by the bandage above her right eye.

"How did you get hurt?"

Anna toyed with the neckline of her hospital gown, a frown darkening her features. "Kyle was walking with me to the mall. I needed to go to the drugstore."

"And?"

"And I tripped. I fell down..." Anna's voice shook.

Cathy reached for her. "I'm so sorry you're hurt. But how could you have hit the ground so hard? Where was Kyle? Didn't he grab you? Surely he didn't let you fall without trying to help."

"Mom! Stop! I don't need you so upset when nothing really happened. I wouldn't have come to the hospital if Kyle hadn't insisted. He did everything he could to help me."

"Where's Chloe? She's your best friend. Why didn't she come to the hospital with you?"

Anna closed her eyes briefly then looked up. "I called Daddy. He told me you'd freak out, but I didn't believe him. I wish he was here."

Irrational anger tore through Cathy. She wanted to scream and throw something. Scott hadn't shown an iota of concern for Anna since he'd left and married another woman. If it hadn't been for Cathy's attempts to maintain a connection between her daughter and her ex, Anna would have known how little Scott cared. But she'd always made a point of reminding Scott of their daughter's birthday and anything new or different in Anna's life. She'd done it all for Anna, and this was how her daughter responded?

Scott had done everything he could to gain custody of Anna, including having a psychologist, Mark Wilson, do an assessment trying to prove Cathy was an unfit mother. She would never forget those days when Mark interviewed Anna and gained her confidence. Anna had been happy that Mark showed her so much attention and understanding. But when he made the case that Anna might be better off with her father, that staying with her mother was not necessarily the right decision for Anna, Cathy had been furious.

As far as she was concerned, the man was a fraud. At the very least he was acting in Scott's best interests, not Anna's.

She shook off the memory. She couldn't stand to be reminded of Scott or Mark. Neither of them mattered to her anymore. The only person who mattered in her life was here in this room.

"Sweetie, there was no need for you to call your dad. He's too far away to be of any help," she said, fighting to keep her voice even.

Seeing the loneliness in Anna's blue eyes and knowing how much she wanted her father to care about her, Cathy eased her daughter into her arms. "It's okay. I'm here and everything will be fine."

She felt Anna's tears on her shoulder. She stroked her daughter's blonde hair gently, loving her as she had never loved anyone in her life. Anna meant everything to her.

A nurse entered the curtained space. "We're taking your daughter for an X-ray, then if everything is okay, she'll be going home."

Giving Anna one more hug, Cathy whispered, "This will be over soon."

Anna's glance was a blend of bravado and uncertainty as the nurse moved to unlock the brakes on the stretcher then pushed it toward the corridor.

"I'll be here when you get back," Cathy murmured, clutching her purse tighter to ward off the chilling thought that in the past few hours so much had changed between them.

In the four years since the divorce, Cathy had watched her daughter blossom into a beautiful, independent teenager. A young woman who was carefree and happy, who shared everything in her life with her mother. She and Anna were best friends. No one, including Scott, could come between them. Not now. Not ever. Anna had always confided in her... always.

Until now. A ball of fear formed in her chest. Fear mixed with foreboding as Cathy waited for Anna's return. They were a team, she reminded herself. They would get through this together.

CHAPTER TWO

*M*ark Wilson took a moment to calm the disbelief and anger building in him as he observed the behavior of these two very difficult parents. For two months he'd been working with this family to give their daughter a chance to express her needs. She was a seventeen-year-old, private-school student struggling to get her parents to accept who she was and what she wanted out of life.

She wanted to go to the University of Michigan and study genetics rather than the Ivy League school they were pushing her to attend. What had started out as a disagreement had escalated into a standoff between the parents, Jessica and Don Parker, and their only daughter, Elaine. He turned to the father whose sullen expression he found particularly annoying today. "Don, do you hear the excitement in your daughter's voice when she talks about the University of Michigan?"

"Yeah, Dad, I would really love you to meet Mr. Duncan, the professor who's heading up all the research I'm interested in."

The father swung his gaze to his daughter. "You can take genetics at lots of different universities, don't you know that?"

"There you go again, Don, trying to belittle what Elaine

wants," Jessica yelled, her face red, tears dampening her high cheekbones.

"Okay, let's give Elaine a chance to explain why she wants to go to the University of Michigan."

As he tried to find common ground, Mark was reminded of another case he'd been involved in, one that had haunted him since he'd offered his opinion four years ago. Just this afternoon he'd received a phone call from the guidance counselor at the local high school, asking him to be part of a meeting involving the young woman from that case. She'd been in some sort of altercation in which she'd been injured. The school psychologist, Ed Jenkins, was ill and he'd requested that Mark attend tomorrow's meeting in his stead.

As Elaine finished her explanation, he turned to Mr. Parker, took a deep breath and used a gentle, inclusive tone when he addressed her. "Can you speak to what your daughter has just said? How you feel about it?"

"What do you mean?"

"Why don't you rephrase what your daughter just told you in your own words? It would give you and Elaine a chance to understand each other better."

As he proceeded to engage with the Parkers his mind kept going to the call he'd gotten. The school had identified recent issues with the teenager that, when combined with the incident today, had the administration worried. She was a high achiever both scholastically and in extracurricular activities but was now getting into fights and not doing well in class.

The student's name was Anna Collins—a name he wasn't likely to forget. His testimony and opinion had nearly resulted in Anna living with her father and leaving her mother behind. After observing Cathy Collins—a mother whose obsessive need for control had manifested in explosive bouts of anger that raised Anna's anxiety—he'd felt compelled to suggest Anna live with the father, who seemed much more easygoing and less controlling.

An outburst from Don Parker forced his mind back to the issues at hand. "I think what I'm going to get each of you to do is to write down the reasons for and against Elaine going to the University of Michigan. I want each of you to give two reasons why it's a good idea and why it's not."

"It's not a good idea," Don Parker said emphatically.

"Just be willing to remain calm and do as I ask," Mark said, glancing at each in turn to get their consent to what he considered to be a very simple exercise. He'd run out of ideas with these parents and was quite frankly willing to admit defeat if something didn't change soon.

As he worked with them, he was reminded of four years before. Anna had been a child struggling with her parents' acrimonious divorce, which made her frightened not only of the future but also of her father moving away and her mother's sudden outbursts. Cathy had been a very driven woman determined to control all aspects of her daughter's life.

He hoped things had changed since then. Still, he wasn't looking forward to meeting her again.

He refocused on the parents in session with him now. He wanted to shout how lucky they were to have a daughter; how good their lives could be if they would only stop and listen to what their daughter wanted out of life.

Instead, he calmly reminded them of the listening strategies they had agreed upon last session.

While she waited for Anna to return, Cathy's loneliness pressed around her like a blanket. She remembered Anna's first day at kindergarten—how impossibly empty the house had seemed when Cathy returned from walking Anna the two blocks to the school...

Her cell rang.

"I got your message, and I'm on my way from Boston."

At the sound of her mother's voice, Cathy's anxiety eased.

"I'll be there in a couple of hours. How's Anna?"

"She's been checked over, a few tests run and I'm taking her home soon."

"How are you doing?" her mother asked softly.

"I'm—I'm worried. Scott called me, and he's angry."

"That man! What is the matter with him?"

Cathy rubbed her forehead, her mind racing over the past few hours. "You know Scott. Nothing's changed."

"Listen, honey. Forget him. You take care of yourself. I'm sure everything will be fine. Tell Anna I love her and I'll see her as soon as I get back in town. In the meantime, if you need anything, my cell phone is on."

"Thanks, Mom," Cathy said, pushing her hair off her face. "Call me when you get home."

"I will."

If anything was wrong with Anna, Cathy would have to get Scott involved, something she dreaded. As usual, she hadn't gotten anything remotely like kindness from him, but maybe if she'd tried a little harder...

She checked for messages. None. Scott could have called back if he was so concerned about Anna.

Why did this have to happen now, when her life was going so well and Anna was so happy? Would Scott use this incident to drive a wedge between her and Anna?

If Scott saw this as a chance to take Anna to join him and his new wife and children, knowing Anna's desire for a family... Cathy took a deep breath to ease the sense of forboding inching its way around her heart.

She was so tired of the pressure of being in charge, of being the one responsible. She'd give anything right now to have someone to rely on, to help her get to the bottom of what was going on in Anna's life. Why hadn't Anna talked to her? Was she in shock? Could she have a head injury? Exhausted, she tilted her head back to keep the tears from sliding down her cheeks.

There was a rustling sound as the nurse approached her. "Mrs. Collins, Anna's tests were normal and she is ready to go home. I'll run through the discharge instructions with you."

Cathy followed the nurse to where Anna sat slumped in a wheelchair, her hands in her lap, her head down.

"Anna has several cuts on her knee, which we've dressed. Those dressings can come off in a couple of days, unless there's further bleeding. Check in with your family doctor if you have any concerns."

"Thank you," she said as her gaze moved to her daughter, seeking signs of how Anna was feeling. Anna had always been such a stoic child.

"We'll get you home and tucked into bed. We'll talk about all this tomorrow when you're feeling up to it," she said, pushing the wheelchair ahead of her.

Anna tossed her long blond hair off her face, stared up at her mother from the wheelchair and squared her shoulders. "What happened was no big deal. I fell and Kyle was there to help me," she said, as if annoyed by her mother's presence.

Cathy saw the shift in her daughter's gaze and had this awful feeling that she was lying. But she didn't know what to say, how to approach her over this. "You could have been seriously injured, Anna," Cathy said.

Anna grabbed the wheels of the chair, stopping it, and jumped up. "I want to walk," she said, her voice matter-of-fact. There was a pronounced limp as she hurried away.

"Anna, wait for me," Cathy called as she followed her toward the entrance.

She caught up just as the automatic doors leading to the parking lot whirred open. "Wait here. I'll bring the car around."

Anna scanned the parking lot. "No, I see it," she muttered, wincing as she stepped off the curb.

Pushing aside her irritation, she followed Anna to the SUV. Cathy clicked the remote door opener and climbed into the vehicle. Anna got in the passenger side and snapped on her seat belt, groaning as she did so.

"Are you okay?"

"It's the seat belt. I hit my shoulder when I fell."

She reached across the seat and hugged her daughter. "Oh, sweetie, I've never been so afraid in my life as when the call came saying you were here."

"Mom, I'm sorry for worrying you. I didn't mean to," she whispered before kissing her mother's cheek.

They held each other for a few moments, their closeness an instant reassurance. If Anna was hiding something, it would work itself out once they were home. She hugged Anna again before settling in and buckling her seat belt. "Let's go home. I'll make a pitcher of peach smoothies and we'll watch a movie together. What do you say?" Cathy turned into the flow of traffic while she watched Anna out of the corner of her eye.

"I'd rather just go to bed." Anna pulled her cell phone out of her knapsack.

"Who are you calling?" Cathy asked as she changed lanes before stopping at a red light.

"Kyle. I want to tell him I'm okay, that I'll see him at school tomorrow."

She was still waiting for her daughter to explain what happened, and all Anna could think about was her friend? "Kyle?"

"Yes, Kyle." Anna put the phone to her ear.

Indignation rose like a balloon to fill the space around Cathy's heart, zapping her already-frayed nerves. "Anna, put that phone away. Now!"

"Mom! I'm calling Kyle."

"No. You're not. Besides, you can't go to school tomorrow. You need to rest."

Anna rolled her eyes. "Mom, stop being so melodramatic. I fell. End of story." She gave a disgusted sigh. "Why are you making such a big deal about it?"

"A big deal?" Cathy glanced at her daughter. "I get a call to come to the emergency room because my daughter has been injured, and it's no big deal?"

Anna smoothed her hair around her cheeks, hiding her face.

"What is going on with you?" Cathy asked, unable to keep the anger out of her voice. "And if you're so anxious to talk to Kyle, why won't you talk to me?"

Anna turned her head so quickly her hair swung out around her face. "Mom! Stop it! See? This is why I called Dad. You're so unreasonable," Anna said.

For a few moments, Cathy couldn't speak. Hurt led the surge, followed quickly by disbelief that her daughter would confide in Scott and not her. "You called your father." She forced the words past her taut lips.

"Because I knew you wouldn't call him, and I wanted Dad to know."

"Anna, I would have called your father after I could assure him you were okay."

"Why can't I call my dad?" she demanded. "I'm going to call him when I get home."

"Do you expect him to come? To leave behind his precious life with his new family and come to look after you?" The second the words were out, Cathy wished she could take them back. "Anna, I'm sorry. I didn't mean to say—"

"For your information, I didn't expect Dad to come here. Not with you hovering around me!" she yelled.

"Anna, I didn't mean to upset you, but you should have called me and told me where you were and what was going on."

"The nurse told me she'd called you and you were on your

way. As for Dad, I just needed to talk to him. Can't you understand that?"

Trying to be calm, she softened her tone. "Of course, I can. Look, let's forget all this and go home. You're safe and that's what matters."

"Mom, there's something else I need to tell you, and I don't want you to be mad at me for doing it."

"What's that?" Cathy asked, her nails digging into the steering wheel.

"Kyle and I are talking about going away on March break. I might go to Dad's—"

"No!" Cathy said without thinking.

"Mom. I have a right to see my father."

"I know. I'm sorry." She took a deep breath. "Anna, we can talk about this later."

Anna slumped in her seat, pressing her palms to her forehead. "I've made you angry, haven't I?"

"Not angry so much as concerned." Had Anna and Kyle started dating? "Is Kyle going with you to your father's house?"

"Of course not. He has family in Phoenix, and he thought it would be fun to visit them," Anna said.

Did Anna's sudden interest in visiting her father have something to do with Kyle? "If you and Kyle are involved, it's okay. I really like him."

Anna gave a long sigh and closed her eyes. "No, Mom. Kyle and I are friends. He's my math tutor, or don't you remember? I wish you'd stop trying to find a boyfriend for me. Really. If 1 wanted a boyfriend, I'd have one. Now, can you stop interrogating me?"

"I didn't mean to make it sound like an interrogation. But this hasn't been easy for either of us."

Anna didn't respond.

The only sound was the hum of the car as Cathy drove carefully down their street and into the driveway. Normally,

Anna would have hit the garage door opener on the visor and made some teasing comment about her mother nearly clipping the cedar hedge along the driveway. Not tonight.

As Cathy pulled into the garage, she was certain of one thing. She no longer believed that Anna's injuries were the result of a simple fall on the sidewalk. She didn't believe that Kyle was an innocent bystander. She didn't believe anything her daughter had told her. It was very clear that there was something going on in Anna's life. Something her daughter was hiding.

Shutting off the engine, she turned to Anna. "Sweetie, you have to understand that I'm concerned about what is going on with you. The injuries the nurse described couldn't have been from a simple fall on the sidewalk. You're too good of an athlete to fall like that. Besides, you have no injuries or scrapes on your hands to prove you put your hands out."

"I'm telling you the truth. Why don't you believe me?"

"Anna, you're telling me that you hit the sidewalk hard enough to hurt your shoulder, your forehead, to scrape your leg and hurt your shoulder. I don't buy it, not for a minute. I need to know what happened."

Anna glared at her, tears flooding her eyes. "I fell. That's all."

There was no way she could let this continue. Knowing what had happened to Anna left her with no choice but to show her daughter how serious this lack of truthfulness was and that it wouldn't be tolerated.

Cathy held the wheel with a viselike grip as she stared straight ahead. "Anna. You leave me no choice but to ground you until you're willing to be honest with me."

Anna's indignant gasp filled the vehicle.

CHAPTER THREE

*A*nna limped ahead of Cathy into the house, dropping her backpack on the kitchen table before heading to her room. Needing answers, Cathy followed her. "Anna, you have to understand. I can't ignore what you've done. I can't."

Anna stopped and stood perfectly still. "Mom, I wish you would trust me on this. I know what I'm doing."

"Would you please explain that statement?" she asked, refusing to accept Anna's determination to shut her out.

Anna turned. "Kyle and I were just walking along, fooling around, when I fell."

"Who else was there?"

Anna's gaze dropped to her hands. "No one. Like I said, we were teasing each other. I stumbled."

There was that evasiveness again, that guarded tone. "Why didn't Kyle grab you? He's bigger and stronger. Why didn't he break your fall?"

Anna continued to study her hands.

A horrible thought occurred to Cathy. No! "Did Kyle hit you?"

Anna stared at her in shock. "Kyle isn't like that," she said.

"Why can't you just let it go? He's my friend—a good friend. He would never do anything to hurt me or anyone else."

Then why did Cathy feel so unsure about Anna's explanation? Something didn't ring true even though her daughter hadn't changed her story. Her head pounded as she considered the possibilities. She peered at Anna's face, the unfamiliar lines of tension evident around her eyes and mouth. Cathy wanted to hug Anna close and tell her that everything would be okay. But would it? Was there something seriously wrong in her daughter's life, or was she simply overreacting? "I love you, sweetie, and we'll work this out. Let's talk in the morning after we both get some rest."

"Mom, I don't want to talk about it tomorrow or any other time. It's over. I promise. Okay?"

Fear welled up in Cathy. "As far as I'm concerned, until you tell me what's really going on, it's not over. But it's up to you. Without the truth, you'll miss out on school and your friends. But if that's the way you want it..."

Anna shrugged, turned away, and went into her room, closing the door behind her.

The closed door and the change in Anna's attitude fed Cathy's fear. Should she go after Anna and insist on answers? Or would that only drive her further away? Should Cathy apologize to see if they could find a way to talk about what happened? They always talked before bedtime. Always.

A part of her wanted to scream in frustration. Another part of her simply wanted to forget everything in the hope that it would all go away.

She locked the house and put the security system on before going to her bedroom. As she passed Anna's door, she listened for any sign that her daughter was still awake. Nothing.

Making her way to her room, she ran a bath and took her cell phone in with her. She'd talk to Gina, get her advice on what all this meant, then try for a little sleep.

. . .

The next morning, Cathy went in to the office.

"What are you doing here? You should be home with Anna," Gina said with concern as Cathy opened the door to the office.

"There's not much point in staying home when Anna won't talk to me." Cathy rolled up the sleeves of the old white shirt she'd tucked into her faded jeans. She couldn't be bothered dressing up this morning. She was too tired, and she didn't have any clients coming in.

To ease her mind away from her problems, she had decided to come in to work and make a list of cold calls. She needed more sales if she was to meet her goal for this year, because now her plan to take Anna on a vacation was even more urgent.

"I'm sorry you've had such a rough time. But if it's any consolation, you and Anna will work things out together. That's how you've always done it, and this won't be any different."

"I hope you're right." She wasn't so sure. Last night she'd finally given up on sleep, gotten up, washed two loads of laundry, made banana muffins then headed in to the office. Cathy had left the house without speaking to Anna, mostly because her daughter hadn't yet emerged from her room. While making the muffins, she'd noticed that most of the milk she'd bought yesterday was gone and the peanut butter was still sitting on the counter. Anna had been up sometime in the night and had eaten her favorite comfort food.

"Anna wasn't anywhere in sight when I left, and I didn't have the courage to go into her room. Quite frankly, I don't know what to say." Cathy tucked her purse under the corner of her desk and turned on her computer.

Gina pulled up a chair next to Cathy's desk. "You've got to stop worrying. You've done enough worrying over the past four years to last you a lifetime. Like I said last night, I've had huge fights with my boys, taken their phones and grounded them on several occasions. They got over it. Anna will, too."

"Anna's never hidden the truth from me...at least not that I know of. As for Kyle, I thought he was trustworthy. He's been at my house dozens of times. Yet he disappeared before I got to the hospital. Why wouldn't he stay with Anna? He's been so attentive to her lately, I thought they were dating. And Anna says they want to go to Phoenix on March break next spring. Doesn't that sound like more than friends to you?"

"It does. Did you know about their plans for Phoenix?" Gina asked.

"Not until last night."

"Are you okay with her going?"

"No. Especially when she won't tell me the truth. And God knows what sort of game Scott will play with her. He's already siding with her about this whole falling-on-the-sidewalk story."

"Do you suppose he's angling to get her to stay with him?" she asked.

"Who knows?"

"Cathy, just remember the same qualities that I admired in you when I hired you, and then when you became a partner, are the same qualities that will get you through this." Gina wagged her finger at Cathy. "You're smart, caring and determined, and you will get through to Anna. It's only a matter of time."

"I hope so," Cathy said.

"Listen, why don't you take the day off? Go shopping and buy something really nice for yourself. You never have the opportunity to do things just for you, and you work harder than anyone else in this office."

"That would be lovely. But I keep feeling I should be doing something about Anna. Maybe I should go home and be there when she gets up. Any other time Anna's had a problem, I've supported her," she said.

"While you're thinking about it, I'll duck across the street and get us coffee. The usual?"

Cathy nodded. "Thanks."

After Gina left, Cathy continued to puzzle over Anna. When her cell phone rang, she glanced at the caller ID. What did the school want? Then she realized what she'd forgotten to do. "Hi, look, sorry. I should have let you know that Anna wouldn't be in class today."

"That's okay. I know about Anna's incident yesterday, and I'm really sorry. But I'm not calling about that, not specifically," said Melody Chapman, the guidance counselor. "We need to talk with you, Mrs. Collins."

Cathy's throat tightened. "Why?"

"Anna's been having...difficulties at school recently."

"What kind of difficulties?"

"That's what we need to see you about."

"Why didn't anyone tell me?" Cathy said, upset that she was only finding this out now.

"We sent messages home with Anna. In hindsight I should have contacted you directly, but Anna's always been such a responsible student..." An uncomfortable silence filled the void.

Always been such a responsible student?

What was this woman saying? Was she implying that Anna's grades weren't good? Or could Melody be suggesting something worse than slipping grades? "When do you want to meet?" Cathy asked.

"Would two o'clock work for you?"

"Of course."

After she hung up, Cathy sat in a state of disbelief. Anna was having difficulties and she'd known nothing about it.

The door whooshed open, flooding the room with chilled

air. "What a long line over there..." Gina stopped. "What's wrong?"

"I just got a call. I have a meeting at the school."

"About what?" Gina's eyes were wide as she placed a cup on Cathy's desk.

Cathy took a sip from the double espresso. "Apparently Anna's having difficulties. But I don't know any more than that. The woman took me so much by surprise I didn't press for details. I don't know what to do. I probably should talk to Anna before I go to the meeting. But the whole business of not telling me the truth yesterday..."

"Is there anyone you could talk to about this?"

"You mean a professional counselor? I went that route after the divorce."

"And it helped, didn't it?"

"Yeah, but that woman has left her practice and moved away."

"What about Margaret?"

"Mom's in the midst of getting a new exhibition up and running in Boston. Besides, she hates Scott."

Gina shrugged. "You need an ally. Teenagers are clever about concealing the truth. You're alone with a young woman who is intelligent and resourceful. Can I help?"

"Not unless you have a magic wand that would erase all this."

"Would a sympathetic ear help?"

"You're already doing that." Cathy stretched her arms up over her head, trying to release the tension in her neck. "I'm going to call Anna and see if she's up. Maybe if I tell her I have a meeting at the school about her behavior, she'll talk to me." Cathy grabbed her jacket and purse and started for the door.

"Call me after the meeting?"

"I will." She dialed Anna's cell phone number, searching for the words she wanted to say.

It went straight to voice mail. She left a message, urging her daughter to call her as soon as possible. She called the house, but there was no answer.

As she got into her car, she redialed Anna's cell. Once again, it went to voice mail. When she called the home phone, Anna's voice sounded sleepy and bored.

"Why didn't you answer your phone?" Cathy asked, fighting to keep the accusatory tone out of her words.

"I don't know where it is. I must have left it in the car. Can you look for me?"

Cathy leaned across the console and checked the floor and the sides of the seat. Down near the door she saw the bright pink cover. "I found it. Why didn't it ring?" Cathy inspected the phone.

"I must have put it on silent mode."

Anna's casual attitude was surprising since she never allowed her phone out of her sight and never turned it off. "I've been called to a meeting at the school."

"What?" Anna yelled. "Mom, why do they want to see you?"'.

"I have no idea, but it seems you might."

"Mom, please, whatever they tell you... I'll be here when you're through with the meeting. I promise to tell you everything."

The pain in Anna's voice made Cathy's stomach ache. "Anna did someone push you down on the sidewalk?"

"No, not exactly."

"Then tell me what's going on," Cathy demanded.

Anna said nothing.

"Anna, I don't know why you simply can't tell me now." Still, she said nothing. Cathy looked at the clock, frustrated at her daughter, at having to go to the school, at this entire situation. "I have to go to this meeting, but you will tell me everything when I get home. Understood?"

"Okay," Anna said, her voice shaking.

When Cathy reached the school, her shoulders felt as if they were trapped in a vise. She rushed up the stairs and down the hall to the counselor's office. She knocked gently.

"Come in," a woman's voice called out.

The sun-drenched office and Melody Chapman's smile were warm and inviting. "I'm Cathy Collins. I'm Anna's mom. I hope I'm not late."

"No. Not at all. I'm Melody Chapman. I'm so glad to meet you." She extended her hand.

Cathy saw the genuine friendliness in the woman's face and knew she had an ally in Melody.

"The psychologist is running a little late, but said he'd be here as soon as he could. Anna's homeroom teacher is out for the day, and I thought it'd be better to have the meeting with only the three of us rather than her replacement. Is that okay with you?"

"Sure. Whatever you think is best." Cathy sat in one of the visitor chairs.

"How have you been?" Melody asked.

"Fine. Good...until yesterday."

"How is Anna feeling after her...accident?"

Cathy heard the pause, subtle yet definitely there. It was almost as if Melody wasn't sure what to label Anna's fall. Accident or something else?

Cathy suddenly didn't want this woman to know that Anna hadn't said anything except that she'd fallen on the sidewalk. Cathy didn't believe Anna's version, but faced with a woman who seemed to know more than Cathy did, she felt an overwhelming need to support her daughter. "Anna's as good as can be expected after her fall."

Melody gave her a sharp glance. "Her fall? Is that what she said happened?"

"Yes. Last night at the hospital."

"There were several witnesses who said she was pushed, but

there seems to be differing versions of what happened. I need to talk to a couple of other students before I can say for sure."

Betrayal hit. She'd been suspicious of her daughter's version of events and now she had proof. Her daughter had been hiding things. And it had been going on for a while. "I don't know what to say."

Melody glanced around as if collecting her thoughts. "Why don't I get you a cup of coffee? What do you take in it?"

"Black, please."

"I'll be right back." Melody slipped out, leaving a quiet space so out of tune with the roar of emotions raging through Cathy.

Why hadn't Anna told her the truth? What was she hiding and where did it stop? When had she decided that Cathy had no business knowing what she was up to?

Cathy had always worried that someday Anna might get mixed up with the wrong crowd. She'd read that the best way to prevent that was to keep the lines of communication open. She'd done that. Every night before Anna went to bed, Cathy had made a point of talking with her, of listening to anything Anna had to say. She'd supported Anna in every way she knew how.

Yet, despite those talks, despite the unwavering support, Anna had become secretive. She swallowed against the lump forming in her throat. Her daughter's betrayal hurt. And the wound went deeper because she was dealing with this on her own. She alone faced the shameful awareness that the teachers, counselor and principal knew more about Anna's behavior than she did.

Scott's accusations about her worthiness as a parent came to her. He would think this was her fault. Scott, who had fought so brutally to get custody of Anna, would gloat if he could see Cathy now. Yet where was he when his daughter needed him? He had moved on, remarried and was happily caught up in his new family. A family that didn't include his daughter. No, he'd abdicated his responsibility for Anna except when he could use her to punish Cathy.

She straightened and shook off those thoughts before they spiraled out of control. She normally didn't feel sorry for herself, but after last night she couldn't seem to stop the feeling that somehow Anna had moved away from her, away from her support and caring. In less than a day Cathy had gone from being a mother who could trust her daughter who could take joy and pride in the person Anna had become—to someone who didn't know what was going on in her own home.

A movement near the door caught her attention. She turned. Instead of Melody, Mark Wilson stood there. "What are you doing here?"

"They called me to sit in on this meeting," he said as he moved to the chair beside her.

Cathy felt her face flush. She intensely disliked this man. He'd nearly taken her daughter from her. "I will not talk about my daughter with you. Did Scott send you?"

He held up his hand. "Please let me speak."

"You have nothing to say to me. I will not have you meddling in my life ever again."

"I'm not meddling, Mrs. Collins."

She wanted to scream and yell at him, but she knew that he'd only see that as further proof that she wasn't a stable parent. There was only one thing to do. Cathy picked up her purse. "I'm leaving," she said, heading for the door.

Melody met her at the entrance, a cup of coffee in her hand. She glanced from Mark to Cathy. "I'm sorry I wasn't here to make the introductions. Cathy, this is—"

"I know who this man is. And I won't discuss my daughter with him in the room." She moved to leave, but Melody stopped her.

"Cathy, I'm sorry. Please let me explain," Melody said. "I didn't know that you and Mr. Wilson knew each other."

Angry and feeling betrayed by the whole world, Cathy turned her back to Mark. "Did Mr. Wilson happen to mention what he did to me?"

"I'm truly sorry," Mark said. He shifted until he was within Cathy's line of sight. "When the school called saying they had an urgent situation on their hands, I felt I had to help. But I can see that you're upset, which means I won't be much help or support. I should have anticipated that you'd feel this way. Again, I'm sorry."

Through her anger she could see that he was sincere, but she didn't care. She still suspected Scott had arranged for Mark to get involved. It didn't matter how he'd come to be here; it only mattered that he not be involved in their lives again. "I don't want you here. Have I made myself clear?"

Melody touched Cathy's arm. "We need to talk about Anna. If you'd rather that Mark isn't part of the conversation, I'll respect that. But your daughter is in serious trouble. The school feels we need to support Anna in whatever way possible. I'm not qualified to give her the help she needs. I want to do what is right for her and for you. That's why I asked that there be a psychologist at this meeting."

CHAPTER FOUR

*M*ark saw the anger in Cathy's eyes and realized that not much had changed with this woman in the four years since he'd last seen her. She was still angry, still determined to have her way and still fighting for control. The things he'd found so unlikable about her four years ago were the same traits that would make helping her daughter a challenge no matter who tried to work with her.

Could she not see it was critical to put Anna's interests ahead of her own? If they were to help Anna, they had to focus on her. He kept his expression neutral as he met Cathy's hostile gaze. When the school had explained the dramatic change exhibited by Anna Collins, Mark felt compelled to do what he could to help. Faced with Cathy's aggressive behavior, he realized that he could not allow this woman to set the agenda. "Your daughter needs your help and support—"

"She has it!" Cathy said, her fists forming balls against her thighs.

Mark held up his hand. "Let me finish. Once I do, I won't say another word. Understood?"

She nodded.

"I'm here for only one reason. I want to help Anna. You do, too. As does Melody. We're all here to support your daughter. Agreed?"

Cathy nodded again, although her expression left him with no doubt about her feelings toward him. Seeing the tense set of her shoulders and the fidgeting movement of her hands, he continued carefully. "It's in your daughter's best interest to get to the bottom of what's going on, wouldn't you agree?"

Cathy made a small sign of assent, anguish visible on her face. He understood how stressed she was. Every parent deserved support in dealing with issues around their children. Cathy was no exception. "Let's try to work this out together."

"Have a seat, please," Melody said.

"As long as you do not try to tell me what I should do," Cathy said to him. "And if I ask you to leave, you will."

Why was she being so aggressive when her daughter was in serious trouble? But maybe Cathy didn't know the full extent of the issues around Anna's behavior. "Agreed."

Mark chose a chair next to the wall, making himself as unobtrusive as possible to ease Cathy's frustration at his being there.

"As near as we can determine, Anna's problems started about a month ago," Melody said after taking a seat. "She didn't show up for volleyball practice one week and didn't offer any explanation. After that she often arrived late or seemed distracted on the court. Coach Cassidy is concerned about her performance on the team."

Cathy straightened. "Anna loves to play volleyball. I'm sorry, but I didn't know about this. I'll speak to Anna."

Mark saw the genuine surprise in Cathy's expression. If she hadn't known about this, there was a communication breakdown between her and Anna.

"I understand your alarm, but there's more. She and Stuart Jameson were yelling at each other outside the classroom after a math test a week ago. A teacher had to intervene. Anna has also left the junior prom committee, something she wanted to be involved with when school started in September. She's been late to class on a couple of occasions, which has never happened with her"

"I don't get it," Cathy said, her voice shaking. "Anna has never, ever behaved this way. She loves working on the junior prom committee, and I can't see her yelling at Stuart Jameson... All I know about Stuart is that Anna doesn't like him very much. But if she yelled at him, he had to have said or done something." Mark watched her struggle to regain control. "I drop Anna off at school most days unless Kyle drives her. How could she be late for school?"

"She didn't say. We asked her to make up the time. She stayed late to do extra math, the class she missed those days, and it was after one of her makeup sessions yesterday after-noon that the incident occurred."

"There has to be an explanation." Cathy rubbed her temples as she mumbled, "This is not like Anna."

Mark wanted to ask if anything had changed at home, if there was anything different in Cathy's relationship with her daughter. But he had promised not to say anything, aware that she might take his questions as an attack on her parenting, as she had four years ago. They needed to gain her cooperation in addressing these issues before he could take any active role.

Melody shifted uneasily. "Based on your reaction, I'm assuming you didn't get the phone call I made to your home, and your cell, after the yelling incident with Stuart. I left a message for you to call me."

Cathy's expression was one of misery. "No. I didn't, but sometimes when I get home late I forget to check messages. And it's been really busy at work and Anna's never had trouble in school..." Her voice trailed off.

Melody continued. "She's had a verbal altercation with

Stuart and was injured yesterday in an incident involving at least one of her classmates. We are still trying to determine exactly what happened and who else was involved. We believe that Anna has problems she hasn't shared with anyone other than, possibly, Kyle Donahue. Is there any reason you can think of that would have caused these changes in your daughter?" She glanced toward Mark. "Has anything happened at home?"

Cathy shot Mark a look before turning her attention to Melody. "I don't know what's going on. Anna is a wonderful daughter. We have a good relationship. She's been fine." She picked up her purse then stood. "Thank you for telling me about this. I'll talk to Anna. I'm sure there's a simple explanation."

Mark had to speak up, to try to get Cathy to see how grave this situation was. "Anna needs help. I can't emphasize that enough. These sorts of changes in behavior can be caused by anything from drugs to bullying. Those are serious issues that have an impact on more people than Anna. We have a responsibility to act in her best interest, and that includes uncovering the facts."

Cathy's gaze swept over him, her disdain evident. "She's my daughter. I'll look after her. I always have."

Could this woman not see Melody's genuine concern? Did she not understand the possible ramifications of whatever Anna was hiding from everyone?

A fleeting expression in Cathy's eyes told him she knew something...something she wasn't willing to share.

He stepped forward to block her route to the door. He held out his business card and concentrated on making his expression nonthreatening. "You are not alone. A lot of teenagers have issues that can be resolved with a little help. You've been given an opportunity here to help Anna before this situation escalates. And you've been offered the support of her school. Why not take it?"

"Does that include your support?" she asked. The defiant tone was in direct contrast to the desperation in her eyes.

He sighed inwardly. "Call me if you need me before the school psychologist gets back."

She turned the card over in her hand slowly as if considering. He mentally crossed his fingers. As much as he didn't like Cathy, he felt empathy for her, for her dilemma as a single parent. He saw a lot of parents struggling to do the right thing by their children. He had to believe that when it came down to it, Cathy would do the right thing by her daughter.

She carefully placed Mark's card in her pocket then stepped around him. Without looking back, she headed down the corridor.

"What was that all about? She clearly doesn't like you," Melody asked after he closed the door.

"I was the psychologist who did the professional assessment of Anna four years ago when Cathy Collins was going through a divorce, and her husband was seeking custody of Anna."

"What! I wish someone had told me. It would have been much better if I'd met with her first or waited for Ed Jenkins to get back."

Why had he agreed to attend the meeting? Had he really believed he could help, given the history between them? It had been a mistake coming here, being part of this meeting. He could not be involved in a case in which his personal bias played such an obvious role. "I've got to get back to the office. If you need me, you have my number."

"I'll follow up with Cathy to see if she's made any progress with Anna. In the meantime, I'll be sure to speak to Ed about the case."

"I hope you can reach out to Anna and help her," he said.

Melody shrugged. "I'll keep trying. I like Anna, but I'm very worried."

Mark left feeling like a failure, feeling guilty that he'd not been able to change anything about Cathy's approach to her daughter. Yet, a part of him wanted to make up for the emotional pain he'd caused in her life. Given her hostility toward him, it was unlikely he'd ever have that chance.

Tears streamed down her cheeks as Cathy searched the parking lot for her SUV. She couldn't remember where she'd parked it. She couldn't remember anything but the words of the guidance counselor. Anna was in trouble, and Cathy had known nothing about it. She should have known before anyone else. Why hadn't Anna confided in her? And what was she doing yelling at Stuart? Cathy had heard rumors about Stuart being involved in drugs from one of the other real estate agents she worked with, and it sent a chill through Cathy.

She spotted her vehicle along the rear fence. She had to get home to Anna. They needed each other, now more than ever. Her little girl...her only child... In her anxiety she nearly walked into the path of an oncoming vehicle that swerved to miss her.

Pay attention!

She climbed into her SUV, closed the door. The heat was suffocating. Rolling down the window, she took a deep breath and tried to calm down.

It had been one of the most frightening experiences of her life. And, once again, Mark Wilson had witnessed her fear and humiliation. Deep inside she realized that he hadn't been there to hurt her, but it hurt all the same to know that he would feel justified in his original assessment of her.

Would Anna have been better off with her father?

No. Cathy would never believe that.

Still, she'd been so rude to Mark. She couldn't seem to stop herself. Yet she had the feeling that he was genuine in his offer of help, and she felt guilty for not being more cooperative. But all that would have to wait. She needed to get her daughter to tell her the truth. Once Anna did that, then Cathy would know what she was facing and how they could resolve it.

She felt a rush of anxiety. She gripped the wheel. There was no way she could drive in this condition. She had to calm down, figure out how she would manage the coming days. She wished she could talk to her mother, but she couldn't. Not before she had a chance to get the truth from Anna. She blew her nose and wiped her cheeks.

She'd felt under siege in the meeting. It had taken every ounce of self-control to sit and listen to examples of Anna's behavior—behavior she'd had no knowledge of. And the way the counselor talked about the incident yesterday as if it were a progression, somehow expected.

Anna's bruises and the anxiety on her face rose in her mind. Her little girl had been injured and abandoned while Kyle—Anna's supposed friend—had sought the safety of his home and family.

Maybe she should call her mother, get her to come over to the house this evening. Anna loved her grandmother, and Cathy needed someone in her corner right now.

She was about to start the car when she saw Mark standing at the edge of the parking lot. Should she duck down out of sight? His eyes met hers. He hesitated, then came toward her vehicle.

Go away!

No such luck. She worked to put a smile on her face and failed. Why should it matter? Mark's opinion of her was based on their past experience. Nothing she could say or do would change that.

She adjusted her seat belt, ready to leave the moment he said what he came to say. "Did I forget something? I have to get home to Anna. She's pretty sore, as you can imagine."

He stood close to the car door, his piercing gaze locked on

her face. She crushed the urge to squirm. She refused to give him any reason to think less of her than he already did.

"You didn't forget anything. I'm just concerned for you."

"Thank you for caring, even if we both know it isn't true."

"Can we call a truce? Anna's been through a rough patch, and it would seem there are still issues to be resolved."

"Are you in touch with Scott these days?" she said, fixing him with a don't-mess-with-me smile.

He didn't flinch. "I met Scott only once, and you remember when that was."

She couldn't let herself believe him. Last night Scott had accused her of not being a good mother. And suddenly Mark Wilson is part of a meeting over Anna's issues at school. In her experience that level of coincidence didn't exist.

She looked straight at him, into his chocolate-brown eyes framed with the thickest lashes she'd ever seen. Her breath caught in her throat at the concern and caring she saw. There was no hostility in his eyes, no judgment in his expression.

"Cathy, I promise I will do anything I can to help Anna. You don't have to believe me, but I'm guessing that right about now you would like someone to step up and help you. For what it's worth, your ex-husband has not been in touch with me." He placed his hand on the window's edge—a strong capable hand, she noted. "I have no agenda, only to help Anna if you'll let me. As I said before, if you need me, I'll be there. You can count on that."

She was caught between his concern and her fear that she would be naive to believe him. "Why does it matter to you? You know I don't like you. And I know you think I shouldn't have custody of my daughter."

Mark wanted to walk away from this irritable woman. He wanted to tell her that her behavior was churlish and immature. Neither action would accomplish anything. He was beginning to see why Anna might not have been willing to confide in her mother, a woman who clung to her opinions despite information to the contrary.

Unless something altered the situation, Anna and Cathy would resolve little over the next few weeks. But he'd just sworn off any involvement with this situation, so why didn't he walk away?

Because you're attracted to red haired women in trouble as your wife had been. You believe you can sway their opinions, change their attitudes.

He almost squirmed at the uncomfortable knowledge that he felt some sort of attraction to Cathy. Wrong time, wrong place, wrong woman.

He noticed her nervous expression. Should he push her to accept his help? Or maybe he could persuade her to listen to her daughter, to encourage Anna to share her feelings. It would make it easier for Anna to be more open.

No. He couldn't be involved. His decision in the counselor's office was the right one. "Okay. Fine. Have a nice day."

She looked surprised. "I—I'm sorry. I didn't mean to be rude," she said, a tiny furrow forming between her blue eyes.

The way she looked at him, the open vulnerability in her eyes startled him. He'd never imagined Cathy Collins would apologize to him. "I understand how difficult this is for you."

"Do you?" she asked.

"Well, not personally, but as a child psychologist I am accustomed to dealing with teenagers," he said, "and listening to their parents."

Cathy hesitated, her hands clinging to the steering wheel.

In that unguarded moment, he saw a woman embedded in a crisis she was struggling to deal with. He wanted to once again offer his support, but she was an adult and she had his business card. All she had to do was reach out to him. Yet, he knew she wouldn't do that. Cathy's pride wouldn't allow her. "Drive safe," he said before turning and walking away.

Cathy watched Mark leave and wished she could have kept him talking to her. How strange was that? She didn't like him. She didn't trust him. Well, maybe she trusted him a little, but that hardly counted. As she focused on his broad shoulders, his long stride, she faced the truth. She wanted to talk to a man who understood what it was like to deal with a teenager in trouble. And he happened to be the only man in her life who qualified.

She needed to unburden her heart, to seek relief from all the turmoil wreaking havoc inside her. But she was also afraid that he'd uncover a flaw in her, in her parenting that would prove she hadn't been the kind of mother she fervently wanted to be. To expose her feelings, her concerns to a man she didn't trust was senseless.

With a sigh she drove out of the parking lot. She followed the tree-lined streets to her subdivision. She loved this street, the only route that led directly to her home. She loved the trees, the shady areas like tiny alcoves along the curbs, the brightly colored town houses and condos. It all seemed so upbeat and inviting, a balm to her worry.

Cathy parked in the garage and shut off the engine. She had stopped at the local bakery and bought Anna's favorite bagels, a peace offering of sorts. She had rehearsed how she'd start this conversation. If all went as she planned, Anna would do the talking.

Sitting alone in the vehicle, her eyes aching from lack of sleep, she wished with all her heart that she didn't have to face her daughter. Not this way with so much at stake. If she were perfectly honest with herself, she wasn't sure she was ready for the truth from Anna.

Knowing her daughter, there had to have been something

pretty serious going on in her life for Anna to behave the way Melody Chapman described.

Yet she couldn't put this off any longer. She grabbed the bag of bagels and headed inside.

In the kitchen she saw the peanut butter out on the counter, along with a loaf of bread, its remaining slices spilling from the plastic bag. A spike of irritation at Anna's thoughtlessness hit. She couldn't clean up after herself? Especially now?

Cathy checked the bathroom, the den, but found no sign of Anna. Had she left the house without telling her? "So much for grounding her," she muttered. She dug her cell phone out of her purse and dialed Chloe's number. Maybe Anna had gone there. Chloe answered on the fourth ring.

"Is Anna with you, Chloe?"

"No," Chloe said her voice trembling.

"Are you all right?" Cathy asked.

"I'm fine." She sniffed and cleared her throat.

"Have you heard from Anna?"

"Yes." She paused. "She called me."

"Did she say where she was going?"

"I thought she was home. We didn't talk very long. She was pretty angry with me."

Chloe and Anna had never had a fight before that Cathy could remember. "About what?"

"You'll have to ask her," Chloe said, sounding upset.

"And you don't know where she might have gone?"

"No." Huge sobs filled the line just before Chloe hung up.

What was that all about? Cathy hadn't checked Anna's room. "Anna, are you in there?" she asked through the closed door, a sickening feeling growing when she received no response.

She eased the door open, expecting to find Anna curled up on her bed, upset at the rift with Chloe. There was no one in the bed. In fact, it was neatly made and everything in the room was in order. On the dresser by the bed, an envelope was propped against a photo of the two of them at the nature park when Anna was ten. The photo of Anna and her father was nowhere in sight.

Her heart pounding with dread, she picked up the envelope and tore it open. Four words were scrawled in Anna's familiar writing: *I've gone to Dad's.*

Stunned, Cathy stared at the note. The words stood out black and hard against the white paper. Panic rose in her throat, choking her. Anna couldn't have left like this. She wouldn't leave without saying goodbye. Cathy's hands shook as she reread the note.

How could Anna do this? She had to know how terrified I'd be.

Feeling faint, Cathy sat on the bed. Anna had said she'd be here after the meeting. What had made her decide to go to her father now? Had she called her father after the argument with Chloe, and he'd seen his chance to get her to his house?

"Why?" Cathy yelled. "Why did you do this, Anna?"

Cathy began to pace, her mind churning. She stopped. Had Kyle been involved in this? Was he planning to leave with her? Anna said they'd talked about going to Phoenix together.

Cathy grabbed the house phone and searched the incoming-call list, checking to see who might have called this morning. Even if Anna planned to go to her father's, someone had to have convinced Anna to leave now, rather than later. She would never have left on her own, especially when she'd promised to be here when Cathy got home.

The list showed that, other than Cathy's call, only Chloe and Kyle had called the house.

If Anna was planning to go to her father's, she'd need money, an airline ticket. Spencer Island was a long way from Phoenix. She'd have to pack... Cathy stared around the room, looking for clues. She opened the top drawer of the dresser, then pulled out the box where Anna kept her babysitting money. The box was empty. How much cash had Anna had in there?

She had to have gotten help from someone. As much as Cathy hated to upset her mother, she called her, but it went to voice mail. She left a message asking her mother to call but didn't leave any information about Anna, A message wasn't the way she wanted her mother to find out that Anna was going to her father's.

Who could help her?

"Gina." Dialing her friend's number, she went into the kitchen, searching for any clues about when Anna might have left the house. Nothing.

"Cathy, how did the meeting go?"

"Oh, Gina, I'm so afraid. I can't find Anna. I came home to find a note saying she was going to her father's."

"Did you call him to see if he's expecting her?"

"I want to know what's going on before I talk to him. I can't deal with him otherwise."

"Do you suppose he sent her an airline ticket?"

"I have no idea. Anna said she'd be here when I got home. She promised to tell me everything. I talked to Chloe, and she doesn't know where Anna is," Cathy said, unable to accept that Anna had left for Phoenix without saying goodbye.

"What did the psychologist say?"

"Who cares? It was Mark Wilson."

"No!"

Cathy sighed. "My luck hasn't changed."

"I'll be right there." Gina hung up.

Meanwhile Cathy searched the house for more clues but found nothing. If she had a ticket from her father, it must have been sent by email. Where was Anna's computer? Her search turned up nothing. Anna must have taken her laptop with her.

Gina came in the back door, pulling Cathy into a hug. "Let's see what we can figure out. Anna couldn't have gone very far," she said as she led the way into the kitchen with her usual take-charge attitude.

"I just can't believe she would leave. Not when she promised to be here. Not when we needed to talk," Cathy said.

"I agree with you. Anna wouldn't leave without saying goodbye. I'm sure she'll be back and you can talk to her then. Let's just stay calm and wait for her. In the meantime, tell me everything that went on at the meeting."

Cathy told her what she could remember in her distressed state.

"Maybe the counselor's right and Anna confided in Kyle. You should call him. Maybe Anna showed up at his house," Gina said.

Cathy did, but no one answered. She left a message for Kyle, telling him that Anna was missing and asking him to call back right away.

Gina poured two cups of coffee, sliding one across the counter to Cathy. "If you're right and Anna's planning to go to her father's, you need to call him."

"And give him another reason to be nasty? Not until I have to. Besides, if she were going to Scott's he would have to have sent an airline ticket to her. I don't think Anna has enough money saved to buy one."

"I think you should contact Mark Wilson."

"You've got to be kidding! How can he help?"

"I don't know, but he works with teenagers—he understands them. He knows she's in some sort of trouble. At the very least, you could bounce ideas off him. To be honest, I don't know what's going on with Anna, but if she's left home, you need any help you can get. If I were you, I'd swallow my pride and call the man."

"I don't know what to do," Cathy said, praying that Anna would walk through the door and say she'd changed her mind about going to her dad's.

"You have to put aside your feelings about Mark. For Anna's sake. What choice do you have?"

Cathy managed to swallow around the hard lump in her throat. She might not like Mark, but he had shown concern for Anna. He was also qualified to assess what might have motivated Anna to take off this way. If he could help find Anna, what she felt about the man didn't matter.

"Okay, I'll call him. What can it hurt?"

"You won't be sorry." Gina began to tidy the clutter on the counter.

Cathy dialed Mark's number, and he answered on the first ring. "Cathy, is Anna all right?"

"Anna's left home. I need your help." The line was quiet. Was he not going to answer? No. He couldn't do that to her, not under the circumstances. "Look, I'm really sorry for how I behaved—"

"Cathy, that's not important. What's important is Anna. I'll clear my schedule and be there in about half an hour. In the meantime, check with Anna's friends. Get that young man—"

"Kyle."

"Yes. Ask him to come to your house."

"Yes," she said, relief flooding over her. She might have to drive over to Kyle's house, or call his mother at work, but one way or the other she would find him.

She hung up and dialed Kyle's number again. He answered immediately. "Mrs. Collins, I got your message. I've been out looking. I can't find Anna. I've talked to her other friends at school, and no one has heard from her."

She was comforted by the fact that Kyle's voice echoed her concern, even though she worried about the fact none of Anna's friends were with her. "Can you come over here?"

"I'll get my mom to drop me off right away."

. . .

46

When Kyle arrived he looked so young, so vulnerable. Cathy put her arms around him. He clung to her for a moment before moving away. "I'm sorry I left the hospital the other night. My mom was on my case for spending too much time with Anna. But Anna and I have had so much going on..."

"It's okay. We need to find Anna. Did she say anything to you? Her note said she was going to her dad's, but she'd need money or a credit card to buy an airline ticket,' she said as they gathered around the island.

Kyle studied his hands.

"Should we call the police?" Cathy asked.

"Let's wait for Mark to get here," Gina said, passing Kyle a glass of milk he'd asked for.

"Did you hear any of the conversation Anna had with her dad?" Cathy asked.

"I didn't, but she told me afterward that she wished her dad were here." He ducked his head. "Sorry, Mrs. Collins. I know that's a sore point with you."

"Please don't worry about it, and call me Cathy."

He offered her a quick smile.

The doorbell rang. Cathy raced to answer it. Mark's calm expression eased her fear a little bit. "Please come in."

They all settled in the living room. The bright sun streamed in through the large windows facing the back lawn, warming the space.

"Anna left a note saying she was going to her father's in Phoenix. But I don't believe she would leave me without saying goodbye. And I can't imagine her going to her dad's, despite the fact she talked about going last night."

"Why not?" Mark asked.

"Because she hasn't seen him for months. He has a new family, and she has always felt uncomfortable even talking about him, let alone going to visit him. He's never made any real attempt to see her, except in the summer for a couple of weeks. After the big deal he made at the custody hearing, he's basically left me to raise Anna."

Kyle cleared his throat, glancing from Gina to Cathy and Mark. "Anna told me she's had several calls from her dad in the past few weeks."

"I didn't know that." Cathy caught the understanding look in Mark's eyes. "Well, if my daughter was going to visit her father, she would need more than just her babysitting money: Oh, wait. I forgot something." She went to Anna's room and checked the old-fashioned jewelry box where Anna kept another stash of money. Empty.

When she returned, Mark and Kyle were deep in conversation.

"Kyle has something to tell you," Mark said.

"What is it?"

"I'm really sorry. I should have said something sooner, but I promised Anna." Kyle scrubbed his face with his hands. "She said her dad was sending her an open plane ticket to Phoenix."

"When?" Cathy demanded. When had Anna's feelings about her father changed? When had they started communicating so regularly?

"Did she mention which airline?" Mark asked.

"No, she didn't. I'm sorry, but she didn't tell me anything other than the fact she expected the ticket to arrive any day now."

"There can't be that many airlines operating out of the Portland airport," Mark offered.

"I don't know what's going on with her anymore," Cathy said, her heart pounding hard in her chest at the extent of Anna's secrecy.

"If it helps any, Anna felt pressured by her father to go to Phoenix," Kyle offered apologetically.

"That miserable man. I'm going to call Scott. He's got a lot of explaining to do." Cathy stood to get her phone.

Mark held up his hand. "That can wait. First, let's find Anna. Why don't we go to the airport and see if she's there?"

Again, Mark's calm demeanor eased her panic. "You're right. I'm just so angry and afraid and mixed-up and hurt."

"I know," Gina said, her voice gentle. "We'll find Anna before she gets to Phoenix. She couldn't have left the house much before you got home."

Mark stood. "Let's go now."

"You're coming with me?" Cathy asked, surprised.

Mark's expression was resolute. "You asked for my help. I'm giving it."

CHAPTER FIVE

Gina volunteered to stay at the house in case Anna returned. The other three took Mark's car to the airport.

"Let me out here," Cathy said when they approached the departures area, impatient to get inside.

"I'll come with you," Kyle said from the backseat.

"I'll park the car and be right in," Mark said.

A rush of cool air enveloped Cathy as they strode through the doors of the Portland airport and toward the gate area. "Only four airlines are showing on the board, none going to Phoenix," Kyle said.

Cathy searched the terminal for any sign of Anna. "I don't see her."

"Let's start with the first airline listed," Kyle said, heading toward the check-in desk. As they moved closer, Cathy spotted Anna standing in line.

Letting out a strangled cry, she strode toward her. "What are you doing here?"

Anna glanced up, a forced smile appearing. "I could ask you the same thing."

"Don't be smart, Anna. Answer the question."

"As I said in my note, I'm going to Dad's house."

"You are not. You're coming home with me. You and I have a lot of talking to do, and I'm tired of waiting around for your explanation. Get your bag and let's go."

"No. And for your information, I don't have a bag. Dad said he'd buy me new clothes when I get to Phoenix. He's even taking me shopping for anything I want."

Fury at Scott blindsided Cathy. In the depths of her anger, she sensed Mark's presence behind her. She turned toward him, saw the compassion in his eyes, and felt a little calmer.

Anna followed her gaze. "I remember you, Mr. Wilson. You told me about playing volleyball when you were in high school. You were really kind to me. But why are you here?"

"I was invited," he said.

"I guess I should thank you for bringing Mom out here so she could be angry with me."

Mark didn't respond, but Cathy was stunned at Anna's words and tone. After all they had been through together, after all their closeness, how could Anna want to be with Scott? She'd shown little interest in visiting him, so why the sudden change?

How could Anna treat her this way? Was this some sort of punishment for all the hours she put in at the office and showing houses? While she acknowledged those absences could make Anna question her place on Cathy's priority list, at the same time the job provided Anna with the lifestyle she enjoyed. If that was Anna's motivation, this immature little stunt needed to end now.

"Let's go, Anna. We're going home," Cathy said, her patience with her daughter gone. When they were in the privacy of the house, they would have this out. She was tired of the hiding and lying.

"Mom, I'm about to check in. We'll have to have this

conversation another time." Anna glanced from Cathy to Kyle. "Hi," she said, a welcoming smile on her lips.

"Hi," Kyle said, going to stand beside her. "Were you going to leave without saying good-bye?"

"I tried to call you."

"I know. But there's been a lot going on. I don't want you to go."

"I don't have a choice. Besides, Dad needs me."

"To do what?" Cathy interjected, seething at the easy way she'd been dismissed. She had no idea she could be this angry with her only child.

"Mom, please stay out of this."

"You need to come home." She grabbed Anna's arm.

"Stop." Anna pulled her arm away.

"Let me talk to her for a minute," Kyle said, barely above a whisper.

"Why?" Cathy demanded.

"Because I need to tell her something."

What was going on with these two? Cathy glanced between the two teenagers. They were totally focused on each other. "Okay, you've got five minutes, and then Anna's coming with me, whether she likes it or not."

Anna took Kyle's hand then followed him to a quiet corner with two empty seats.

"Hey, what's all this about?" Kyle asked. "You're leaving without talking to me? I thought we had a deal, that we'd stick together and figure out what to do. Did your dad really call?"

"No. I had a fight with Chloe, I can't believe she's defending Stuart when she saw what he did yesterday. She won't tell people what he did to me, how he bullied you and me. And after what he did last night—"

Reliving those awful minutes made Anna shake. She rested her hand on her knee and winced at the sudden pain. She'd been awake most of the night with pain, had heard her mom talking to Gina and she was so sorry for all the worry her mother was going through because of her. "I'm afraid of what will happen. I can't tell Mom because she'll be so upset. I don't know what else to do. Going to Dad's will give me a chance to think things through."

"Why did you bother calling Chloe?" Kyle asked.

"She's my best friend. I needed to—" She pressed her fists into her forehead. "I am so angry with her. I just needed to get away. I have that ticket Dad sent me, so..." She shrugged.

"Your mom didn't know about that ticket."

"No, she didn't. You told her?"

"Mr. Wilson said I needed to help with anything I knew. Your mom really cares," Kyle offered, taking her hand again.

"So that's how she ended up here. You told her," she said, hurt that Kyle did it.

"I had to. I don't want you to go. You need to face these bullies. You can't run away and ruin your school year, miss out on volleyball and all your friends."

Anna wanted to believe him. But if her mother found out that she was gay, that her perfect daughter wanted to come out, to speak up at school...who knew what she'd do? She loved her mother, but she couldn't face her anger. Not until she figured out how she could deal with everything that was going wrong in her life. Her dad's place would give her a little time to work things out. She hadn't told him anything, but she was sure he'd understand when she did. "I'm sorry. I called my dad. He'll be waiting for me. I can't let him down."

"What about your mom?"

Anna knew only too well that her mother would be really upset with her over going to her dad's. But she was so tired of her parents not getting along. Did they know that she needed both of them? If only they'd try a little harder to be friendly with each other, things would be better.

"Mom? She grounded me like I'm some little kid. Besides, she made it clear she doesn't trust me, or you, for that matter. I could tell by the look on her face last night that she didn't believe our story about me falling."

"Can you blame her? It was pretty lame."

"I know."

"What can I say to convince you to stay?" Kyle asked. "How can I help you when you're half a continent away?"

Anna sighed and closed her eyes. "You've already helped me so much. I'm so thankful you were with me when Stuart pushed me. If you hadn't been there I would have been seriously hurt." She hugged him close, wanting to remember this moment.

What she couldn't tell him or anyone else was that if things worked out with her dad, she planned to move to Phoenix, start over and find her place in the world. Being gay wasn't a crime; it was simply the way things were. She couldn't go on denying it.

"If you go, I'm going with you."

Startled, she stared at him. "You can't. You have to stay."

"I have relatives in Phoenix. I'll stay with them. Mom and Dad will understand that I'm taking a break. They're cool with whatever I do."

"No! You're not coming with me."

"Anna, if you're ever going to be able to face your life, you need to get the school to stop Stuart from bullying you. You can't do that from Phoenix."

"This is silly. You can't just take off'

"Isn't that what you're doing?"

"It's not the same," she muttered.

"If you stay, we could work together on this. We both know that Stuart and his friends won't stop bullying people and will use any flimsy excuse for what they're doing. If we don't stop them, who will?" Kyle asked.

Late yesterday, Stuart had been waiting outside the school gym when Anna left her math class. He'd harassed her and threatened to tell the whole school she was gay. Not believing him, she'd walked past him out to where Kyle waited. They'd ignored his taunts as they walked toward the mall, until Stuart had hit her, knocking her to the ground.

"What could we tell the school that they'd be willing to believe? Stuart will deny that he followed us to bully us. He's popular—do you think they'd believe us over him? And what if we tell on Stuart and they get the police involved? He'll say it was all a mistake, that he never meant to hurt me. Then my mom would want to know why we didn't tell the truth in the first place. I'm sure she knows that I lied about last night. She kept asking me all kinds of questions about how I fell."

Anna wished she could simply go to her mom, tell her the truth and have it over with.

But that wouldn't work, at least not for now. Her mom would make a big deal about it, be angry, upset and go all protective on her. Especially because her mom didn't like Stuart, because she was convinced he did drugs. If she found out Chloe was dating him, she'd flip, then talk to Chloe's parents and the school, and this whole big mess would get worse.

Anna wanted to tell her mom that she was gay, that she was being bullied, but she couldn't disappoint her mom, who thought she was straight and that Kyle, of all people, was her boyfriend.

Her mom had worked so hard to give her a good life. She knew all that. But lately it felt like her mom didn't understand her, didn't know what she had to endure every day at school.

"Look, I need to get away, to get things clear in my head. You can't go with me. I need you to stay here. See if you can convince Chloe to help us." Chloe had been with Stuart when he pushed Anna. She still couldn't believe that her best friend wouldn't defend her. "She's so sure she's in love with that jerk, and I can't get her to listen. But she might listen to you."

"I've already decided that if you won't let me come with you, I'm going to the police. You can't be the only one Stuart is bullying."

"You can't go to the police."

"Why not?"

"Don't you remember how we got into this mess?"

Stuart had been going out with Chloe for about two weeks when he cornered Anna in the corridor and hit on her. She'd made it very clear she wasn't interested in him, that she and Chloe were friends. When she rebuffed him, he accused her of being a lesbian. Anna had told him to get lost and to mind his own business. He told her he would make her pay.

"Yesterday changed everything. You know that, right?" Kyle asked. "We need to take action. He's not going to stop otherwise."

"He will if I'm not here," she argued.

Kyle leaned back and stared up at the ceiling. "I'm going with you. End of story."

"I wish I'd never told you," Anna grumbled.

"Why?"

"This is my problem. You didn't have to be involved."

Kyle turned to her. "But I am involved. I've got an idea. Mark seems like a good guy. He might be able to help us. He was part of the meeting at the school."

"How do you know?"

"He said so."

Anna glanced at her mother, saw her worried expression and felt really sad. Anna didn't want to hurt her mom. She loved her very much. She just didn't know how to cope with what was happening in her life. She loved school. She wanted to play volleyball, be part of school activities. But Stuart's bullying isolated her... She was on her own to defend herself—except for Kyle, of course. As much as she wanted to tell everyone she was gay, she was afraid of how people would respond. What if her friends reacted the way Stuart did?

"My mom doesn't like Mark because of what happened during the divorce. I'm surprised she let him come here."

"I don't think she had a choice. She was too worried about you. He's doing his best to help you and your mom."

"But Mom hates him."

"Maybe, but he might be able to help us. Will you give it a try? Would you do it for me?" he asked, a grin of encouragement on his face.

Anna loved Kyle like a brother. He had been her friend since fourth grade. She trusted him completely. Maybe she should take his advice. In truth, she didn't want to leave home, her friends and especially Kyle. And she didn't want to cause her mom more worry. Sighing, she glanced toward her mother, who appeared to be deep in conversation with Mark. "Okay, but you're going to owe me big-time," she teased.

"Thanks." He put his arm around her shoulders. For the first time in a while, Anna felt like she might be able to sort this mess out.

Mark arrived from parking the car to witness Anna's rudeness toward her mother. Her defiance and cockiness contributed to the tension and distrust between the two of them, and he understood how hard it would be for Cathy to remain in control. He had to admit that the Cathy he'd known wouldn't have held her composure so effectively, and he admired her for doing the best she could in a difficult situation. Underneath Anna's bravado, he suspected, lurked a teenager who felt trapped between her parents. But if Anna left, she would still be in trouble when she returned, and Cathy would be worried and anxious the entire time. He saw the struggle in Cathy's eyes and wanted to reach out to her, to reassure her that there was still time to convince Anna to stay home and face whatever was going on.

But was he prepared to be part of this? It could take hours of his time, and for what? He wasn't officially assigned to the case, so he'd be acting in an unofficial capacity. Cathy might have been willing to have him along in her moment of desperation, but he doubted that she'd cooperate long enough for him to make an impact on Anna's behavior.

Seeing Cathy's reaction to the news Anna intended to visit her dad moved Mark. Scott had blindsided Cathy and played on his daughter's insecurities—actions Mark thought were deplorable. A father who really cared about the welfare of his daughter would not put her in this difficult situation with her mother.

A deep compassion for Cathy filled Mark. She needed support—perhaps more than she knew—and he could provide it.

She turned to face him, anxiety evident in her deep blue eyes. "What do we do now?"

"We wait and see," he said. It seemed like a platitude, but they could only wait to know the outcome of Kyle's discussion with Anna.

"That seems to be all I do," Cathy said, her easy tone sounding forced. She was silent for a moment then asked, "Where did I go wrong?"

"You could provide all the support and the most stable home life in the world and still have your teen act out." He wasn't sure his words were as reassuring as he wanted them to be, so he sought to explain. "They have all those crazy hormones running amok, and there's an incredible amount of pressure on teenagers—pressure to do well in school, to succeed in extracurricular activities, to fit in with their peers. Because of their age and inexperience, they have fewer tools to deal with issues that arise in their lives than adults do. As adults, we sometimes forget that."

"I believed there were no secrets between us. Now I know that's not true, and I hate how it makes me feel."

"Like a loser parent?" How many good parents had sat in his office and confessed the same thought? So many parents believed if they did the right things, said the right things, put their kids in the right activities, they could protect their kids and avoid messy, painful situations. Clearly Cathy belonged to this group.

"How did you know?" she asked, meeting his gaze.

"Trust me when I tell you, you're not alone. Teenagers are trying to be adults, learning to take charge despite their fears and inexperience. They make mistakes—some bigger than others, some with severe consequences—and parents blame themselves." Was he helping her? He didn't want to sound too clinical, but he wanted Cathy to understand what she was experiencing wasn't unusual. She wasn't a bad parent simply because Anna was in some sort of trouble.

She held his gaze for a long moment, and he let himself be open to her scrutiny. Let her see that he was being honest and not judging. Without warning the space between them felt charged as awareness of each other crowded in.

No, that's not what he wanted here. It was inappropriate for so many reasons.

Cathy looked away, breaking their connection. Feeling as though he'd been granted a reprieve, Mark struggled to get his attraction to her under control. Wrong time, wrong place, wrong woman, he reminded himself for the second time that day.

. . .

Needing to regain her equilibrium, Cathy glanced away from Mark's compelling brown eyes. How could she be attracted to Mark when he'd caused such havoc in her life? Yes, he'd been supportive today and she'd been glad to have him with her, but that didn't change the situation between them. Did it?

Holding hands, Anna and Kyle strode toward them. "They look like they've come to some sort of decision," Cathy said.

Anna's hug came as a total surprise to Cathy. "Mom, I'm not going to Dad's house. At least not right now."

Clutching her daughter, Cathy breathed in the scent of green-apple shampoo, remembering the first time she'd brought it home and Anna had proclaimed it was the only shampoo she'd ever use. Cathy had been so close to losing this closeness, to losing her daughter.

"Thank you. I'm so relieved," she whispered, forcing a steady tone into her voice as she smoothed her hands over Anna's hair. For the moment, Cathy's anger and frustration with Anna was swept aside. "You'd better call your father and tell him you won't be on the flight."

Anna released her. "I need my cell phone. Do you have it?"

"Right here." Cathy pulled it out of her purse.

Without saying thank you, Anna grabbed it and walked away.

"Anna, have you forgotten your manners?" Cathy said, embarrassed that her daughter could be so rude and behave as if she was the only person on the planet. Had she been like this all along, and Cathy was too blinded by her false mental picture of their relationship to see the real Anna?

Cathy's rebuke was ignored as Anna had a friendly, laughter-filled exchange with her father, Cathy noted with disquiet.

Anna slid her phone in her pocket as she approached. "There. Dad's okay with me coming later."

Of course, Scott would be. She was well aware that his role of supportive parent had a shelf life about of one week. This sudden, cozy relationship with her father was one more thing Cathy wanted to get to the bottom of. Her daughter had a lot of explaining to do. But not here.

"Let's go," Cathy said, trying to control the anger seeping through her.

"Okay. Kyle and I have a huge science assignment due on Monday, so can he stay for dinner?"

Cathy wanted to say no. She was tired of Anna putting her off, of avoiding their long-overdue discussion. She searched Anna's face for any clue as to what was going on. Cathy could hear Melody's warning that Anna's grades were slipping and felt as though she was in an impossible position.

What if she said no then Anna did poorly on the assignment? How much further back would that put her academically? Would delaying their talk another few hours make that much difference in uncovering the root of her issues? Probably not. "Okay." Cathy nodded.

Anna smiled at Kyle. "Time to head home, then." They started toward the exit.

What did Anna think there was to smile about here? Did she assume her disappearing act and lying would be forgotten?

Mark moved to follow the teenagers, but Cathy hung back, working through what had happened and how she would deal with it. Could Anna and Kyle have come to an agreement about how they would explain their behavior? If that was the case, Cathy needed an ally. Anna had suddenly become good at changing the subject, of making Cathy feel she was out of order to ask questions. Cathy wanted someone there, someone whose authority Anna would respect.

Would Mark help her? He'd certainly eased the situation today, and despite her wariness of him, Cathy had to admit he'd been very kind and caring. Maybe having someone like him at her side when she talked to Anna would shift things around in her favor.

She caught up with him. "You said you'd be willing to help me any way you could. Could you help me find out what is going on with my daughter? Would you stay for dinner?"

He locked his gaze on hers. That frisson of awareness crackled between them.

"I'll stay, but you should know Anna may want even less to do with me than you. If that's the case, I won't be of much benefit to you."

"And if I'm willing to take that chance?" she asked, suddenly aware of how much his answer mattered to her.

"Let's give it a try," he said.

CHAPTER SIX

he warming scent of lasagna in the oven brought back memories of other Fridays when Anna would hang out in the kitchen, full of stories about what her friends said and did, how her day at school had been, what one of her teachers had said or how close a volleyball game had been.

Where had all that gone?

Gina had met them at the door, saying that she had to go home but was pleased that Anna had been found. Gina's gaze had taken in Mark standing next to her. Cathy had a pretty good idea what her matchmaking friend was thinking—that if Mark had come here, there was a chance they were willing to talk to each other. To Gina, talking was the first step in a relationship. But Gina didn't understand how little Cathy wanted to do with Mark, even though she welcomed his support tonight.

Sitting in the family room, Anna and Kyle huddled around Anna's laptop while Mark volunteered to set the table. That was usually Anna's job, but Cathy appreciated his offer and the distraction his presence offered.

"The table's ready. Anything else?" he asked.

"A magic wand. One flick of the wrist so all this never happened," she answered.

He shrugged. "If life were that simple."

Cathy lifted the pan of lasagna from the oven and set it down to cool a bit before serving. "I plan to be perfectly calm and in control about all this. Anna is going to explain her behavior."

"Let's decide first what you want to know."

"Well, the truth about the incident yesterday would be a good place to start," Cathy said, feeling her stomach knot at the thought of the potentially awful things her daughter had covered up with her story about falling. "I must be the dumbest mother on the planet."

"No, you're a mother who chose to believe and trust her daughter."

"What if Anna refuses to tell me what's going on, or she announces that she wants to live with her father?" As difficult as the past few hours had been, Cathy could not imagine her life without her daughter.

Mark's gaze met hers across the kitchen island. "I don't know what will happen. She may not want to tell you, but as long as she believes you're listening, it may encourage her to be more open."

"How do you know that?"

"Because it's clear you're very close." His intense look made her want to squirm.

"But if we're close, why won't she talk to me?" She occupied herself with gathering serving utensils, trying to ease away from the sense of intimacy that seemed to have appeared from nowhere. "Never mind. You can't possibly answer that. I guess I'm just worried that something else will go wrong."

"Anna is probably as scared as you are. And because of that she may tell you what she thinks you want to hear," Mark said.

"Then, what do I do?"

"Try to understand what she's going through. Try to figure out what's real and what's not."

Bracing her hands on the counter, she faced him across the island. "She obviously is going through something she isn't willing to share with me. Why didn't I see the signs that she was skipping school, missing volleyball, all those things Melody talked about?"

"Cathy, every parent has doubts about their abilities. You're going through a difficult time, but it's not impossible."

Not impossible? Did he have any idea what she was going through? She was in danger of losing her daughter to an ex-husband who would destroy the relationship Cathy had carefully cultivated with Anna. Not only was Anna's well-being at stake, but also Cathy's identity. If she wasn't Anna's mother, who was she? How could Mark even understand that?

Mark was getting involved more deeply than he'd planned when he'd agreed to dinner. It wasn't so much what Cathy said as the fact that he wanted her to say more, to confide in him. The expressions moving across her face made him want insight into her thoughts so he could ease her burden. He wanted Cathy to share her feelings, her life. He wanted to be involved. But that was a boundary he couldn't afford to cross.

If he were to help Anna, he needed to park his attraction to Cathy and keep their relationship on a professional level. "What you need to do is to let Anna know you're listening to her," he said, watching her response. "Don't interrupt her if you can help it. I know that's difficult when a teenager says something outrageous or something that you don't believe, but you still have to try. I know you feel at a disadvantage given what has been going on these past few weeks."

"That's an understatement," she said, her insecurity evident on her face. Her words didn't have that usual sarcasm, which gave him hope that Cathy might be able to keep the conversation with Anna going. Maybe it would help her if he told her about his own experience with his siblings. It was worth a try. "I have three sisters, and I didn't get along with any of them."

"Why was that?" she asked.

"Because I felt responsible for them. My mom was a single parent, and because I was the oldest, I babysat my sisters a lot. I hated it. I wanted to be with my friends, and instead I had to look after my younger sisters, who showed little or no respect, especially as teenagers. They would tattle to Mom about things I'd said or done. I never had a normal conversation with any of them until I went to college. I guess I needed the distance to gain perspective. And it helped that I didn't have to look after them."

"Your opinion is that I need to gain a little perspective on the situation."

He met her questioning gaze and realized she was serious. He couldn't let her down with a casual, off-the-cuff remark. "I think you're too hard on yourself. It may take more time to get the conversation going with Anna than you think. If it does, don't be discouraged. And don't blame yourself."

"You really believe I can do this?" she asked as she reached across the counter, touching his hand, a quizzical expression on her face.

Her touch was warm. Her red hair shining in the light, making him want to touch it.

Why had she touched him? She hadn't even been aware she'd reached for him until she felt his skin under her fingers. Cautiously she glanced at him to see his response. He seemed not to have noticed. Act normal, she told herself. If it didn't bother him, don't let it bother you.

"So, we'll eat then talk?" she asked, assembling the salad with quick movements.

She was so aware that there was zero reason to daydream about Mark's personal appeal. Her dating skills were nonexistent, and she was hopelessly inadequate in the small-talk department. Sure, she could talk with potential buyers and sellers, but that was business.

She knew her strengths and weaknesses all too well. Whatever she was feeling where this man was concerned would be pointless to pursue. She couldn't ignore the past and how his recommendation had left her feeling inadequate at a time when she had already feeling low and insecure. Those wounds couldn't be erased by a few kind words and a couple of hours of shared concern.

"Dinner's on," she called, studiously ignoring him as thoughts tumbled around her head.

"I'm starving," Anna said, sweeping into the kitchen with Kyle trailing behind her.

Watching Kyle and Anna, two teenagers she'd once believed told the truth, she despaired at finding the words to start a painful discussion.

She joined them at the table just as the phone rang.

"Ignore it, Mom. Whoever it is can leave a message."

"But it might be important." Although the day had been unproductive workwise, she still had a responsibility to her clients.

"Why can't you let a ringing phone simply ring?" Anna asked, giving one of the dramatic sighs she'd become so proficient at. "I thought you wanted to talk."

"I do." She glanced at the caller ID. "It's your father."

Anna's smile vanished. "He wants to talk to me, not you, Mom."

Cathy kept her gaze on her daughter as she picked up.

"Cathy, what did you do to Anna?" Scott's tone was vicious and accusatory.

"Thanks for telling me you had invited her to Phoenix," she replied, surprised at her response. During her years of marriage to this man, she'd seldom said anything even faintly confrontational to him.

"She's a big girl. If she wanted you to know she was coming here, she would have told you."

"Don't ever go behind my back again," feeling uneasy. She was aware that everyone at the table was listening to what she said.

"What in the hell is going on with you? There's no need to be so difficult," he said, indignant. But his indignation no longer counted in Cathy's world. "And while we're issuing ultimatums, don't ever hang up like you did in the hospital. I have a right to know about my daughter. You don't get to play gatekeeper. No wonder she wants to live with us."

His words cut deep. "In your dreams, Scott. Anna has no interest in living with you." She looked straight at Anna, who had the good grace to look embarrassed, telling Cathy that her daughter had said something to encourage Scott's ridiculous idea. "Anna is fine."

"Put my daughter on the phone."

He'd been nasty like this before, and she'd let him get away with it. Not anymore. She wanted to yell at him, stamp her feet and hang up on him, but nothing would be accomplished except convincing Mark she was a raving lunatic.

"Scott, your behavior is hurtful and inappropriate," she said, remembering the words she'd rehearsed during one of her counseling sessions during the divorce. "Until you can speak civilly to me, we have nothing to say to each other. You may speak to Anna, but I expect you to act appropriately."

Feeling empowered, she didn't wait for Scott's response and held out the phone. "Your father wants to speak to you."

When she'd practiced those phrases years ago, she had never imagined actually using them. At the time Scott had been so domineering she couldn't picture a time she'd feel strong enough to call him on his behavior.

But she said them. And she was proud of herself.

Take that, Scott!

"Dad?" Anna put the phone to her ear, acutely aware that her mother, Mark and Kyle were listening to every word she said.

"Honey, did your mother put you up to this?"

Why had she agreed to go to his house? When he had originally sent the open ticket, she'd been over the moon at the thought of seeing her dad and getting to know her half-sisters. But hearing her mom tell him he was being mean reminded Anna how he could be. Did she really want to be on the receiving end of that, especially after Stuart's bullying? Dad probably wouldn't treat her that way, but she still felt uncomfortable. "No, Mom didn't know," she said, meeting her mother's gaze.

"Well, it doesn't matter. I'll meet the same flight tomorrow afternoon."

"I'm not sure I can go tomorrow," she said, fixing her gaze on Kyle.

"What do you mean? You promised me you'd visit. Cindy and I are counting on you. You said you wanted a chance to get to know her and spend some girl time together."

She couldn't imagine doing girl things with anyone but her mom. Anna was old enough to know that she and her stepmother would never be mother-daughter close, but she couldn't tell her father that—he wouldn't understand. He'd been so excited about her visit, and she'd been thrilled to get the ticket from her dad—her ticket out of the mess here. Originally, she'd planned to talk it over with Mom and maybe use the ticket to visit at Christmas. Getting grounded and having Mom go nuts on the parenting front had made Anna want to get away.

But now things were different. "I know I said I'd come, but Dad, would it be all right if I came once school is out, maybe Christmas or for New Year's?"

"Honey, I know your mother's listening to every word you say, and God knows I understand how suffocating that can be, but we need you. Regine and Michelle, your twin sisters, need you."

"But Regine and Michelle are too little to even know me. I really enjoyed the photos you sent," she said, hoping to soothe him. She didn't want to fight with her dad.

Her mother suddenly approached. Placing her hand over the phone, Anna whispered, "I'm trying to talk to Dad."

"Ask him if he wants you to babysit."

"No," Anna said.

"Ask him what you're going to be doing while you're there," she persisted.

Frowning at her mother, she put the phone to her ear. "Dad, are you still planning that trip to Palm Springs for us?"

"Yes. We've got it all arranged. You can spend lots of time by the pool and we'll have dinners out. How would you like private golf lessons?"

Her mother raised her eyebrows as if to prompt her.

Anna rolled her eyes, but asked, "So you have someone to watch Regine and Michelle?"

"Well, you want to get to know your sisters a little better because, thanks to your mother, you haven't had a chance. You wouldn't mind keeping the sweeties occupied while Cindy and I have the occasional game of golf, would you?"

"Are you in a tournament, Daddy?" Anna brightened. She hadn't seen her father play for years, and he was good. He'd been club champion the year before he'd moved away.

"We both are. Unlike your mother, Cindy believes it's possible to leave her children and enjoy her life. It means that the two of us have a life together."

Did he mean that golfing was his way of getting away from her when she was a kid? She didn't dare ask him, but still she wondered. Her dad hadn't been around much when she was small, but lots of dads were busy. Besides, she hadn't had to worry, because her mom had always been there.

"Come on, honey. Say you'll come. We want you here, and I promise no curfews. How does that sound?"

No curfews?

"Can you and I go to Flagstaff while I'm there? I've been studying the Grand Canyon, and it would be really cool if I could take some photos, maybe even some video for YouTube."

"Sure, anything you want," he said, and in the back ground she could hear her sisters' laughter, children she didn't know except through their photos and FaceTime.

And her dad had told her before that he wanted to make up for not being around when she was younger. "Okay, I have a few things I need to do here before I can come, but why don't I call you later next week?"

A long silence ensued, an embarrassing interlude during which she fended off her mother's whispered comments about not going to Phoenix. Anna wondered for a second if her mom was right about the reason her dad wanted to see her.

No. Not true.

She had promised her dad, and she needed to see him. He would understand and be there for her. And if things went as badly at school over the next week as she expected them to, she would need the chance to escape even more.

"That means you won't be here this week, or be able to go with us to the golf tournament. Your mother really got to you, didn't she?" her father said, his voice low, thick with anger.

"What? What do you mean, Dad?"

"Your mother is up to her old tricks. Put her on the phone."

Why did they have to be like this? Why did they have to fight? And worst of all, this time it was her fault. "Mom, Dad wants to speak with you," she said, feeling totally awful.

CHAPTER SEVEN

*C*athy recognized the redness around Anna's eyes as the beginning of tears, and her heart rose in her throat. Her daughter was hurting from something her father had said. Scott couldn't get away with causing Anna any more pain. Whatever had caused the change in Anna's behavior this past month, her daughter didn't deserve to be treated badly by her self-centered father. She wouldn't let this go—not this time around.

She took the phone from Anna. "Scott, do not expect Anna to babysit while you and Cindy play golf."

"Mind your own business."

"She is my business, and she will not be your babysitter. She is still in school and her summer plans are made. If you want to visit her here, fine. But she's not going to your place."

"Have you forgotten our agreement? I have her alternate holidays and two weeks in the summer."

"This is neither a holiday nor the summer," she said, her tone firm and strong. She couldn't believe that she was standing up to him—or that it felt so good.

"Stop being so difficult. Anna told me about the accident

and your behavior. I'm going back to the judge and getting her away from you."

"You wouldn't do that. No judge would look at a petition from you," she said, realizing that Anna was now old enough to have a say in the custody decision. The thought chilled her—she was no longer secure in what Anna would choose.

"Just watch me. You may have succeeded in keeping her with you, but that can all change. Anna has a say in what happens, and after the way you behaved at the hospital..." He let the words hang between them.

Once Scott was angry about something, he would not stop until he got his way. Anna might see Scott's bid to have her with him as proof of how much he loved her. Even if he didn't get custody, he could make everyone's lives miserable, not to mention the damage he could do to her fragile relationship with Anna. "Anna and I have things to talk about," she said speaking calmly as the old familiar anxiety buffeted her confidence.

"I'm sure you do. Think about what I've said. If you let her come as we'd planned, I'll forgive and forget everything else." He hung up.

Knowing Scott the way she did, she guessed he must have played on Anna's yearning to be part of a family again, to recover the life she'd once had. "Anna, you have no obligation to babysit your father's new children, and he has no right to ask."

Anna chewed her lip and raised her chin in defiance. "That's not what he wanted."

"Okay, if you're sure," she said, deciding to follow Mark's advice and keep the conversation between her and Anna going.

But this didn't mean she would let Scott hurt Anna. Not ever.

. . .

Mark could feel the anger welling up in him. It seemed evident Scott was selfishly still trying to take Anna away from her mother, and it sickened Mark. He'd seen the devastation caused when parents fought over custody, and he'd naively assumed that Scott was following the terms of their parenting agreement.

He watched Cathy as she sat down at the table. He wanted to reach out to her, to tell her to stand firm, to commend her for remaining calm during what had sounded like an unpleasant conversation.

He was beginning to see that she had cause to be angry. In the past, the way she'd handled her anger had been the problem. But this evening she'd shown that she had developed coping strategies that allowed her to constrain her feelings.

He admired her for that. Although he'd worked with children for his entire professional life, he'd never really had to impose discipline or set limitations. His job was to suggest actions and strategies, not enforce them. And he'd certainly never dealt with child-rearing conflicts with a spouse. He sensed the best course of action in this moment would be to calm everyone, to get them focused on eating and let the tension ease. When they felt calmer, they could talk. "Should we reheat our lasagna?"

"Good idea." Cathy moved to pick up two plates while Mark grabbed the others and headed to the microwave.

Once the servings were warm, they started to eat. Mark engaged Anna and Kyle in conversation, discussing safe topics such as their favorite Instagram videos and sporting events. After a bit of awkwardness, the teens became livelier and the mood lightened.

He glanced at Cathy and noticed the way her shoulders had relaxed and the tightness around her mouth was absent. Good. His instincts had been correct. He took a certain pride in making the situation better—however temporarily—for Cathy.

Then, deciding that pleasing her might be dangerous territory, he concentrated on the teenagers.

Cathy watched the ease with which Mark talked to Anna and Kyle. Mark truly understood teenagers, keeping to topics they'd find relevant without seeming patronizing or fake.

Before he left this evening, Cathy would ask his advice about how to deal with Scott and how to protect Anna from his schemes. It would be good to have a professional opinion again. The counselor she'd seen during the divorce had helped her formulate strategies to deal with Scott's behavior back then. But things were different now. Anna was older, able to make her own decisions and less likely to accept her mother's position on issues, which meant that Cathy had to consider a different approach. And because Mark had proven helpful in the past few hours, she was more inclined to seek his advice going forward.

Smiling across the table at Mark, she asked, "Would you like more lasagna?"

"Thank you." As she served, his gaze was so intent it seemed he could see everything about her. Even while she was uneasy with the sensation, it sent a thrill through her.

Wanting to focus on something other than the handsome man across from her, she glanced at her daughter and Kyle. They seemed to be enjoying themselves, chatting about school and Kyle's plans to try out for the basketball team in November.

"Mark, have you talked to my dad lately?" Anna asked.

The question startled Cathy because, much to her embarrassment, she'd accused him of the same thing.

"No, I haven't. Why do you ask?" he said. His smile made the question nonthreatening.

"I really want to see my dad."

"That's reasonable," Mark said, a look of understanding in his eyes. "I'm sure something can be worked out."

Anna flicked a glance toward Cathy. "Wish someone else understood that."

One...two...three... Cathy waited until she reached ten before lifting her fork to take a bite. As she chewed, she gave herself a pat on the back for not rising to Anna's bait.

"Did you know Anna is a really good volleyball player?" Kyle asked.

"I can believe that," Mark said, giving Anna his full attention. "I played varsity volleyball in school. Great game."

"Would you be willing to give me a few pointers?" Anna asked.

"I'm sure we can find time, although I'm pretty rusty. It's been a while since I played."

"I'm trying to get better around the net."

Although Cathy had played volleyball in high school, Anna had never once asked for her help. She struggled to not feel left out and hurt.

"I can help you with that." He seemed to think for a moment. "Maybe we can get three others on your team together and really work out your moves near the net."

"Awesome." Anna smiled at Mark. "When do you want to do it?"

Cathy wasn't about to be sidetracked by Anna's enthusiasm to play volleyball with Mark. She wanted answers. "Anna, before you make plans to play volleyball, we need to talk about what happened to you. Being sent to the emergency room is serious, and you promised to explain what happened."

Anna looked across the table at Mark, her smile engaging. "We were walking and Kyle was teasing me."

"You fell so hard because you were joking with Kyle?" Cathy demanded. "I don't believe that."

"I made a mistake, and I admit it," Kyle said, rubbing his

palms over his thighs. "I should have caught Anna before she hit the sidewalk."

Cathy ignored Kyle. "Not good enough, Anna. You told me before I went to the meeting at the school that you would tell me the truth when I got home. Instead, I find you at the airport ready to leave for your father's. That is not a responsible, mature way to behave." Cathy paused, reining in her hurt and sense of injustice.

It was so difficult to do as Mark had suggested, but she wanted to try. She wanted to prove that she could listen, could be understanding. Deciding to change topics, she asked, "Anna, why did you and Chloe have a fight?"

Anna glanced at her plate, picked up her fork and put it down. "It wasn't really a fight."

"Chloe was crying on the phone to me about something you and she talked about."

"Mom, can this wait until after we finish eating?"

"Is this another excuse?" Cathy asked.

Kyle rubbed his chin, pushed his bangs up off his forehead. "This is my fault. I was teasing Anna and didn't pay attention when she tripped. I'm sorry for all the worry I've caused."

Anna looked up to exchange glances with Kyle, tears glistening in her eyes. She opened her mouth as if to speak then stopped, focusing again on her hands.

"Are you okay, Anna?" Cathy asked, seeing her daughter's reaction.

"Sure. Just a little tired from all that's happened with Dad and stuff"

One minute she was cocky and sassy, and the next she was quiet and compliant. Cathy wanted to blame the shifts on being a teenager, a phase Anna was going through. But she couldn't. "Anna, Kyle's given his explanation but not you. You have not been honest with me. And you've been rude to me. You're not leaving this house until I have an explanation."

The tension in the room pulsed to life. No one met anyone else's gaze. Cathy regretted asserting her control, because it had killed the potential for getting answers. Yet she knew Anna was lying.

Cathy looked to Mark for support, but he was studying Anna, seeming deep in thought. She needed a cue from him to know how to continue. Should she back down or continue to stand her ground? Her frustration growing, she stared at her plate as if the food would offer clarity.

Mark leaned back in his chair, the action causing everyone to look his way. "This might be a good time for me to leave, as you clearly have things you have to work out," he said.

What? Did that mean he wasn't going to help her or offer support where Anna was concerned? The realization deflated her. She had been counting on his help. She really had.

Feeling the familiar rush of anger, she fired a look at him. "I agree," Cathy said. "I'll walk you to the door." She stood and went to the front door. The sooner he was gone, the sooner she could talk to Anna. If he wasn't going to help, there was no reason for him to stay.

When she opened the door, he didn't move to leave, and his closeness was a little unnerving. "Cathy, I know this isn't easy for you, but try not to get too angry with Anna and Kyle."

"What do you mean?" she asked, uncomfortably aware his words felt like more criticism.

"What I'm saying is, you need to get to the truth, but you might not get it if you're angry."

"But I am angry."

"I know you are," he said in a soothing tone. "It might be better, though, if you can contain it while you seek answers." His glance was more assessing than caring, and no wonder. He had nothing to lose in all this. He was a psychologist trained to ferret out any information he could from his clients.

But no one in this house was his client. As she looked up

into his deep brown eyes she felt silly for entertaining the idea that she would seek his help in dealing with Anna. As far as she could see he'd done his duty, answered her urgent call and now wanted to leave her to deal on her own. He'd been at that school meeting because he was available, not because he was the right person to help her address Anna's issues. She didn't owe Mark anything. "Mr. Wilson, I understand your professional interest in my daughter, but I'd like to point out that being a parent and being a psychologist are two different things. I can look after my daughter."

"Not if what I heard in the meeting with Melody is true. You don't seem to be aware of what's going on in your daughter's life."

His words hurt. She lashed out at him. "You don't know anything about my relationship with Anna. You walk in, watch for a bit, then convince yourself you know what's going on. How can you be so unfair?"

"All I'm saying is that you might learn more if you put your anger on hold and listened to your daughter."

With that he walked out of the house. And not a minute too soon, as far as Cathy was concerned. She would do what needed to be done, and that started with getting the truth out of Anna and Kyle.

She was tempted to slam the door but stopped herself. She would not reinforce his belief that she had anger issues. A strange pain rose, settling around her heart. She wished someone cared enough about her to see how much she needed support and understanding. A moment of sheer loneliness assailed her.

Mark seethed all the way home. Few parents frustrated him the way Cathy Collins did. There were moments in the past few hours when he'd felt close to her, as if they were working as a team to solve Anna's problems. Then, with little warning, she'd begun treating him like a complete outsider.

He remembered what she'd been like when he'd first met her. The anger she'd shown, much the same as tonight. She clearly didn't see that her anger wasn't helping her relationship with Anna.

Yet something about the woman drew him to her. What was it? She was abrasive and driven, angry and openly hostile toward him. Yet he had to admit that when she'd stood up to Scott, when she tried to get answers from Anna, Mark had admired her strength and tenacity.

He remembered how his mother had struggled to be treated fairly after his father left. She'd fought to be recognized as a hardworking woman dedicated to raising her children well. And maybe that was what he admired most about Cathy—her spirit and determination to keep trying: Seeing her struggle alone and clearly without the support of her ex-husband reminded him of his mother's efforts to make a life for him and his sisters without the support of his dad.

Pulling into his driveway, he remembered the expression on Cathy's face as she stood at the doorway. Bereft and sad.

He'd seen the vulnerability in her eyes after the call from Scott. She obviously had concerns about her daughter living with Scott in Phoenix. Were those concerns only about her own loss, or did she have serious worries about Scott's behavior?

An empty feeling slid through Mark. Would he have had the same issues if he had teenager? Would he be facing similar circumstances? Deep regret, the kind he hadn't experienced since Maria's death, swamped him.

He shouldn't have walked out on Cathy the way he did. It wasn't enough to leave all of this to Melody Chapman and the school psychologist, Ed Jenkins, to deal with. Sure, he didn't agree with Cathy's approach with Anna, but she was right. He wasn't a parent. He had no idea how he would have reacted in similar circumstances.

One thing he did know was that he shouldn't have left Cathy tonight. For reasons he still couldn't quite work out, he had been unsure of his role. He wasn't their psychologist, and Cathy didn't trust him as a friend. Yes, she had asked for his support, but he'd lost sight of that when she'd started pressing Anna for answers and Anna had stonewalled her.

Was that why he'd left? His attraction to Cathy clouding his perspective, he hadn't trusted himself not to overstep? And Cathy was wary enough of him that she'd freeze him out the moment he made a wrong move. Of course, he'd already made the wrong move and she had frozen him out.

He had to fix this. As soon as possible.

With Mark's parting words ringing in her ears, Cathy returned to the kitchen to clean up. As she loaded the dishwasher, she could hear Kyle and Anna in the family room sharing a laugh. How could they be so lighthearted when Anna was clearly in some sort of trouble? It wasn't a rational thought, but Cathy felt they were mocking her with their laughter.

The kitchen tidied and the leftovers put away, Cathy walked into the family room to find Kyle and Anna sitting together on the sofa, their laptops open on the coffee table. "Anna, it's time to talk."

"Give us a minute," Anna said, holding up her hand.

"You have ten more minutes to wrap up, then we talk." While Cathy hadn't been able to keep the reproach out of her voice, she thought she was being reasonable.

"Kyle and I are working on an assignment," Anna said, a frown forming as she glanced up. "You remember I have this assignment due, don't you?"

"No more excuses. Ten minutes." Cathy sat, watching the

clock, silently counting the minutes. When the time was up, she strode across the room and closed the laptop. "Start talking now."

"Why do you have to be like that?" Anna cried, her face flushed. "Kyle and I have lots to do, and we're way behind on our project."

"And yet you were prepared to leave for Phoenix today. If you don't take your assignments seriously, how do expect me to?" Anna remained stubbornly silent. "Anna, either you start talking or Kyle leaves."

"Why can't you be more like Dad?"

As much as she ached to launch into a litany of Scott's bad behavior, Cathy refused to engage in the same old argument. Scott could be lighthearted and smart because he never took responsibility for anything, especially raising his child.

She decided to turn her attention to Kyle. "What really happened yesterday?"

Kyle glanced from Anna to Cathy. "A couple of the kids in our class were fooling around and bumped into Anna. If I'd been quicker, they might not have knocked her over."

"What do you mean?" Was Anna being bullied? Was that what Kyle was trying to say? She'd read that one of the signs indicating your child was being bullied was changes in behavior.

"They were mad at me," Anna offered slowly.

"Why were they angry with you?" Cathy asked, the need to protect her daughter surging.

Anna looked at her hands. "I...did something they didn't like."

"Which was?" Cathy pressed her, needing the full story before she could take any action.

"Some of my classmates don't agree with my beliefs."

"That doesn't give them the right to bully you."

"Mom, please give me a little time to deal with this. It's

something I can manage myself. Really." Anna looked up, her gaze imploring her to understand. "You've always said that I needed to take responsibility for my actions. That's what I'm going to do next week at school. I know I shouldn't have tried to run away from it.

Seeing the unguarded look on Anna's face Cathy's heart ached for her daughter. If only Anna would share her thoughts, her worries... "Why don't you let me help make this easier for you?" Cathy said, her voice gentle.

"Let me try first. Then if I can't manage..." Anna shrugged.

"Anna, whatever it is, I'm more than willing to go to the school on your behalf. Bullying is wrong."

"Mom, please let me deal with this. You can trust Kyle and me to work things out. We know we can handle this if we have a little more time."

Seeing the look of regret in Anna's eyes Cathy pulled back. Even though every mothering instinct told her to press her daughter for answers, she knew she had to allow Anna this opportunity to fix the situation.

If that didn't work, then Cathy would step in. And heaven help anyone who got in her way.

The next Monday, Cathy drove Anna to school, checking each cluster of students as she passed them, wondering if they were involved with bullying Anna. She was more and more convinced that she should go to the principal with her suspicions, but if Anna and Kyle simply denied her allegations, her efforts would be pointless. "Why don't you invite Kyle to dinner tonight?"

"Not if you're going to interrogate him," Anna said.

"I won't interrogate him. I simply want to get to know him a little better. What's wrong with that?"

Anna pointed her finger at her mother. "I know why you drove me to school today. You've donned your daughter-protector suit," she teased. "I appreciate that, Mom, I really do.

But let me do this on my own, okay?" She opened the car door and got out. "Kyle and I have to get together after school to finish our social-sciences project."

"I thought you had volleyball practice this evening."

"I'm skipping volleyball tonight."

A few weeks ago, it would have been unheard of for Anna to miss a single practice. "I can pick you up from school."

Anna chuckled. "Mom, stop worrying. I'll see you tonight when you get home."

That evening Cathy got home from work later than she planned. Kyle and Anna were huddled in the den. "What's going on?" Cathy asked.

Anna looked up, a guilty expression on her face. "I had a call from Dad today—Kyle was with me when he called."

"Your father called you at school?" Cathy struggled to keep her tone even.

"I told him I'd call him back when I got home. I didn't want to talk to him with my friends around."

"Did he say what he wanted?"

Anna shrugged. "I won't know until I call him back. He really wanted me to come to his place when I talked to him last night. I'm sure it's about that."

Cathy was tired of talking about Scott. Tired and disappointed that the man who was critical of and domineering with her, who ignored his daughter for long periods of time, had suddenly come between her and Anna. With a sigh of resignation, she said, "Anna, I'm not stopping you from seeing your father. The next time you talk to him, find out when he wants to come here to visit you."

"Why can't I go visit him? It would be so much easier. He already sent me the ticket. Mom, I need you to understand something. I can't handle the fact you two can't get along, and I can't take any more fighting between you."

Cathy had thought she'd hidden more of the animosity

between her and Scott from Anna. Cathy had never intended for anything like that to come between them. "I'm sorry, Anna. You're right. I need to let you decide how to work it out with your father. Just tell me what you're planning to do—ideally before you make any commitments. Okay?" she asked, the old familiar urge to fix Anna's life nearly getting the better of her.

"Okay." Anna smiled as she reached for her mother, her arms going quickly around Cathy's neck. "I love you, Mom."

"I love you, more," Cathy whispered into Anna's hair, surprised and pleased by the hug.

She'd missed Anna's affection. What she'd give to have back her sweet daughter the one who confided everything in her! She sighed inwardly. Truly, she wanted everything good to come Anna's way, despite the hard time they'd been going through recently.

Anna slipped out of her arms, and returned to lean against the counter. "Mom, is it still okay for Kyle to stay for dinner?"

"Of course. As long as he calls his mom and gets permission."

"Thank you, Mom. You're awesome."

Anna and Kyle remained in the family room, huddled together. Were they more than friends? She cautioned herself not to get her hopes up as she went to her bedroom to change. As she walked down the hall, it struck her.

She always did what was expected of her—from dinner to diapers to earning a living. When anyone she cared about was upset, she tried to comfort them despite her own feelings, her own needs. For once she'd like to be the person who was being comforted. "Fat chance of that," she muttered, pulling off her suit jacket.

CHAPTER EIGHT

*T*he following day Cathy stopped at the local market to pick up a few essentials. Since last evening her thoughts had been on her realization that her life revolved around striving to be what others expected of her. She did the right thing to please everyone on the planet but herself.

Maybe she was feeling a little sorry for herself, but wasn't she entitled once in a while? Since Scott had left, she'd learn to manage her life and to care for Anna. And she'd done it mostly on her own. Surely that counted for something.

Pulling her cart close to the vegetable displays, she reached for a couple of paper bags and began to select carrots and a bunch of radishes, along with fresh string beans—all of Anna's favorite veggies. As she filled each bag, she popped them into the cart next to her, her thoughts on how to enjoy her day.

She turned to put one last bag in her cart when she spotted her purse sitting in a different cart behind her...and Mark coming toward her, clutching an eggplant and rutabagas in his hands.

For a moment he looked surprised, then smiled. "I see we

both like vegetables," he said, his glance moving from her eyes to the cart and back again.

"Oh, I put my vegetables in your cart. I'm sorry," she said, feeling a little foolish. After the other evening, he probably wasn't thrilled about seeing her again. Yet his expression gave nothing away.

"Not a problem. I probably shouldn't have left my cart beside you."

Did that mean he'd seen her? Had he been watching her? She had to admit to being pleased at the possibility. "Do you always shop here?" she asked, wondering how she'd missed seeing him before today.

"No, but I had a meeting a couple of blocks from here."

His dark blue shirt and faded jeans looked good on him—sexy. The hint of stubble was appealing in a Ryan Gosling sort of way. She had to admit he was attractive and would be pretty hard to resist. Not that she'd ever be in the position to find out, given everything between them, she thought ruefully.

"Where's your office?" She wanted to keep talking to him, wanted to make amends for what she'd said the other day.

"On Maine Street, about four blocks from the Arts Theater," he said, his gaze on her, making it impossible to look away.

"You're a long way from your office," she said, liking the way he looked directly at her, making her feel valued.

"And for your information I'm not checking up on you." He gave her a smile that started a warming sensation deep inside her body.

"I didn't think that for a minute," she said. Although it might have been nice if he had.

"Thank you for the great meal the other night. You make awesome lasagna."

"Anna likes it," she offered, basking in the compliment but uncertain as to how to keep the conversation going. Was he as uncomfortable as she was? He didn't seem uneasy...but maybe he was better at hiding his feelings. She would have sworn he wasn't interested in her welfare, yet he made no move to end their conversation.

As she stood next to Mark, a thought hit her. Why couldn't she have a little time to simply enjoy meeting someone in the market on a lovely afternoon?

Feeling attracted to a man for the first time in so long served to remind her of what she missed most about marriage. Spending time together—just two people sharing their day, loving each other without condition. The longing for something she would probably never have made her blink and look away.

"Is everything okay?" he asked, genuine concern in his voice as he moved the cart to step into the space next to her.

She met his inquiring gaze and wondered how it would feel to be part of a couple again, to have someone care exclusively for her.

"Really, everything's fine," she said. As they stood quietly facing each other, an awkward silence between them, he wondered: Hadn't he always been drawn to people who were alone?

As a child he'd always felt alone...solitary, drawn to others who felt the same. As much as he loved his three sisters, the pressure of being in charge, of being responsible for them, had kept a barrier between them. Baby-sitting had also prevented him from hanging out with his friends. Going to college hadn't changed that feeling very much, because he'd studied hard to succeed and prove that his mother's financial sacrifice for his education was not in vain. Eventually being alone became easier than opening up to others and allowing himself to be vulnerable.

So many habits could linger in a person's life long after they'd outlived their purpose. He knew that better than anyone. His work had become a habit, one that put an objective distance between him and others in his life.

Was Cathy his chance to engage, to break the habits of a lifetime? He wanted the opportunity to be involved with someone, and he sensed that she might be receptive to the idea.

"Do you suppose we could start over?" he asked. "Maybe get to know each other better? You and I haven't had the easiest relationship so far, and I take responsibility for at least part of that. I realize that you're not a fan of mine, but I honestly believe that your heart's in the right place where Anna's concerned."

Her eyes shone with appreciation. "I've put my heart and soul into raising her."

"You have. I can see that."

"While Scott did little or nothing where Anna was concerned," she said, her voice rising.

"I'm sorry that what I did hurt you."

"Anna and I have been together since the day she was born. While her father was off doing his thing, I was home looking after my daughter. And you—"

Four years later and she still responded with anger. Nothing had changed, and he was a fool to let his attraction blind him to that. "Look, I'm sorry. This isn't helping either of us."

She swiped a strand of hair from her face, looked away and looked back at him. "I'm sorry, too. I shouldn't have attacked you. I really didn't intend to. I'm worried about Anna, and everyone seems to have an opinion or idea, but no one seems to have a solution. And I still can't get any answers from Anna, because I'm afraid I'll drive her away."

Her anxiety and honesty were genuine. He sensed that she wouldn't play games. Yes, her anger issues were still present, but she was making an effort to chance. That he could admire.

Despite her antagonism toward him at times, he liked her willingness to try to work things out.

He had once thought her irresponsible with her insistence that Scott was to blame for her issues with Anna. But witnessing firsthand how much anxiety Scott created for his daughter and Cathy, Mark was beginning to understand why she might believe that.

You're never too old to learn, Wilson.

"I've got an idea. Why don't we finish up here before someone complains about us blocking the vegetable aisle then go have a coffee?" he asked.

She smiled. "I'd like that," she said. "And I'm sorry. Truly sorry. Talking about Scott does that to me."

They quickly finished their shopping and before long were seated at a cozy table in a nearby café.

This was his chance to apologize for the other night and make things right between them. Her outburst in the store had shown she still harbored resentment toward him, and he wanted to give her a reason to let that go.

"Cathy, I owe you an apology for the other night at dinner." She looked wary but met his gaze. "I shouldn't have left. You asked me to support you, and I didn't. I left when you probably needed me the most. And I—" The words seemed to stick in his throat. "I wanted to jump in to say a lot of things that weren't my place to say. I mean, I'm not your family's psychologist and I'm not a personal friend. Yet I wanted to guide your conversation, act as your counselor. I wanted to put the words in your mouth rather than let you find your own way with your daughter."

He didn't want to admit this next part. It was bad enough that he had just told her he thought her approach to her daughter was wrong. Once he admitted the rest, it would change the dynamic between them and he would be open in a way he rarely allowed himself to be. He owed her the truth, though. Or at least as much of the truth as he understood.

"More than that, though, I had the urge to interrupt with my personal feelings. I wanted to stand beside you as a friend and show Anna what her behavior was doing to you. That was not my role and, honestly, I was uncomfortable with how protective I felt toward you. Those feelings were entirely too personal for the situation between us, and I was confused about why I was there. I left, but immediately I knew I'd done the wrong thing. I abandoned you when you needed support, and for that I'm sorry."

Her eyes searched his face as if looking for proof that he meant what he said. Slowly a smile began on her lips, reaching toward her eyes. "Thank you," she said. "It did feel like you deserted me, and I assumed it was because you disapproved of how I was handling Anna. It's good to know there was more to you leaving."

"There was. Definitely." He took a deep breath. "I don't know what to do about these feelings I have for you. I don't even know what to call them, except that I know they're more than professional. Maybe nothing has to be done right now. Maybe it's enough, for the moment, for you to know."

She nodded but said nothing. Her expression was contemplative, but he couldn't detect any sign she rejected his confession. Good. They could figure out their relationship—or whatever they called it—as they went.

"You know, sometimes I feel as if my life is one long treadmill. When I was a kid, I had a hamster that spent all night getting off and on the little exerciser in his cage. I finally had to move the cage out of my bedroom so I could sleep. And here I am, practicing the life habits of a hamster."

"Lots of time I feel that way too. But I never considered I was behaving like a hamster."

"We have something in common. Imagine that," she said, chuckling.

The sound of her laughter felt so liberating. "What would you say if I invited you to go fishing?" he asked.

"Fishing?" Longing flashed in her eyes, followed quickly by a look of resignation. "But what about your job?"

"Don't we deserve a break?"

"I really shouldn't. I have so much to do."

"But maybe what you really need is time to think. You said yourself that you are searching for a way to approach Anna. It might happen when you're doing something totally unrelated. Why not give it a try?" he asked.

Looking him straight in the eye, she said "Okay, why not? I haven't a clue on how to fish, but I'd love to go fishing."

CHAPTER NINE

*B*ack at her house, Cathy held the phone tucked against her shoulder while she put the groceries away. "Am I crazy for doing this?" she asked Gina.

"No. You deserve a little downtime. You're working way too hard. It will do you good to concentrate on something different, like not jabbing a fishing hook into your finger. It will give you a focus other than your daughter," Gina said, chuckling. "Can't wait to hear how you make out."

"We'll know pretty soon. He's due here any minute," Cathy said as she put the last item in the cupboard.

"Is this a first date?" Gina asked.

"It's not a date. We're going fishing." Still holding the phone, Cathy went to her bedroom and started yanking clothes out of her closet, looking for jeans and a shirt that would be appropriate for fishing. She looked for an outfit that said sexy in a subtle way. She and Mark might have gotten off to a rocky start, but his invitation today made her feel better about herself than she'd felt in so long. "I've never fished before."

"I doubt you'll get much fishing in. Want me to keep an eye on Anna?"

"That would be great. She's supposed to come straight home from school today."

"Tell her I'll pick her up and bring her here for dinner. My boys will be here as well, so they can all catch up."

"That would be wonderful. Thanks so much."

"Not a problem. We love Anna."

"I'll pick her up when I'm done."

"And don't you rush back, hear me? You and Mark enjoy yourselves."

"Don't count on that. Seems we're better at fighting." The call waiting ping on her phone sounded. "Gotta go. I got another call."

"Hope it's Mark, and happy fishing," Gina said.

Cathy took the other call, and was thrilled to hear her mother's voice.

"Where are you?" Cathy asked, expecting her mother to say she was leaving again for an exotic, faraway place to paint some famous person's portrait.

"I'm home. Edna is cleaning, and I've been busy." She hesitated. "I want to see you and Anna, especially since she had her fall. How's she doing?"

This was not the time to talk about her concerns over Anna. She wanted to do that in person. "She's doing fine, back at school."

"And you?"

"Busy. I'm hoping to make my sales target this year."

"And you will. I have total faith in your abilities."

"Thanks, Mom."

"I'm wondering if tonight work for you and Anna to come to dinner?"

She snatched a pair of socks from the drawer, sat on the bed and pulled them on. "No, we can't. I have a previous commitment."

"I had really hoped you could," Margaret said, wistfully.

Cathy hated not pleasing her mother. Chances were that her mother wanted to see them before she left for another assignment. Margaret's New York agent kept her extremely busy immortalizing people in portraits.

And Anna needed to connect to family—there was always the possibility she'd open up to her grandmother. Maybe she should cancel her fishing plans and have dinner with her mom tonight. It would give Anna a chance to be fussed over by her grandmother.

Here you go again, doing what other people want you to do, not what you want to do.

But maybe she could do both. "Okay, why don't Anna and I come over this evening? Maybe around six thirty?"

"That would be wonderful, darling. See you then."

Cathy quickly finished changing then glanced out her bedroom window to see Mark's BMW pull into the driveway.

She moved toward the door, making a quick call to Gina to rearrange their plans. Knowing Anna was probably still in class, Cathy left a hurried message on her phone.

She set the alarm then locked the door. As she approached the car, Mark got out and came toward her, the sun glinting off his black hair, his T-shirt emphasizing his muscular chest.

"It's only fair to warn you," Cathy said as she climbed into his car, "I can't fish. I've spent my entire life on dry land."

"I don't care," he said, starting the car. "You sit back and relax. We can always go for a walk on the beach if you'd rather, but let me work my fishing magic on you first."

"I'm all yours," she said, glancing at his handsome profile, surprised at how much she meant those words. Mark was being kind to her, and she appreciated his effort.

"Sounds tempting." He gave her a long, sideways glance that warmed her belly and made her glad she was sitting down with a seat belt around her. Otherwise she might have jumped the console into his lap—not a very cool move and perhaps a bit premature.

Deep inside she knew she'd never reveal how she felt. She couldn't risk that kind of exposure. To do so would threaten her control over a situation, over herself. As sweet and kind as he had been for the past few hours, she couldn't let her guard down around him.

Still, she noticed the strength in his hand that rested on the console between them. She had the sense she was safe with him. How easy it would be to grow accustomed to such a feeling, to rely on it...

"Tell me about this place where we're going to fish," she said.

"I've only been there once, but I enjoyed it." He described the beach, the fishing pier, the way the sun slanted off the water and the bad sunburn he'd gotten that day. Cathy traced his profile in her mind, delighting in the way he looked over at her as he talked, his gaze catching hers. "I forgot to bring sunscreen," she said.

"I have a tube of every strength available."

"Glad someone plans ahead."

His brown eyes locked on hers. "I'm willing to bet you don't do much that isn't planned."

"Haven't had much choice in the past few years."

He pulled into the flow of traffic heading to Murphy's Cove. "I hear you. If you ask me, it's time to change all that for both of us."

"You feel overworked, too?" she asked, curious to know more about him.

"Seems like I've worked all my life—or at least once I started babysitting my sisters. Not my idea of fun, but my mom needed my help."

"I envy you having sisters. I'm an only child," she said.

"Not many of my friends envied me growing up. My sisters ate into my social life and teased me unmercifully. But it all worked out in the end. We're great friends now, even though we all live in different parts of the country. My mother worked long hours at two jobs. I went to college on a scholarship."

The thought that he'd worked the way she had made her feel close to him, made her feel they had something more in common. "Can I assume you also want to run away from it all?" she asked.

"Yeah. But where would I run? And the truth is I love my work."

She understood that, as well. Even though she resented what Mark had done to her years before, Cathy didn't doubt for a moment that he believed in what he was doing. "I'm glad I took your business card a few days ago," she said.

"Me, too."

Feeling more at ease around him, she luxuriated in the coziness of the vehicle as they drove toward the coast. Her senses were treated to a kaleidoscope of fall colors, broken occasionally by homes tucked into spaces framed by tall evergreens.

A little later, he slowed the vehicle and turned into a narrow parking spot adjoining a pier, its long wooden planks glowing in the afternoon sun. "All you have to do is relax and enjoy yourself. I'll take care of the rest," he said.

Cathy opened the door to a blast of fall heat. "Where do we go?"

"Follow me."

He got the gear out of the trunk and took the rods in one hand, the tackle box in the other, and started down the pier at a fast pace.

"What's the big rush?"

He laughed, a deep throaty sound. "Sorry about that. I guess I am a little excited."

The planks rumbled beneath her feet. She turned to see a truck bouncing along the pier as it made its way to a fishing boat tied at the end. "I've lived in Spencer Island all my life and I've never been on this pier."

"Glad to know I can offer you a new experience." Mark put his gear on a bench and began putting bait on the hooks.

The sun warming her, Cathy watched what he was doing. Growing up, she'd had no opportunity to fish or do anything like that. Her mother believed that galleries and museums were the best way to spend free time, to educate Cathy on what the world's art collections proved about society. Although she came to appreciate her mother's efforts, as a young child she had felt constrained and often bored while touring a museum or gallery.

Being outside, seeing the gulls swoop and sway, she reveled in adding a new experience to the long list of things she'd never had the chance to do. But that would never happen with Anna. Her daughter would have every learning experience possible in life, as well as learning about the art world—Cathy would see to it. Once they were over this rough patch, everything would be fine.. just fine.

Turning her gaze to Mark, she was startled to find him looking at her. He was so gorgeous-something she hadn't really noticed until recently—and he had chosen her to go fishing with him. Feeling the attraction building, she searched for something to say. "What can I do?"

"You can hold that rod for me while I get mine ready." He worked swiftly and competently, and before long, he closed his fishing tackle box. "Are you ready?"

"Sure, but be prepared—you may be pulling fishing line out of my hair."

"I look forward to the opportunity to run my fingers through your hair in search of fishing line," he replied, leaning toward her, the heat of his body blending with hers. She fought to keep from swaying into his broad chest. She wanted to touch his face, feel the texture of his skin beneath her fingers. His body was so close...too close.

Suddenly uncertain, she retreated and concentrated on the rod she held. She couldn't look at him for fear he'd see her need.

"Let's fish," he whispered in her ear, making her neck tingle in pleasure.

"Okay," she said, her voice sounding like a gasp.

He showed her how to cast, how to hold the rod and what to do should a fish take the hook. His powerful hands guided hers.

An old man meandered over, watching Mark's instruction. "You'll make a fisherman out of her yet," he said.

"I'll certainly try." Mark held her hands, his scent wafting around her, coaxing her into the curve of his arms.

"Hmm. This is nice." Her heart opened, her spirits lifted as she spoke the words into the intimate space between them.

He didn't say anything. He simply gazed into her eyes until she felt uncomfortable and turned her head away.

"Am I too close?" he asked.

Words of denial were on her lips, but she saw he would not be put off or lied to. "A little," she murmured.

"Want to tell me about it?"

Feeling protected in his arms, she tried to explain. "I haven't dated since the divorce. Well, except for an occasional night out with someone a friend recommended. Trial by terror, I call it, because none of it felt right to me."

"And what would you prefer?" he inquired quietly as he took the fishing rod from her hands and put it aside, before sitting down on the bench, giving her his full attention.

"Someone who treats me well, who shares my interests, who loves me and my daughter."

He patted the bench beside him. "He'd also need to be someone who gave you room to be who you needed to be."

"What do you mean?"

"Someone who doesn't force you to live your life his way, someone who allows you to be your own person. I'm guessing here, but I suspect that being your own person has been something you've had to work on."

How did he know?

She had fought hard to be someone other than a famous artist's daughter. And when she'd married Scott, he'd insisted on being the center of attention in the marriage, leaving her little opportunity to express herself other than as a wife and mother. "I wanted Anna to grow up in a family with two parents who loved her. I didn't have that. My mom was always busy with her art, and I never knew my dad. He died in a car accident before I was born."

"My dad wasn't around, either." He paused. "Having heard your side of a conversation with Scott, is it possible he bullied you, that he still bullies you?" he asked, watching for her reaction.

She gave him a wry smile. "You sound like Gina."

"Do you think she might be right?"

Her first thought was to excuse or explain Scott's behavior. She'd always been so quick to come to his defense, to take responsibility for how he acted. "I don't know if he's a bully."

"You're sure?"

"Is that how you see me? As a victim of bullying?"

"How you see yourself is what's important," he countered. "Do you resent Scott?"

"Why are we talking about Scott?" she asked, hating that the mention of her ex-husband had upset her.

"Sorry." Mark gazed out across the water, and she felt a chill flood her heart.

Words of explanation were on her lips, but she held back.

Mark had been kind to her. They were having a lovely afternoon. She felt safe around him, safer than she had for a very long time. "What I feel about my marriage doesn't matter anymore," she said, watching his face intently.

"Cathy, you have every right to feel what you're feeling. Just so you know, I was angry for you when Scott called, and I saw your reaction to his words. Being angry is a natural response, but sooner or later we have to face what made us angry."

She'd never had anyone talk to her like this before. Her first instinct was to lash out, to defend who she was and how she managed her life. Mark couldn't possibly know what she'd gone through with her ex. "I didn't come here to talk about my shortcomings. I came here to enjoy the afternoon. I thought you did, too."

He leaned in. "Did you just tell me to butt out?" he asked, hugging her close.

She soaked in his touch, feeling calmed. "A few days ago I would have yelled at you instead of saying what I felt."

"You should give yourself credit for your honesty about how you feel."

Surprised and pleased by his comments, she faced him. "While we're on the subject of behavior, I want to ask something. How did you cope with your sisters as teenagers and not remember how moody they can be?"

"I don't know. Maybe because I was young, too," he said, his gaze on her, unnerving her.

She felt so vulnerable, so exposed. Where was this leading? "It's not easy for me to talk about all of this. You see, I've always felt I didn't measure up." Oh! She didn't mean to say that, not at all. She didn't want him to know how uncertain she felt when it came to relationships, and having her relationship with her daughter under his scrutiny was enough for her. "Maybe we could leave all this, maybe concentrate on today?"

He touched her hair, ran his fingers along her cheek.

"Excellent suggestion," he whispered, his lips moving slowly, purposefully along her chin to her mouth. He kissed her, wrapping her in his embrace.

Lost in his arms, she clung to him, never wanting this moment to end.

CHAPTER TEN

*H*is kiss, so gentle yet so possessive, had opened up a whole new world. She felt different in a way she couldn't describe. As he stroked her cheek and looked into her eyes, she knew she would remember this moment long after today.

"We probably should get going," he said, still holding her close.

His touch distracted her; she struggled to answer. "I suppose so."

She could still feel his lips on hers as he loaded the trunk. She'd never been kissed the way he kissed her. Never with such care and tenderness. She felt adrift in a place of beautiful sensation.

She was finely attuned to him—his easy grace as he moved to open the car door for her, his confidence, his patient acceptance. It all held her spellbound. As if in a trance, she got in and fastened her seat belt. The feeling of intimacy in the narrow space after he climbed in swept all worries and troubles from her mind...until her phone rang.

"Did Anna call you?" Gina asked.

"No. Why?"

"She asked to go to your house to wait for you. She said she wanted to get ready for dinner."

"Thanks for letting me know, Gina. We're on our way back now," she said, her life swooping in to steal the moment.

"How's it going?" her friend whispered.

She glanced at Mark, who had been quiet since they'd gotten on the highway. "Nice. Really nice."

"Okay. See you at work tomorrow. Say hi to Margaret for me."

"Will do."

As they drove the rest of the way home, Mark asked her about the real estate in Spencer Island.

"Are you interested in buying a home?"

"For now, I'm happy in my condo."

"Sorry for asking the question. Hard for me to leave my work behind," she replied, scrambling for something intelligent to say. It was as though she couldn't keep up with the complete reversal of despising him to...wanting him.

"In case you didn't notice, I'm trying to make conversation," he said, squeezing her hand where it rested on the console.

"Me, too." She didn't move her hand from his.

He smiled and held her hand just a little tighter.

When Mark pulled into her driveway, she spotted Kyle's red Toyota parked there. He and Anna sat on the front steps, their heads together in conversation.

"I didn't realize that Kyle would be here," Cathy said as Mark turned off the car.

"Is he here a lot?" Mark asked.

Anna shot off the step and ran toward the car, a scowl on her face. Cathy got out. "Hi, what's up?"

"Mom, where did you and Mark go?"

"Fishing. I left you a message."

"About Gina picking me up and you going fishing before we

went to Gram's." Her glance swerved to Mark and back to her. "You don't fish."

Surprised by the anger in Anna's question, Cathy asked, "What's going on?"

Anna marched off toward the house without answering as Mark came around the car. "Does she object to you going fishing?" he asked.

Anna had been incredibly rude, once again embarrassing Cathy. But after the past few days, she'd almost come to expect this kind of behavior. "That's the way Anna is these days—sweetness and light one minute, surly and demanding the next," Cathy said. She glanced his way, suddenly aware of him, of their date, and how much she enjoyed it.

"I'd like to invite you in for a drink," she said.

"I'd like to come in," he countered.

"I'm just not sure... I mean."

"You're worried about what your daughter will think?"

"Yes. Things seemed to be in such chaos. I don't want to upset her."

"But you need to have an honest conversation with her."

"Honest conversation? That's next to impossible when all I get from her is attitude."

"Have you told her how you feel?"

"You mean like today? Will I tell her that she's rude, that she shouldn't have invited Kyle here without talking to me first? Especially when she knew I wouldn't be here?"

He shrugged. "Do you suspect them of something?"

"Yes. No. Maybe. I'm tired of being the one who has to correct Anna's behavior. Her father plays the good parent and I'm left to pick up the mess." She'd had a wonderful afternoon with a gorgeous man for the first time in ages, yet now she had to deal with Anna's attitude. "Then people like you come along and tell me I have anger issues. You would, too, if this were your child."

Damn! She hadn't meant to say that. She had seen a different side to him, had relaxed her barriers against him and had felt sexy and attractive in his arms. Then she'd ruined it by criticizing him. "I'm sorry. I didn't mean that."

He turned to her, his broad shoulders shielding her from the house, a momentary reprieve from the argument she knew she would face with Anna.

Mark felt the distance forming between them and was disappointed. Although the drive home had been a little awkward after the phone call, the afternoon had been perfect. Kissing Cathy had been in a league all of its own. He hadn't planned to kiss her. Most of all, he hadn't expected to feel about her the way he did, the way she made him feel...good about himself.

And he was pretty sure she'd felt the same way.

During the afternoon he had felt connected to Cathy in a way he hadn't felt with someone since his wife died three years ago. He'd invited Cathy to go fishing because he wanted her to have a break, but once they got to the lake he'd been surprised to realize how much he enjoyed being with her, teaching her to fish. She'd been quick to catch on, too. They seemed to fit well together, to talk easily.

Talk. He shouldn't have talked to her about serious stuff—a dumb move. Hardly the move of a man intent on enjoying the company of a beautiful woman. They were out to enjoy themselves and he'd offered her advice...on bullying, of all things.

No wonder she was annoyed with him. He would have been, too. "Look, I shouldn't have offered my advice. I had no right to. I didn't mean to interfere in what is going on between you and Anna."

She glanced away. Was she upset with him?

Not wanting to embarrass himself any further, he pulled his

keys from his pocket. "I had a great time, but you have to work things out with your daughter. My being here may only make that more difficult,' he said, trying for a neutral tone. He didn't feel neutral. He wanted to go into the house with her to explain what he'd said and why he'd said it. But, once again, he wasn't sure of his reasons, and that was the strange part. For a second time he decided he'd be better off to simply step away.

"Fine," she said, feeling that he was leaving her to face the situation on her own. Again. Why couldn't this man understand how she was feeling? Did he not see that she was afraid of facing her daughter alone? Was this her fate—to be attracted to men who left her to deal with the tough stuff on her own? "Thank you for a wonderful afternoon," she said, not meaning it nearly as much as she would have a little bit ago.

"You're welcome." His gaze met hers as he took her hand, allowing her to believe, for a fraction of a second, that he might kiss her again. Her body flooded with warmth at the thought.

Instead, he turned, got in his car and drove away without another word.

The hurt was so unexpected. An hour ago, she'd been happy in his company, feeling upbeat and ready to enjoy life. Now she was fed up with life and with Mark. Disgusted, she went into the house to face her daughter.

Kyle and Anna were watching TV in the family room.

Standing at the kitchen sink, staring out at her backyard and the petunias that needed weeding, she debated what to say to Anna. Why should she say anything? No matter what, there would be an argument, and Kyle would be there to hear all of it. And her mother was expecting them to arrive and spend a pleasant evening of smiling and pretending that everything was just fine.

At least Cathy would have a nice dinner prepared for her.

She couldn't fix Anna's attitude or Mark's opinion of her anytime soon. And maybe she didn't want to. Everyone expected her to find the solution, to be the parent, the adult, to put aside her own feelings. Not tonight. She deserved a little mothering of her own.

Besides, as the therapist she'd seen during the divorce had said, the only person Cathy could fix was herself. To date, she'd done a really lousy job of it. "Kyle, I assume Anna told you that she and I are going out to dinner," she said over the sound of the TV.

"Yes, she did." He rubbed his palms on his thighs as he peered out under his bangs at Anna. "I'd better go."

"Mom, don't be rude." Anna turned to Kyle, rested her hands on his shoulders and hugged him.

"I'll talk to you tomorrow," Anna said, loud enough for Cathy to hear.

Tired and frustrated, Cathy waited while Anna saw Kyle out. As he pulled out of the driveway, Anna turned on her mother. "Why can't I have a normal life like every other teenager I know? Kyle's my friend, and you're being ridiculous."

"Anna, let's sit for a minute and talk." She indicated the kitchen table and waited until Anna took a seat—fortunately with minimal theatrics. "You don't seem to get it. I'm responsible for you. The past few days have been really difficult for me. When I asked about what was going on and if I could help, you wanted more time to deal with it. But that hasn't stopped me from worrying about whether I'm doing the right thing and whether you'll be okay. I know this is probably not what you'd like to hear. But I am really worried about your safety. As for Kyle, he has two parents to look out for him. You have me."

"And Dad."

"That remains to be seen."

"What about your date with Mark? When were you going to

tell me about that?" Anna asked, her voice low, her cheeks flushed.

"It wasn't a date. We had a few hours free and decided, on the spur of the moment, to go to Murphy's Cove. He offered to teach me how to fish."

"Yeah, right," Anna said, her tone derisive.

"Anna, I've had enough for one day. Your behavior toward Mark was uncalled for. You owe him an apology."

Anna chewed her lip. "Do you care about Mark?"

"I haven't figured that part out yet."

"Then why did you go fishing with him?"

"Because I'm tired of working all the time. I needed a break. I don't see the harm in that."

Anna didn't speak for a few moments as she continued to chew her lip, her eyes on Cathy. "I'm acting really awful, aren't I?" she asked, putting her arms around her mother. "I don't have a problem with Mark, Mom. I think he's kind of cool. You deserve a life, and I'm sorry I embarrassed you. I will apologize to Mark the next time I see him."

Surprised and delighted, she smiled at her daughter, love surging around her. "I suspect you're behaving this way because of what's going on with you and Kyle. Why don't you tell me about it?"

"Kyle and I are working out the stuff about my fall."

"That's all? You're working things out?" she asked, focusing on not being drawn into another argument.

"You always told me that you and Dad tried to work your problems out. Why can't I be allowed to do the same? Who knows? Maybe I'll be better at it than you and Dad were."

She hadn't expected the comparison but there was a certain logic. "It was different where your dad and I were concerned. We were married."

"So? Kyle and I are friends, and we need time to work out our problems with a few of our classmates."

"Okay, but this can't go on forever. I will give you one more day, then I want some answers. As for your father, nothing has changed where he's concerned. He can come here to see you when he wants to. But you're not his babysitter."

"I think you're jealous of Dad's happiness and you won't admit it."

Shocked, she stared at her daughter. "Where did you get a notion like that?"

"Because you're always trying to keep me away from Dad."

"That's not true."

"I want to go and stay with them. I want to get to know my little sisters. Dad wants to see me, to include me in his family."

She was tired of taking the blame, and Anna was old enough to face the consequences. It might mean that they were late for dinner at her mom's, but this simply could not continue. "Why don't you call your father right now? Tell him that you'll come for a three-day weekend. This Friday is development day at school, so you won't miss classes. And while you're talking to him, make plans for this summer's vacation."

Anna's face brightened. "Mom, that sounds great. I could go on the Thursday night and come back on Sunday night in time for school on Monday."

Cathy realized her daughter really did want to visit her father—this wasn't a scheme to get back at Cathy or avoid whatever was happening at school. Anna would be so disappointed when she tried to get a commitment from her dad. But she to face up to reality, not the fantasy world she insisted on building around her father. "Call him now."

Anna jumped up. "Sure. They have a room ready for me and everything. I can't wait," she said, charging down the hall to her bedroom.

Cathy waited, hoping she was wrong about Scott, that for once in his life he'd put someone else's needs ahead of his own.

Regardless of how she might feel about him, Anna had clearly decided she needed to see him, and that was all that mattered.

Watching the minutes tick by, Cathy had decided to check on Anna when she appeared, her face blotchy and red.

Cathy saw the quivering lips, the agony on her face, and gathered her daughter into her arms. "Are you okay?" she asked, stroking her hair, holding her close.

Anna erupted in sobs as she clung to her mother. "Dad doesn't think— Dad says it's not— He doesn't want me there for a weekend! He wanted me there for a couple of weeks so he and Cindy can go out and do things by themselves. I'd have to miss school. I can't do that right now."

"I'm so sorry."

"Cindy doesn't think it's a good time, and Daddy doesn't want to upset her. She didn't do well in some silly golf tournament and she's upset about it. I asked him when would be a good time, and he said he'd have to get back to me."

So now he was blaming his new wife for his lack of interest in Anna. What a surprise!

Anna wiped her cheeks and moved out of her mother's embrace, making her way to the table. "What am I going to do? I made them mad by not going when he said, and now Cindy doesn't want me there."

She had no advice for her daughter that wouldn't put Scott in a bad light, and as much as he deserved it, Cathy couldn't add to the hurt Anna was feeling.

"Would you talk to Dad, get him to reconsider? Maybe I could go a couple of days next week. And I guess I could babysit for Cindy."

"I don't think your father will listen to me. Besides, it's not a good idea for you to miss school right now. You want to get your grades back up." All true, but those words would do nothing to soothe her daughter's hurt. "How about this? When the school year is over, we'll take a vacation to Phoenix together and you could visit with your dad for a few days. After you've seen him and his family, you and I will travel around the state."

"Would you really do that, Mom?" she asked, her voice filled with gratitude as she smoothed away the tears on her cheeks.

"I'd do just about anything for you, sweetie."

"Anything?" Anna smiled. "Okay. Get out of those fishing clothes, Mom. We're going to be late for Gram's dinner."

Was it all over so easily? Maybe now was all that mattered. "I'll be ready before you are."

Her mother lived in an older neighborhood on the road to Cranberry Point, a place with towering pines and a view of the ocean. As they pulled into the driveway, Anna cried, "There's Grammy. And she's got a puppy!" Anna was out of the car before it was completely stopped, her feet skidding on the gravel as she made her way across the space. She knelt and gathered the puppy into her arms.

Margaret, her ankle-length purple dress swirling around her, laughed and clapped her hands. "Come here, darling child."

Anna, with the dog trailing behind her, came over to Margaret. "I love your dog."

"Thank you," she said, hugging Anna while she rocked her back and forth, the pup yipping at their feet.

A dog. What was her mother going to do with a dog?

Remember your promise to yourself? You're going to enjoy your evening. Margaret's problems aren't yours.

"It's a chocolate Labrador, right?" Anna said, untangling herself from the hug.

"Yep. A male, because they make better watchdogs."

"What's his name?"

"I thought you could name him," Margaret answered, crouching to pat the puppy with Anna. The dog licked first Anna's face and then Margaret's, all the while emitting whines of happiness.

As her mother rose, stretching out her arms to Cathy, there was a look of such profound loneliness in her eyes that Cathy could hardly believe what she was seeing. Margaret had never been one to succumb to loneliness or admit to missing anyone. Her mother had always been so strong and determined to live her life her way. And yet, at this moment, Cathy could have sworn that her mother had doubts...fears.

"Darling, I'm so glad to see you."

"Me, too," Cathy said, walking into her mother's arms, feeling the strength of her touch, responding to her warmth and love. The scent of L'Air du Temps—her mother's signature perfume—settled over her.

For the first time since she'd married and left home, Cathy wanted only one thing—that Margaret would stick around and be part of their lives, rather than travel so much.

"I've got dinner ready if you'd like to eat now," Margaret murmured, patting Cathy's cheek so gently, so slowly and with so much feeling, Cathy was forced to turn away before she broke down and cried.

"What's going on?" she asked after composing herself.

Margaret didn't answer, instead starting toward the house, her long skirt outlining her legs as she walked. "Let's eat, then Anna can name the puppy."

"I've already done that," Anna said, hefting the puppy up on her shoulder to be rewarded with a slew of dog kisses. "I'm calling him Butch Cassidy, after Mom's favorite character in Butch Cassidy and the Sundance Kid. Don't know why she likes such an old movie." She ducked another onslaught of doggy kisses. "But there's no explaining the tastes of old folks."

"I'm not old," Cathy exclaimed.

"Got ya. And I didn't even try," Anna said triumphantly, holding the dog up in front of her. "Hi, Butch."

"Butch it is," Margaret agreed, chuckling.

Cathy suddenly realized what her mother was doing by

getting this dog. She wanted Anna to have a pet, something Cathy had refused. It was probably selfish on her part, but her days were too busy to be responsible for walking a dog.

Inside, there were huge candles in large glass pots flickering everywhere, giving the main room a magical feeling. The walls were covered floor to ceiling with paintings done by friends of Margaret's. How many hours had she spent gazing at these paintings? Cathy loved the reminder of her childhood.

Anna squeezed past them into the kitchen. "Where are Butch's food and water bowls? He's starving."

"That's a great name for a dog, don't you think?" Margaret whispered as she put her arm around Cathy's shoulder.

"Anna has wanted a dog for a long time."

"You think I got that dog for Anna?" her mother asked.

"I do, and don't deny it," she said, but she could hardly be angry. It made perfect sense, and it provided an opportunity for Anna to spend time with Margaret. "There's only one problem."

"And that is?"

"You'll be away most of the year, and we'll have Butch." She didn't have a clue how she'd manage a dog, given their schedules. But seeing her daughter so happy, she'd find a way. The kind of joy evident on Anna's face had been absent for far too long.

"I believe I have a solution," Margaret said.

"Such as?"

"Let's have dinner, and I'll explain." Margaret went to the kitchen, a galley style with all the amenities.

"What can I do?" Cathy inquired, noticing that the mahogany table was set with the best silver and Margaret's Spode china. "Wow, the table looks gorgeous. What's the occasion?"

"Isn't Butch the perfect occasion, Mom?" Anna asked,

hugging the dog as she sat on the cream sofa in the main room next to the dining room.

"It would take more than a dog to bring out the good china." Cathy glanced at her mother, who stood beside the kitchen counter, a pensive expression on her face.

Margaret lifted the casserole from the oven, and holding it carefully, she made her way to the table and put the dish on an insulated mat.

Her eyes bright with excitement, she said, "I've got good news. I'm not traveling anymore. I've decided that if people want me to paint their portraits, they can come here. I've worked hard, my reputation is solid and I'm tired of being away from my family." She wiped a strand of graying hair from her forehead. "And my family is here—the two of you."

Cathy and Anna exchanged surprised glances. "Are you serious? After all this time?" Cathy asked.

"Sit down while I tell you all about it." Margaret pulled the salad from the fridge and sat at the head of the table. "Anna, put Butch in his kennel in the laundry room, will you?"

Anna did as she was asked, washed her hands then took her place at the table. "So, let's hear it, Gram. What's the plan?"

"Anna, your mom has always had to live around my crazy schedule, and now I want to be here for her, and for you. I'm not getting any younger, and before I miss out on everything going on in your lives, I've decided to change how I work. My agent isn't all that happy, but he'll manage. Besides, he's made lots of money off me while he got to stay home with his family." She raised her crystal wineglass. "To a new life."

Cathy peeked at Anna, and her daughter's face was radiant. "What do you think, Mom? Isn't this great news?"

Cathy felt a rush of excitement at the thought of her mother being around all the time, being a part of their lives. She raised her glass. "This is wonderful news. To a new life,' Cathy said before taking a sip of the dark red wine.

They ate their meal punctuated with Anna's excited stories of what she and Butch would do together, how she wanted to take Butch to obedience school. "Mom, we'll check all this out when we get home, right?"

"We will." Cathy wiped her lips with the Irish linen napkin as she let the idea of her mother being around full-time sink in. "You'll be able to have sleepovers at your gram's anytime you want."

"And when you're tied up with work, I'll be able to invite Gram over to our house, with Butch, of course. We'll make chocolate-chip cookies." Anna gave a satisfied smile, rubbed her tummy and got up from the table. "If it's all right with you guys, I'm going to take Butch for a nice long walk."

Margaret smiled. "That's a wonderful idea. Have you got your cell phone with you?"

"Yes. Why?" Anna asked as she took the leash off the hook at the back door and fastened it on Butch's collar.

"Just in case you need us. Butch may want to run, and you could end up in the next county."

Anna laughed—a lovely, melodic laugh that Cathy hadn't heard in far too long. She realized now how big a mistake it had been to deny Anna her wish to have a dog.

"See you later," she murmured, happy at the thought that her daughter would spend the next little while doing something she loved.

"Let's sit out on the deck and watch the sailboats moving into the harbor," her mother said.

They sat in well-weathered Adirondack chairs. Below them, the lawn stretched toward the ocean. The wide expanse of water rippled and glistened in the half-light. "It's so beautiful here." Cathy breathed in the scent of lavender wafting from the herb garden along the side of the house, the wind in the pines, birds calling.

"It is, and someday it will be yours."

Where was this coming from? Her mother never talked this way.

"What is going on, Mom? Are you worried about something?"

"I'm setting up a trust fund for Anna's education. And I'm redoing my will, naming you my sole beneficiary. I want to look after you and Anna."

"Are you sure you're not hiding something?" Cathy asked.

"No, I'm looking after business, something I've not done well over the years. But my accountant says I need to start planning for the future."

"That's great, Mom, especially after the week I've had." She explained her concerns around Anna, Kyle and the accident.

"Cathy, I'm sorry you've had to go through all this. But this proves how important my decision is. With me around more, I'll be able to help you with whatever is going on in your life. I want to be a better mother and grandmother."

Cathy had become so accustomed to making her own decisions, being responsible for her own life over the years, she didn't know how to respond. "I'm happy for you, Mom."

She needed to think, to take this all in. So strange and so unexpected. Her mother could be pretty forceful when she wanted something. What if she wanted to be much more involved in Cathy's life? Or Anna's? Scott meddling in Anna's life, and her mother suddenly retiring might mean a whole new round of conflict over Anna's activities. It was too stressful for her to deal with right now. "Mom, I'm really sorry, but after the week I've had I need to go home."

Margaret looked startled. "I understand, darling. You've always been someone who needed time and space to sort through your feelings. Maybe Anna could stay with me tonight?"

"I don't know. She has school tomorrow and a project due next week."

"Can I ask her? I could drive her over to pick up her things at your house and bring her back here."

"Sure. Go ahead and ask her."

When Anna returned Margaret asked her if she'd like to stay overnight, Anna hugged her grandmother. "I would love that. Can Butch sleep with me?"

"Now, we don't want to get Butch into any bad habits, do we?"

"No, we don't, I guess," she murmured, her expression downcast.

Margaret, her face suffused with love, whispered, "Okay, just for tonight."

Anna's cry of happiness brought a loud bark from Butch.

"We'd better go, Anna, and get your things organized for your sleepover."

On the drive home, Anna hummed a happy tune. "You like Butch?" Cathy asked, knowing the answer but needing the sound of her daughter's voice to break the endless train of thoughts roaring through her mind.

"I love Butch, and I can't wait to take him to obedience class. I'm going to be the best dog trainer ever," she said.

As Cathy listened to Anna's plans for Butch, her daughter sounded like her old self. If a dog was what it took to bring her daughter back to her, the dog could move in with them. Grateful to finally feel at peace with her daughter, she vowed to focus on their lives together, on Anna's plans for college, on their plans for Thanksgiving weekend just a few weeks away. They would have a huge dinner at her mom's and maybe stay overnight just for the fun of it.

Focus on the good...and pray the rest went away.

CHAPTER ELEVEN

*T*wo days later, Mark got a call from Melody Chapman. She was still concerned about Anna's behavior, and the school psychologist was not yet back to work. She'd called Mark to get his recommendations on what to do.

"Anna had another argument yesterday with Stuart Jameson, and it escalated to a yelling match," Melody explained, adding that Stuart was a difficult student. "Before classes ended, Anna left with Kyle. I need to speak with Mrs. Collins, but she hasn't returned my call. I get the impression she doesn't welcome any interference in how she raises Anna."

What could he say? He had that impression, too, although he suspected Cathy had deeper motivations than he'd initially assumed. Mark promised to look into it, although he didn't have any idea how he'd do that.

This wasn't his case, and his only involvement was his complicated relationship with Cathy. And although he felt he understood her better as a person, he wasn't convinced that he could be of much help in the continuing situation with Anna, especially if Anna's behavior at school was not showing noticeable improvement.

Complicating matters further, he had feelings for Cathy. After he'd left Cathy's house, he'd wished he could start over with her. Again. He wanted to erase the awkwardness of their goodbye. Especially because he could still taste her lips, could still remember how she felt in his arms.

The problem was he didn't want to see her to talk about issues with Anna. He wanted to spend time with Cathy. But he couldn't, not after he'd promised Melody to help. Damn it! Reluctantly, he called Cathy.

When she answered she sounded out of breath. "Did I bring you away from something?" he asked.

"Just lugging laundry to the laundry room. I've never seen so many dirty clothes. I'm thinking about buying disposable clothes for Anna, if such a thing exists," she said, a warm chuckle filling the connection. "What's going on with you?" she asked, her tone hopeful and upbeat.

"I wonder if you and I could meet sometime today or tomorrow? I'd like to talk to you about Anna."

"Why? She's doing okay."

Was that disappointment or suspicion he heard in her voice?

He didn't know how to answer that without putting Cathy on the defensive. Besides, he preferred to see her in person, just to be sure she was okay. Then he'd tell her what Melody had said. "Have you talked to Melody Chapman?"

"No. She called, left a message asking me to call. I assume it's about another meeting. I'm going to call her back when I'm finished cleaning the house. Anna really does seem to be doing better, not wanting to go to her father's place..."

"Could we talk?"

She sighed. "Only if you're willing to come here. I've taken the day off to...catch up with things..."

"I'll be there in a few minutes." He had a client coming in shortly after four today, so he had to be quick.

When he got there, Cathy was waiting at the door. "What's so urgent?" she asked.

She looked beautiful with her hair held back from her face with silver clips, her jeans fitting over her slender legs. "I wanted to see how you were doing."

"I'm flattered." She met his gaze, color rising in her cheeks. She motioned for him to enter. "Anna's grandmother got a dog, and that's all Anna can talk about."

"That's great. And how's she doing in school?"

She turned to him, a quizzical look in her eyes. "Is something wrong?"

"I had a call from Melody. It seems that Anna was in another argument yesterday."

"What? Why am I only finding out now? And from you?" There was a hard tone in her voice and he saw signs of anger. Understandable, but he knew that if she couldn't get past her anger, Anna wouldn't receive the kind of support she needed.

"Melody did call you."

She deflated a little. "I should have called her right back. Who was Anna arguing with?"

"Stuart Jameson."

"No. Not again." Her voice rose. "Anna told me she was done with him after the other incident. Melody knows that Anna had never had any trouble at school before, or else I would have been in her office at some point before all this. Stuart is the problem here, not my daughter. Why is the school calling me? Why aren't they taking action against Stuart?"

"I'm sure they've been in touch with his parents," Mark said calmly.

"If you ask me, the school is practicing appeasement." She picked up the phone. "I'll call the school. I don't know what I have to say to get them to address this."

How could he encourage her to not let her anger dictate how she acted with the school? Not only did it make her relationship with her daughter more complicated, it affected how the school staff responded to her. "Would you like me to go to the meeting with you?"

"Anna is still in some kind of trouble, isn't she?" She paused as if in thought. "We talked about it, and she wants to work it out on her own, but if she's had another run-in with Stuart, she isn't working it out."

She rubbed her forehead, her expression anxious. "I'd like to talk to Anna first before I meet with the school. I want to hear what went on from her." She glanced up at him, her expression one of worry mixed with resignation. "Could you stay?"

He'd left her alone to cope twice before, and she still trusted him to support her. If he didn't have faith in his abilities to make a difference in Anna's life, he had to go now and not come back. That way, Cathy could find someone else to rely on.

If he stayed, he might be able to turn the situation around. Seeing Cathy's wary expression, he knew he could be making a big mistake. But his heart told him he had to be there for her or get out of her life. And if he stayed, he'd have to cancel his four o'clock appointment. "Certainly."

"Thank you so much," she said.

He rescheduled the appointment while Cathy made coffee. They talked idly until Anna came home twenty minutes later.

"Mom, who's here?" she asked, stopping abruptly when she saw Mark.

There was something in the way Anna looked at him—disappointment, maybe. "I came to talk to your mom."

"About what?" Anna asked.

"About you," Cathy said. "Did you get into a fight with Stuart Jameson?"

"When?" Anna asked, dropping her backpack near the door and shedding her hoodie as she came into the room.

"The school called. to say that you were arguing with Stuart again. Is it true, Anna?"

"We were talking too loud in the hallway, that's all," Anna said.

"Why would you have anything more to do with the likes of him?" Cathy demanded.

Mark watched the anger flare and stepped in. "I hear Stuart is a bit of a bully. What were you and Stuart talking about?"

Anna slouched against the island. "Stuart is going out with my best friend, Chloe. I was trying to find out what their plans were for the weekend."

"Why didn't you ask Chloe?" Cathy interjected.

"Because Chloe and I aren't talking much these days. Since she started dating Stuart I hardly see her, even at school. She's usually off with Stuart in his car."

"And her mother's okay with that?"

Anna shrugged. "Who knows? Besides, her mother does whatever her stepdad says."

"But you've been friends for years. Is it upsetting you? Do you want to talk about that? I'm worried it's affecting you more than you know, because your grades are down. And what about volleyball? Did you go to practice today?" Cathy asked.

Even though Cathy's words were expressing her concern for her daughter's well-being, her tone of voice was harsh and accusatory. With each sentence she'd gotten louder, her anger more evident...and a bit fearsome.

Anna hunched her shoulders as she looked at Mark. "Can you please tell my mom that sometimes I just don't feel like going to practice?"

She was clearly not telling the whole story. He knew from Melody there was more happening at the school than a simple disagreement, and being too tired for volleyball. "Cathy, I suggest you call the guidance counselor and set up a meeting as soon as possible."

"What? You don't believe me?" Anna demanded.

"That's the whole point. I do believe you. We both do. We need to hear your side of the story," he said.

"Whose side are you on?" Cathy asked, turning her attention to him.

Seeing the anxiety in her eyes made him wish he hadn't decided to stay. Anna might accept his help, but Cathy still didn't trust him. "I'm not on anybody's side. I simply believe there are issues here that need to be addressed."

"Mark, this isn't fair. We need to—"

"To do what? Let this continue?" he demanded, impatient with both mother and daughter. "We can either talk this out with Mrs. Chapman and help Anna get her life back on track, or we can watch Anna's marks get worse and her drop out of more school activities."

Anna glanced from one to the other. "I don't really see the problem. Every kid in my class has had an argument with Stuart. Arguing is his favorite thing to do." She turned to her mother. "I told you I'd handle this."

"Then why is the school calling me?"

"I don't know," Anna said, her head bowed.

"I'll call the school," Cathy said, resignation in her voice. "Maybe Melody can see me today."

Watching Cathy, Mark was concerned that she never seemed to be able to get information from her daughter. Once again Cathy's anger and her daughter's evasiveness had blocked any real communication. Cathy was clearly unable to really confront her daughter, and each time Anna got into a difficult situation she didn't confide in her mother.

Melody agreed to see Cathy, and Mark insisted on joining her. Being with her at the meeting meant she wouldn't doubt who he was supporting.

.　.　.

They left Anna at home and drove to the school in separate cars. Cathy would have liked to travel with him, to express her appreciation for his help. He could have walked away as he had before, but he'd stayed and put up a fight to get her to see things the way they were. He was right about her approach to Anna. Each time she came close to getting answers, she let her daughter off the hook.

"I'm so pleased to see you, Cathy," Melody said once they arrived at her office. She indicated they should sit on the sofa near the window. "Okay, I'll get right to the point. There is something going on between your daughter and Stuart Jameson. I think it has to do with Chloe Ferguson, but I'm not sure."

"Anna says that she and Stuart had an argument, that Stuart argues with everyone."

"That could be true."

Cathy shifted in her seat, her agitation growing. "What do I do?" She turned to Mark. "You saw how evasive she is when I ask her about anything."

"Has this evasiveness been going on for long?" Melody asked.

"No. Just the past few weeks." She glanced from Melody to Mark. "I want you to understand that Anna is not like this. She has always been truthful with me. She and I have always been able to talk, until recently."

"I believe you," Mark said, turning to Melody. "Anna has not said anything, other than she wants to deal with Stuart on her own. To me, this suggests she's afraid to seek help from the school, afraid of what her friends will say or do."

Mark articulated what Cathy wanted to say, and so much better than she would have managed in her agitated state. "Thank you," she said to him. Two words she meant with all her heart.

Melody directed her attention to Cathy. "Okay. Here's what we're going to do. I'll talk to her homeroom teacher. I'll speak to Stuart and Chloe, and then I'll get in touch with the school psychologist, Ed Jenkins, who is due back next week. I think the best way to proceed is for you, Anna and I to talk about this. Get Anna to understand that she's not alone, but that she has to tell someone what's going on."

Relief flowed through her. "Kyle Donahue may know, but he's very loyal to Anna. I'm sure he wouldn't tell me anything without asking Anna first."

They talked a little longer, and Cathy found herself watching Mark as he spoke in such clear terms about his concern for Anna. Regardless of how she had first felt about him, it was clear that the man really cared about children, especially Anna.

As they walked out of the building, he turned to her and asked, "Would you like to go out to dinner sometime?"

"I—I don't know. Are you sure?" she asked.

"It would only be dinner. I'll tell you about my home life."

"Your home life?"

"I share my condo with a couple of cats."

"Cats? You?"

"Why not me?" he asked, his eyes crinkling in a smile.

"Do you practice your psychology techniques on your cats?" she asked.

"If I had, they might be much better behaved," he said, touching her arm as they walked across the parking lot.

She was aware of how good she felt with Mark by her side.

He opened the car door for her. "I meant what I said about dinner."

If she'd been a cat, she would have purred in happiness.

CHAPTER TWELVE

a few days later, Cathy entered the office, her feet hurting in her high heels, her back aching, but she didn't care. She had just sold a million-dollar home to a young couple who owned a computer software company. She had spent a full day looking at three carefully selected houses in their price range. All her planning and work had paid off in the biggest sale she'd ever made. And after what she'd been through with Anna these past few weeks, she was happier than she'd been for long time.

Life was back on track. She'd had a call from Melody saying that Anna was doing better but that she still wanted to meet. They'd set up a meeting between the three of them for Monday, which meant that she had tomorrow and the weekend to enjoy.

Cathy believed that Butch had something to do with the change in her daughter, as she'd been spending every minute she could with the puppy. Anna insisted on going to Margaret's house each night after volleyball practice. Anna was spending less time with Kyle. Although Chloe hadn't reappeared in Anna's life, Cathy had begun to believe that the worst was over. She was almost looking forward to the meeting with Melody.

Gina glanced up when she entered the office. "You did it. I can tell by the look on your face."

"The look of someone who can now afford to take her daughter on a nice vacation. Are you talking about that look?" Cathy asked playfully.

"You bet."

Cathy kicked off her shoes and put her feet up on the desk. "I could really get to like this lifestyle."

"Couldn't we all? So does this mean a celebration?"

"I haven't had time to think about a celebration. I'm still back there watching the couple's enthusiasm over the house. The closing is next Monday—that's how much they want it."

The phone rang. Cathy leaned forward. "I've got it." She had already worked over seven hours today but was ready to keep going. "Town and Country Realty, how may I help you?"

"You sneaky bitch! Why won't you let Anna come here?"

When had Anna talked to Scott? The last conversation Cathy was aware of had taken place over a week ago, and Anna had been in tears afterward. "Scott, you're yelling at me."

"I just called Anna, and she says she isn't coming."

"I didn't know that."

"Like hell you didn't," he yelled, forcing Cathy to hold the phone away from her ear.

"Scott?" Gina mouthed.

Cathy nodded.

"Are you there?" Scott yelled again.

"Stop shouting, Scott." She recalled the therapist recommending not engaging with his accusations until he calmed down. She'd suggested Cathy draw attention to his behavior, stating what she wanted him to change, until he listened.

"I will when you tell me how you're going fix this."

He had lowered his voice, so she decided to talk to him.

"You didn't want Anna to visit you and Cindy last time she talked to you. What changed?"

"My wife and I would like to take her to a resort for a few days."

"You mean you want her to babysit while you and Cindy play golf," Cathy replied.

"Yeah, leave it to you to take Anna's side on this," he said, his voice low and calculating.

"Well, whose side would I be—"

The line went dead in her ear. "He hung up."

"Great. You don't need that bully ruining your day. What'd he want this time?"

She sighed. "You were right all along. He'd promised Anna a vacation, failing to mention she'd be babysitting most of the time. All I can say is thank you, Butch."

"Should we call this the Butch effect?" Gina asked, closing her computer.

"Absolutely. Who would have thought a dog, of all things, could change so much in my life? Whatever it takes to keep peace at my house, I'm doing," she said, giving a double thumbs-up to her friend. She stretched her neck. "I could stand a break from all the parenting stuff."

Gina sighed. "How well I know."

The phone rang again. Cathy held up her hand. "I'll take it. It might be Scott." She picked up the receiver. "Town and Country Realty, how may I help you?"

"Hi, Cathy, it's Mark."

"Hi, Mark." She hadn't heard from him since they'd parted company in the school parking lot the week before. She'd expected him to call, and hearing his voice thrilled her. "How are you?"

"I'm fine. What's new with you?"

"I just made a big sale."

"Congratulations. That means that what I'm calling about will fit right in."

She held her breath and exchanged glances with Gina. "Which is?"

"I want to take you out to dinner this evening."

His deep voice played straight to her eager heart, making her pulse pick up speed. "I'd love to go out. Will your cats be there?"

He laughed. "No. That's for another dinner date. Where would you like to go?"

"Anywhere is fine as long as I don't have to cook."

His chuckle made her feel happy and pleased. "When should I pick you up?"

She glanced at her watch, saw the mess her nails were in and did a rough calculation. "How about eight?"

"I'll be at your door by eight."

Cathy put the phone down gently, her head still swimming with the excitement of an evening with a man she was seriously attracted to. "I've just been handed the perfect way to finish off a successful day."

Gina grinned. "Don't tell me. You're going out on a date?"

"With Mark Wilson."

"How long has this been going on?"

"I'm not sure anything is going on, but I'm about to find out."

"This is a great chance for you to celebrate."

"And go out with a normal man." She pulled her ponytail tighter. "It would seem there are a few of them out there, and one of them wants to take me out to dinner." She propped her chin on her hands, enjoying her first real moment of excitement in weeks.

"What are you going to wear?" Gina asked. "And please don't tell me you're not going to buy something new. Out celebrating with a handsome man is huge."

"It is, isn't it?"

"Then, what are you waiting for? Go shopping and make a night of it. You deserve a little fun. On one condition, of course."

"That would be?"

"That you give me all the details tomorrow morning. If Mark turns out to be someone special, it will be my turn to celebrate."

"I've got a better idea—why don't you come downtown with me and help me find something?"

"I'd love that." Gina continued to make plans as they left the office and drove through the afternoon traffic. Her enthusiasm added to Cathy's excitement.

Wasn't it funny how when her life seemed to be falling apart in one area, it was getting so much better in another?

Later that evening, goose bumps danced up her arms as she entered O'Toole's Restaurant with Mark at her side. She felt beautiful and sexy in the peach silk blouse and chocolate-brown pants. She'd smudged her nail polish in her rush to get ready, but walking beside him now, somehow a messy manicure didn't matter.

As the waiter led them to their table, Mark's fingers pressed ever so gently into her spine, sparking a mix of surprise and pleasure. As he leaned closer, his very male scent wafted around her. She glanced at him, admiring the way his dark hair curled around the collar of his white shirt.

When they reached the table, he held the chair out for her. Watching the grace with which Mark moved to the other side of the table and sat down, she considered herself lucky. She just happened to be sitting across the table from the handsomest man in the room, a man who commanded the attention of every other woman in the restaurant.

He smiled at her as he rested his arms on the table, his sleeves rolled neatly, showing off his tanned forearms. She hadn't noticed the muscles before, probably because the last time she'd seen his arms she'd been busy figuring out how a fishing rod worked.

She was suddenly aware of how brown his eyes were, so focused on her she could barely breathe...and those lips. The memory of his mouth on hers left her scrambling for control.

"How was your day?" Mark asked.

"I sold a house—my biggest deal yet. The commission will allow me to take Anna on a vacation somewhere nice."

"That's fantastic. And a vacation sounds like a great idea. Where would you go?"

"We've never been to Disney, so we may go there. We also talked about Arizona."

The waiter took their orders and Mark asked for a bottle of champagne to celebrate her success. After the waiter uncorked the bottle and poured two glasses, Mark raised his glass to her. "Congratulations to my favorite real estate agent."

"Thank you. I am really happy that things are turning around for me, and for Anna."

Mark watched mesmerized by the way Cathy's fingers caressed the stem of champagne flute. If someone had told him a few weeks ago that he'd be having dinner with Cathy Collins, the woman he'd dubbed Ms. Angry, he would have laughed. He wasn't laughing now. He was intrigued. No, make that charmed by her attention, her eagerness as she described her day.

Yet, as pleased as he was for her success, he had a hard time keeping his gaze away the way her red hair lay along the edge of her chin, the swell of her breasts under the smooth fabric of her blouse, the pouty softness of her lips.

He tried to focus on her story about the couple who had hit

it big in the software business and were setting up their offices in Spencer Island and needed a home. Instead he imagined what it would be like to kiss her, undress her, make love to her.

"I've been talking about me. Now it's your turn. Do you like being a psychologist?" she asked.

"Do I like it?" he repeated, struggling to pull his brain away from the fantasy pathway he'd been following. "Being a child psychologist is...difficult at times, but extremely rewarding, as well. My problem is that I tend to take my job too seriously, which has created problems for me in the past."

Her gaze was direct, her interest evident. "I can't imagine what it would be like to work with teenagers all the time. But I admire anyone who can. Why did you become a psychologist?"

"I loved children. I went to college to become a psychologist. My wife was a psychologist." Why had he brought Maria into the conversation? As he looked into her eyes, he realized that he wanted to share his life with Cathy.

"Tell me about her," she said gently.

"My wife died giving birth to our daughter three years ago," he said, his tone flat, without emotion, the memories tearing at him.

She reached across the table and took his hand, her face showing compassion. "I'm so sorry. That must have been awful."

Mark laced his fingers through hers. "It was. But time has helped me get past the worst of the pain." He raised his gaze to hers. "I'd rather not talk about it tonight. I don't want to ruin our first date with my sad story. This is a time for celebration."

"You told me you had cats, and I've been waiting to hear about them," she said with a smile.

He kept her hand in his, unable to let go. "Growing up, we always had cats. Mom wanted us to have pets, and cats are low maintenance. Jericho and Lazarus are SPCA graduates, brothers, and the best estimate of age the vet could come up with was that they're almost five years old."

"How did you pick the names?"

He shook his head slowly at the memory. "I'm a creature of habit. This is the third pair of cats named Jericho and Lazarus."

Her laughter was musical. He felt crazy happy to be able to make her laugh.

"So, tell me what they're like."

"You have to see them to understand. They run the household. I do as I'm told."

Cathy tilted her chin as she laughed. "I'd like to see that."

He wanted to sit right here and hold her hand all evening. "Tell me how you got into real estate," he asked, wanting to learn everything he could about her.

"I'm really lucky that Gina took a chance on me," she said, partially distracted by his hand on hers.

The touch made her yearn for something she'd refused to even consider—that there might be a man who could care for her. Someone who was capable of genuinely caring, and who was honest enough to be open and willing to share. If her divorce had taught her one thing, it was that a relationship had to be a mutual give-and-take. That honesty and sharing had an important role in the love and acceptance that made a relationship special.

"Gina had just left the big national real estate firm she'd been working for, and wanted to start up her own. I was amazed that she wanted me in her new company. I wanted to prove that she'd made the right decision by taking a chance on me. Then, she made me a partner. I'm so lucky in that respect."

"And you are friends, as well."

"We are. When you work hard in the same office, you learn

to depend on each other. After that it's easy for a friendship to form."

Their food arrived, and the scent of fresh rosemary and the rich flavoring of the lamb roast tantalized her senses. How long had it been since she'd had a date as nice as this? She couldn't remember...

"How's your lamb?" he asked, putting his fork down.

"It's the best I've had in a long time. And you?"

"I've never tasted anything this good." He pointed to the artfully arranged veal dish he'd been eating. "I do a lot of cooking at home. I think I'm pretty good, but this is excellent."

"You cook?" she asked, pleasantly surprised by his admission.

"Of course. One of these days I'll invite you over for dinner and you'll see."

"And don't forget my date with Lazarus and Jericho," she teased. She couldn't help imagining what his home was like, how he looked when he was cooking, what could happen after the meal...

It would be lovely to have someone she cared about, someone who could make her laugh and had the potential to entertain her and give her a chance at a social life. At this stage in her life, that was all she really wanted...wasn't it?

Cathy was savoring a bite of lamb when Sally Jones, another real estate agent, arrived at the table. Sally was a petite blonde with a heart of gold, an entertaining woman who loved gossip.

"Hi, Cathy, how are you?" Sally asked as her gaze honed in on Mark.

"Fine, thank you, Sally. This is Mark Wilson."

"So nice to meet you," Sally said, her flirty smile having little impact on Mark, secretly pleasing Cathy.

They chatted for a few moments before Sally slid into the chair beside Cathy. "Look, I know this is not the time or place, but I'm going out of town tomorrow. Before I go I need to tell you something."

"What?" Cathy asked, wondering what juicy bit of gossip Sally wanted to divulge.

Sally leaned closer. "I know you've had problems with Anna, and you probably don't need any more, but I saw her downtown the other night. She and a tall boy—Kyle Donahue, I believe—were with that Stuart Jameson kid."

Shocked, Cathy looked to Mark to see his expression mirrored hers. Sally had to be mistaken. Anna had been at home all week. "What night?"

Sally's face creased in thought. "It was Wednesday night last week, because I was coming back from a hospital board meeting. I was on Lower Water Street near the dock, and there they were. I nearly hit Kyle when he jumped away from something Stuart held in his hand."

Cathy felt the blood drain from her face. "Are you certain?"

"Absolutely. I was going to stop and offer Anna a ride, but she and Kyle walked away. I had planned to call you at the office and tell you, but I was afraid that you'd think I was meddling. Seeing you tonight, I decided to tell you. Hope you don't mind," Sally said, her voice contrite.

Wednesday night. Cathy had left Anna at home working on an assignment while she did a few showings. Kyle had arrived just before she left, and everything had seemed fine. "No, not at all. Thank you for telling me. I appreciate it."

With that, Sally moved on. Cathy's appetite gone, her thoughts on Anna, she stared at Mark. "This can't be true. Anna... I never thought to check on her. How could I be so dumb?"

"You're not dumb. You're dealing with a teenager."

"What am I going to do?" she asked. Fear and anger choked her. What had her daughter been doing that night?

"You're going to have to talk to her."

"You're right. "I'm going home and we're having it out. This is the end of the road for me. I've done everything I can to help her, to be understanding, and this is how she shows her appreciation."

Mark waved the waiter over. "Can I have the check?"

"Certainly, sir," the waiter said.

Mark reached across the table, taking her hand in his. His skin was warm, his touch so appealing. "I'm going with you."

"You don't have to."

"But I want to."

She met his gaze and recognized something she'd been searching for all her life. Someone who was willing to be there for her without being asked. "I don't know what's going on, but Stuart Jameson is bad news. He's totally pampered and spoiled by his parents."

"It happens." Mark paid for their meals, then said, "Are you ready?"

She nodded. "By the way, thank you for dinner."

He put his arm around her shoulders and pulled her close. "We'll do this again, and next time we'll really celebrate. What do you say?" He smiled at her, creating a warmth close to her heart.

It would be so wonderful to stay in his arms, to take delight in being with him. All she'd ever wanted was a happy home with children and a man who loved her.

She allowed herself several precious seconds while she leaned into his arms, letting his strength shield her from the betrayal she felt at the hands of her daughter.

When they arrived at her house, Cathy spotted the lights on in the den. Kyle's car was parked on the street. "I don't want to go in and confront Anna with this. I'm so angry right now," she said, staring at her front door, remembering better times, moments of sheer joy, all the memories tied up in her beautiful daughter. "How did this go so wrong?"

He took her hand in his, the warmth of him reassuring her. "Let's wait and see what she has to say," Mark said, his voice consoling.

She stared at her house then pointed to the flagstone path that led to the backyard. "We had Anna's first birthday on the patio out back. There are so many memories in this house, so many good times," she said.

"And there will be good memories again." His eyes met hers, creating an intimacy, a sense of togetherness that filled her heart.

In the span of a heartbeat, she knew. She could love this man who sat so quietly beside her, encouraging her to do what had to be done. "I'm so glad you're here with me," she said.

"I am, too. We can't put this off any longer. Anna is probably wondering why we haven't moved from here," he said.

"You're right. I'm ready when you are."

He got out, went around the car and opened her door. "We're in this together," he said as he reached for her hand.

CHAPTER THIRTEEN

ollowing Cathy toward her house, Mark was very anxious. It had been a long time since he'd let anyone close to him. Yet in the past few weeks, his life had shifted in an unfathomable way.

And now he had unexpectedly found someone he cared for, someone he hadn't expected to care for. Yet, each time he saw Cathy, he felt a bond forming between them, a sense that they were reaching a point of togetherness, of need that couldn't be explained by friendship alone.

He'd never met a woman so completely driven by her need to be a good person, to be seen in a positive light by others, always seeking proof of her self-worth—only to come up against a situation that was beyond her control.

He understood better what drove her, shared her need to protect and care for Anna.

Sensing Cathy's distress, he smiled at her. "You can do this."

"I needed to hear that," she said.

He could only imagine what she must be feeling right now, knowing that she had to confront her daughter with evidence of her lies and evasion. The professional in him knew this meeting was overdue. The part of him that had begun to see Cathy as more than a friend wanted to shield her from a potentially difficult discussion. He wanted to reassure her all would work out, but he knew that was his optimism talking. There was a real possibility this conversation could make things worse between Cathy and Anna before anything would improve. But he was here to help Cathy through whatever happened.

Cathy put her purse on the kitchen counter, calling out to Anna as she did so.

"We're in the family room, Mom," Anna said.

She walked purposely into the room, fixing her daughter with a stern gaze. "At dinner tonight, someone informed us you two were seen on Lower Water Street late on Wednesday evening a week ago."

Anna leaned forward, tucking her hair behind her ears. "We weren't doing anything wrong."

"You sneaked out of the house. That's wrong. You met up with someone you know can't be trusted, someone you've been having problems with at school. I'd say that's wrong, too."

"It wasn't that way at all," Anna said, twisting a strand of her hair.

"So meeting with Stuart late at night was a social event?" Cathy asked, not giving a damn how sarcastic she sounded.

Anna looked at Kyle but said nothing.

Cathy glared at her daughter. "Anna, why did you sneak out to meet Stuart, of all people? And don't lie to me again. I've had it with your lies and lack of respect."

Anna glanced at Kyle then at her mother. "Mom, you don't understand what's going on."

"That's the whole point," Mark interjected. "You two owe Cathy an explanation. Are you into drugs? Sleeping together?

Having unsafe sex? What is it? What in hell is going on between you two?"

Kyle rubbed his palms along his thighs, his gaze swinging from Cathy to Anna. "I don't want you to be angry at us."

"Well, I can't be much angrier than I am right now," Cathy muttered.

There was a long silence that Kyle finally broke. "We can't go on like this, Anna. Tell them."

Apprehension grabbed Cathy. As if sensing her disquiet, Mark moved toward her, his hand reaching for hers. She squeezed his fingers.

Anna leaned back, emitting a long sigh as she scrubbed her face with her hands. "I'm gay."

Cathy choked. "You're what?"

"I'm gay. I didn't want you to find out this way. I wanted to tell you when all this was over, but I can't let you blame Kyle for what's going on here. He's the best friend I have, and I'm sorry he's mixed up in all of this."

Cathy sank onto the sofa and gripped the edge, struggling to remain focused in spite of the emotions crowding her. Of all the reasons she'd come up with to explain her daughter's behavior, she'd never considered that Anna might be gay. How had she missed this?

And yet...Anna had never talked about boys, about dating, safe sex or anything like that. Cathy had been ready with all the information she could find, wanting to guide her daughter through the initial relationship pitfalls. When Anna hadn't asked questions, Cathy had assumed she and Chloe were talking. Chloe had had several boyfriends, had talked at length about them over the various meals she'd had here. Anna had said nothing, and still Cathy hadn't considered that Anna might be gay. Cathy had simply assumed that, like herself, Anna was a late bloomer, that with all her school activities she'd had little time or inclination to be involved with boys.

"That's quite a secret to carry around," Mark said, settling close to Cathy on the sofa.

Acutely aware that Anna was waiting for her to say something Cathy struggled to find the right words. "Anna, how long have you known?" she asked, realizing too late that what her daughter needed was her support and understanding, not a question.

"I have never been interested in dating boys. I like them. They're my friends, but that's all," Anna said, her voice calm.

Kyle focused his attention on Mark and Cathy. "Anna told me about a year ago. She wasn't trying to keep a secret, she simply hadn't decided when the best time would be to tell anyone other than me."

"This has been so hard. Everyone at school is talking behind my back,' Anna said, her voice growing more unsteady with each word.

Cathy clutched Mark's hand as she leaned toward her daughter. "Why didn't you tell me sooner? I would have understood."

"I didn't know how. And I didn't want to worry you."

"Worry me? Why would you being gay worry me? It's the secrets that do that,' Cathy said, her voice shaking. "If you're mixed up with Stuart, it's serious. Tell me the truth."

Mark gave her a cautionary glance.

"I have to know," she whispered to him.

"I'm being bullied at school because I'm gay. Stuart is one of the ones doing the bullying. We met with him Wednesday night to try to get him and his friends to stop."

As their eyes met, Cathy crossed the room, her arms extended, her heart breaking for her daughter. "Oh! No! I'm truly sorry you felt you couldn't tell me. I should have paid more attention to what was going on in your life."

Anna stepped into Cathy's embrace, returning it with a strong hold. She poured all her love for Anna into the hug.

When they broke apart, they settled onto the sofa together. "I'm sorry, too, Mom."

Cathy pressed her daughter's head against her shoulder, in awe of how brave she was to accept who she was and stand true to herself. Anna's strength filled Cathy's heart to overflowing. "Don't be. You have nothing to be sorry for."

Cathy looked at Mark, his smile encouraging her. There was a lot to say, a lot to get straightened out if they were going to help Anna through this. "You are not in this alone anymore," she said, kissing Anna's forehead. "Mark and I want to help, so please, tell us what's been going on."

Anna eased out of her mother's embrace. "It started after volleyball practice about four weeks ago. When I came out of the locker room, Stuart was waiting, taunting me about being gay. He tried to push me around, but I didn't let him. When one of his buddies showed up, I left.

"I don't know how he found out, or if he simply made a good guess. Kyle's the only one I've told. We've talked about how I might handle anyone at school finding out. I decided that I would not hide over this because if I started now, I would spend years hiding from who I really am."

"Do you know how brave you are?" Cathy asked.

Anna gave her a shaky smile.

Kyle spoke up. "Stuart started following us around. The incident on the sidewalk was with Stuart and Erie Sanford."

"Why didn't you tell anyone?" Mark asked, a frown of concentration on his face.

"I didn't want to cause any more trouble. I thought that if I ignored them, they'd go away," Anna said. "I convinced Kyle not to tell anyone."

"Why not tell someone at the school? The principal or psychologist?" Mark asked.

"If I accused Stuart and his friends of bullying and word got out around school, there would be so much talk. If Coach

Cassidy found out, I was afraid that he might not be very understanding. I didn't know what to do. It was all such a mess, and Stuart wouldn't leave me alone."

A sudden wave of protectiveness rose through her at Anna's words. "Anna, why didn't you tell me about Stuart, about your plan to meet him?"

"I was afraid that you'd be angry. I didn't want to upset you."

In that moment Cathy saw clearly how her anger had caused her daughter unnecessary pain. Whatever it took, she would learn to control her anger. "But I would have helped you."

"After you were done yelling at me, or before?" Anna asked.

"Anna!"

"Be honest, Mom. You would have been angry, and I couldn't face that with so much going on. When we met them Wednesday night to talk, we felt we had no choice. But they were as mean to Kyle as they were to me. We should have known we couldn't change their minds."

"You could have been hurt," Cathy said. "You left yourselves vulnerable by going to meet them alone."

Mark spoke up. "Bullying doesn't go away on its own. Bullies are cowards who prey on people they believe are more vulnerable, people who won't fight back. We're going to put a stop to this. We'll go to the police if necessary."

"What if we tell the school or the police and the bullying gets worse?" Anna asked.

"Stuart threatened to come after us if we told anyone," Kyle said.

"I'm afraid," Anna said, wrapping her arms around herself and sinking into the cushions.

Her daughter looked so fragile. Cathy stroked her hair, remembering when Anna was a little girl and would come to her with her childhood problems, seeking her mother's help with whatever had upset her. Problems that now seemed so small. "Anna, we'll work this out. You and Kyle will not be hurt again by this."

"Mom, it's okay. I should have trusted you. Now I've dragged everyone into this mess."

Anna's troubled gaze broke Cathy's heart. "I'm sorry that I wasn't easier to talk to. I should have been more willing to listen."

"I appreciate all the concern, but I don't see where the school or the police can help," Kyle said. "You don't know Stuart. I think the teachers are afraid of him and his family."

"Mark, isn't there a program of zero tolerance at the high school?" At his nod, she looked at Anna. "We'll all speak to the principal and insist the administration take action. These bullies have to be stopped. There could be other students involved. You may not be the only victims."

"I'm not a victim," Anna said, her tone forceful.

"Yes, you are," Mark said, sitting across from Anna. "You are a victim of bullying, and it won't stop until it's forced to stop. That means getting others involved and taking action."

Anna chewed her lip in concentration. "That reminds me of something. There was a girl in my class who was dating Stuart, and she stopped coming to school last year just before exams in June. She'd been complaining that her stomach hurt and she couldn't concentrate. I heard the other day that she is going to a private school out of state. Maybe he was threatening her, too."

"It's possible. Regardless of whether anyone else is involved, we will make this stop. You will not have your school years ruined by these people. That's final," Mark said.

"Anna, I agree with Mark. We need to do something."

"I'm done at school if people find out that I'm gay and I can be bullied,' Anna muttered.

"There's always Mrs. Chapman, our guidance counselor. She's cool—all the kids like her. Maybe we can meet with her quietly without the whole school finding out," Kyle said, frowning.

"We'll go with you," Cathy and Mark said in unison.

Anna sat up straight. "I'm not sure that's such a good idea. What about this? Why don't Kyle and I go first and see what Mrs. Chapman says?"

Seeing the worried expression on Anna's face, Cathy squeezed her hand. "I'm sure the school is prepared to handle this sort of situation. If not, we will find a solution on our own."

"Like what?" Anna asked.

Cathy exchanged glances with Mark. "I might have to consider private schooling. I'll talk to your father if needed."

"Definitely not, Mom," Anna said emphatically. "Dad can't know about this. He would be upset with me, and after the last time we talked..."

How well Cathy remembered that awkward phone call...not to mention the scathing one she'd received today. "Okay. We won't tell your dad, but we are going to do something about this. You're my daughter, and this has to stop."

Anna smiled. "Mom on the warpath."

"You haven't seen anything yet," Cathy said, trying to lighten the mood. "Okay, we'll go along with your plan to talk to Mrs. Chapman."

The relief on Anna's face was palpable.

"Maybe it's time we all got some rest," Cathy said.

Minutes later Cathy walked out to the car with Mark. "Thank you."

He unlocked the door, turned to her and pulled her gently into his arms. "You're welcome," he said, kissing her.

She moved into his embrace, her head spinning with emotion—elation and gratitude in equal measure.

His hands moved soothingly over her back, his forehead pressed to hers. "You're not alone, Cathy. I'm here."

"I wish you could stay," she whispered, the strength of his body, the easy way he held her, both frightening and reassuring.

"I will some night soon. But you need to be with Anna."

As he eased away from her, she slid her hand into his. "Promise me?"

"I promise."

A few hours later, unable to sleep, Cathy got up and went to the kitchen for a glass of water. The clock on the stove glowed 3:00 a.m. Her mind wouldn't stop replaying the evening and what Anna had to have gone through these past weeks.

Although she'd been very clear that something had to be done, Cathy wasn't sure what the best approach would be. Leaning against the counter, she drank slowly, focused on tomorrow and what it might bring. She needed at least a couple of hours sleep if she was going to be able to go to work.

She put the glass in the dishwasher and checked to make sure her cell phone was plugged in. On the way to her room, she heard Anna sobbing as she spoke urgently to someone. Her heart lurched in her chest, fear rising. She eased the door open. "Anna, what is it?"

Anna was curled up on her bed, clutching the phone to her ear, the stain of tears darkening the pillow under her head. "I gotta go." She ended the call and tucked the phone under her pillow.

"Anna, why are you on your phone at this hour?"

"I was checking with Kyle about something," she mumbled.

"Are you all right?" Why did she ask such a dumb question? Of course, she wasn't all right. Moving to sit on the bed, she gently tucked the comforter around Anna's shoulders, smoothing the fabric over her bony shoulders, an old habit from the days when she would crawl into bed with her daughter to help her get to sleep. "What can I do?"

"Everything's a mess." Cathy scooped Kermit the Frog off

the shelf over her head and tucked him next to her, a gesture so familiar, so much a part of Anna's childhood. How much about her daughter had changed, and yet how much had remained the same.

"Whatever it is, you can tell me."

Anna stared at the wall as Cathy tucked a long strand of blond hair behind her daughter's ear, willing Anna to share what was bothering her.

"I just got a really nasty text message."

"Who would do that, and at this hour?"

"I'd left my phone on because Kyle was going to call me so I could get up early to study. I'm not certain who sent the text, as I didn't recognize the number, but it had to be someone at school."

"What did it say?"

"I—I can't tell you."

"Anna, I need to know what's going on. Did you save the message? Who sent it?"

"It doesn't matter."

"Yes, it does. This can't be allowed to go on."

"Mom, please, you don't understand what it's like at school for Kyle and me."

Her heart ached for Anna, for her fear and loneliness. "How long have you been getting these text messages?"

"For a while."

Anger rose through Cathy at the thought her daughter had to face cyberbullying in addition to the incidents at school. Where were their parents in all this? Didn't they know their kids were on their cell phones doing things like this?

But she hadn't known that Anna was on her cell phone tonight. She'd assumed Anna was asleep. "I wish I'd known about this."

"And what would you do?" Anna asked, her eyes stark.

"I don't know, but I wouldn't let you face it alone. Why don't I go with you to talk to the counselor at school?"

"Mom, Kyle and I are going to see Mrs. Chapman. Give us a chance, will you?"

"No, not if this is going to continue. The school needs to know just how far this bullying has gone."

"Don't you know how embarrassing that would be for me? To have you follow me to school?"

"I want to be sure we get this straightened out before it gets any worse. Anna, this is really serious."

Anna's gaze shifted from Kermit to Cathy. "Are you saying you don't trust me to meet with the guidance counselor?"

"I trust you and I admire your attitude. I'm only trying to get some sort of resolution to the problem before you get hurt again."

"You'll only make things worse if you show up at the school. Let Kyle and I talk to Mrs. Chapman tomorrow. I'm sure she'll help us. If she doesn't, then we'll do whatever you and Mark want us to do."

CHAPTER FOURTEEN

The next day, Cathy regretted that she hadn't insisted on going with Anna to the meeting with Melody. Cathy had watched Anna leave with Kyle and wished she could protect her from whatever happened today. After they left, she'd gone in to work, but her anxiety and sleep deprivation from the night before had made her unable to concentrate.

She'd come back home spent the past hour cleaning the counters and scrubbing the kitchen floor to keep busy. Surely Anna would call as soon as the meeting ended.

The doorbell rang, making her jump. She scrambled to answer the door. "Mark," she breathed in relief. His wide shoulders and warm smile were a welcome sight.

"How are you doing?" he asked, pulling her into his arms, the solidness of his body steadying her.

"I'm okay. I just wish they'd call or get back here or something," she said.

"They will," he said.

"Would you like a cup of coffee?" she asked as he followed her to the kitchen.

"Will it help to calm your nerves?" he asked.

"Probably not."

"You need to be doing something, is that it?" he asked, glancing around the newly scrubbed space, a wry grin on his face.

She liked the intimacy shining in his eyes. "I clean house when I'm worried."

"So that would mean you've got the cleanest house on the block," he replied, stepping out of the way as she filled the coffeepot with water. "You don't have to make coffee. We could simply sit and talk until they get home."

He was being so kind, so thoughtful, exactly what she needed in the circumstances. "I'd like that—"

"Mom," Anna called out as she and Kyle burst through the back door.

Cathy nearly dropped the coffeepot as she raced to her. "What's going on?" she asked. The sight of tears on Anna's cheeks wounded her. She wrapped Anna in a warm hug. "I'm so glad you're home. Mark's here. We're about to have coffee."

"In the middle of the afternoon? Were you that worried?"

Anna and Kyle sat at the table and Kyle started talking. "Chloe wouldn't come with us to see Mrs. Chapman. We asked her to, but she refused."

"Why did you need her?" Cathy asked.

"We thought she might support us when we explained everything." Anna made a dismissive gesture as if to say Chloe's refusal wasn't a big deal, but Cathy knew otherwise.

"Chloe thinks Stuart isn't a bad guy. She didn't believe us when we told her about Wednesday night on Lower Water Street," Kyle said.

"She's dating him, that's why," Anna said quietly.

Cathy reached across the table and took her hand. "What happened with Mrs. Chapman?"

"I told her about Stuart and Eric Sanford, about the fall, that they were both there and about trying to talk to Stuart on

Wednesday night. Mrs. Chapman...she seemed surprised." Tears slid quietly over Anna's cheeks as she spoke.

She swallowed, swiped at her cheeks and continued. "She said that Eric had never been in any kind of trouble that she knew of. I thought she didn't believe me. Especially when she wanted to know if there were any other witnesses."

"And you said?" Cathy asked, trying so hard to control her anger at the unfairness of it all.

"That Chloe wasn't willing to step forward and tell what was going on."

"Did Mrs. Chapman say anything to show she supported you? She certainly didn't hesitate to tell me what she thought where you were concerned."

Anna touched her mother's arm. "She was helpful in the end, Mom. It just took a little time to get her to understand what was going on. When I told her I'm being bullied because I'm gay, she said that the school would get to the facts and that I'm to tell her if there are any other incidents. In the mean time she would meet with the principal." Anna shrugged. "At least that part is over. I guess we have to wait and see. It was pretty awful, having to tell her everything. I wouldn't have gotten through it without Kyle's support." She smiled at him. "He was awesome."

"Anna, honey, I'm so sorry you had to go through all that. It's so unfair."

Anna stared at her hands. "Mom, what if Stuart doesn't stop?"

"Did Mrs. Chapman say anything else?" Mark asked as he sat next to Cathy.

"No, not really," Kyle answered, a frown on his face.

The wariness in Anna's eyes worried her. She couldn't imagine how she must be feeling right now. "Anna, I will go to the principal or the school board if I have to. In the meantime, I'm driving you to school and picking you up."

"No, Mom. Kyle has promised to drive me to school and back. I don't want Stuart and Eric to see you dropping me off. They will know I'm scared and that you're scared. It will only make things worse."

Mark squeezed Cathy's hand. "Anna's right, Cathy. The school now knows what's going on. Stuart and Eric will be called in and made aware of the accusations against them."

"And then what?" Cathy demanded.

"Cathy, please try to stay calm. I'll contact Mrs. Chapman to follow up. There won't be any more incidents if I can help it. And if there are, we'll deal with it. In the meantime, Anna needs to get on with her school life."

Anna jumped up and went to hug Mark. "You're awesome." She glanced over at Cathy. "I've got a lot of homework to do to catch up. I'd better get at it."

"Don't you want something to eat?"

"I'm not really hungry—maybe later. We'll work in my room and give you and Mark a little space." Before Cathy could react, Anna went to her room, Kyle trailing along behind her.

"Cathy, are you okay?"

Could she tell him how Anna's behavior made her feel? Could she trust him not to belittle her feelings or accuse her of being selfish? The way Scott had? She forced the memories of her ex-husband away and took a chance. "I feel awful."

"Why?" Mark asked gently.

"Because I want so much for Anna. I do everything I can for her, and yet—" she looked into his wonderful warm eyes—"and yet she hugged you, called you awesome."

"And you're hurt," he murmured, touching the nape of her neck.

She nodded, unable to trust her voice.

"Cathy, you have every right to feel the way you're feeling. But I don't know if you should place so much emphasis on her hugging me. Sometimes children take their parents for granted."

"Do you think she was upset when I got angry?"

"What parent wouldn't feel angry when their child is being threatened?"

"That's not how you felt a few weeks ago," she reminded him.

"That's because I know you better now, and I care about you. Anna's upset. You're upset. This is a very stressful situation." He put his arm around her. "You'll get through this, and then you and Anna can talk about how all this made you feel." He kissed her, his lips lingering on her mouth, driving her crazy with need.

"Anna is struggling. You are too," he whispered close to her ear.

"Why do you always say the right things?" she asked, soaking up his warmth. "Why do you never get angry?"

He held her hand. "When Maria wouldn't listen to me about her addiction to pain killers, I was furious. I said things that hurt both of us. I created a division between us that we never healed."

Seeing the sorrow in his eyes, she kissed him, offering him comfort. "It is so awful when you can see the problem but not be able to do anything about it."

He sighed. "I couldn't find a way to get through to her. She hid her pills and never confided in me again."

"I'm so sorry."

"Me, too," he whispered, pulling her closer. His gaze held hers, his sadness reflected in his eyes.

She'd never felt so close to another human being as she did to Mark. "Can you stay for a while?" she asked.

"I'd like to, but I have a session that I can't cancel. I would if I could," he said, his eyes roving over her face, his smile warming her. "Remember I'm cooking dinner one night soon."

155

"Promise me?"

"I promise. We'll set the date very soon."

She followed him to the door. "What can I bring?"

"You." He pulled her against him, his kiss knocking any sane thought from her mind. "I make the best pasta. You'll see what an amazing cook I am." He tapped her nose playfully.

The following Monday, Anna had the best time she'd had in weeks. Sweat rolled down her back as she tipped the last ball over the volleyball net, the final shot in the game. The cheer of the crowd was exhilarating, pushing the burn of her leg muscles to the back of her mind. In the seats under the windows, Kyle sat clapping wildly.

Surrounded by teammates as they jostled one another onto the court in celebration, Anna searched for her mother. She wished she hadn't had to tell her mother she was gay. She couldn't help feeling she'd let her mother down. All the times her mother had made quiet inquiries, dropped little hints about a boyfriend, Anna had had to pretend she didn't hear her or outright not answer her.

Mrs. Chapman had said there was a meeting today with the principal. Her stomach ached at what might happen when the school took action against Stuart and Eric.

Would everyone turn against her for reporting them? If Stuart was angry, he would tell everyone about her. If he hadn't already. Regardless of Mrs. Chapman's concern and support, Anna was afraid of what it would be like once the word got around.

"Great game," Kyle said as he strolled up to her.

"Thanks. Have you seen my mom?"

He glanced around. "No, I don't think so. I've got my phone. Do you want to call her?"

Her mother was probably busy at work. Since she reached

her sales target, she'd been determined to beat it so that they'd have a great vacation. She probably hadn't noticed the time, but she'd be all upset when she realized she missed the game. "She's probably roaring into the parking lot as we speak. What are you doing tonight?" Anna asked.

"I have to get home. My mom wants me to mow the lawn, and I have an economics test tomorrow."

Anna had stopped showering at the school because she didn't feel comfortable in the locker room. "I'm ready to leave when you are."

They walked out of the building into the late afternoon heat. She didn't see her mother's car. "Can I get a ride home with you?"

"Sure."

"I going to cook dinner for my mom tonight," she offered as they crossed the parking lot.

"Hot dogs and doughnuts?" he teased.

She faked a scowl. "That's the kind of attitude that *won't* get you asked to a meal at my house."

They reached his car and she tossed her sports bag in the backseat and rolled down the window after they got in. "So, what are you going to make for dinner?" he asked as he put the key into the ignition.

Anna didn't answer because her gaze was locked on a spot just beyond his shoulder.

"What is it?" He turned his head. Stuart was bearing down on them, a cruel smile on his face.

Anna swallowed over the lump in her throat. Fear ballooned around her heart.

"What do you want?" Kyle demanded.

Stuart braced his hands on the door, hostility oozing from him. "Well, hello, Mr. Donahue and Ms. Collins. I haven't had a chance to thank you both for getting me dragged into the principal's office. You know that being accused of bullying has never happened to me before."

Anna wanted to tell Kyle to drive off. She'd had enough of Stuart. She hated violence and fighting, but if she had to, she would fight. It was better than feeling like a victim every day.

Kyle gripped the steering wheel, glancing quickly at Anna. "Don't be afraid. I'll take care of this," he said, before taking a deep breath. He squinted up at Stuart. "I don't have all day, so if you have something to say—"

Stuart kicked the side of the car. "Get out and fight like a real man. Defend your gay friend. Let's see how that goes."

Cathy drove quickly along the ring road that framed the school grounds. She and Gina had met with a company relocating to town that wanted to contract them to help their employees find housing. It was a huge opportunity to grow their business.

Cathy hadn't wanted to miss Anna's game, but she'd felt she had no choice. She'd apologize when she picked Anna up, and they'd go out to dinner to celebrate. She'd texted Anna to say she'd be late but didn't get a response, which meant that her phone was probably in the bottom of her gym bag.

Cathy had briefly called Mark to tell him about the potential new clients, and he'd been excited for her. It felt wonderful to have someone to share news with, especially because he'd been so pleased for her.

She pulled into the school parking lot, spotting Kyle's red Toyota and steering toward it. As she got closer, she could see Anna running around the front of the car toward...Kyle and Stuart. Even from a distance she could see that something was wrong. Something about the way Kyle and Stuart squared off...

Anna ran toward Stuart, her hands raised. Cathy hit the gas. Tires squealed on the pavement as she clutched the wheel.

Barging between Anna and Stuart, Kyle reached for Stuart,

just as Stuart turned and pushed him into the driver's door. Cathy hit the horn long and hard, causing the three teenagers to glance her way. She hit the brakes, shut off the engine and jumped out. "What is going on here?"

"Stuart came after Kyle," Anna said, breathing hard.

"I did not. I was just talking to him. You were going to hit me and Kyle was, too. You saw it, Mrs. Collins, didn't you?"

While his story was technically true, she definitely didn't believe he was an innocent party in this matter. "Stuart, move away from them this minute," she said, striding toward them, her heart hammering in her chest. "Are you all right, Anna?"

"I'm fine. I wanted to hit him so bad, Mom."

"Anna, this is wrong. I'm sure you have your reasons, but violence is not the answer." She turned to Kyle. "What got into you two?"

Kyle slumped against the driver's door, his eyes never leaving Stuart. "I'm in trouble now, aren't I? But he threatened to go after Anna if I didn't get out of the car."

"And I didn't want Kyle to face him alone, so I got out with him. When he said I was trash just like my mother, I was so angry," she said as she flexed her fingers, staring at her hand as if it belonged to someone else.

Kyle shook his head. "Then he said my father was a liar and a cheat, and he knew some parents that were going to sue my dad." Kyle shoved away from the door and went over to Stuart. "You leave us alone, Stuart. We're not bothering you."

"We'll see who's bothering who. I'm going to the police. You and your bitch buddy, Anna, assaulted me—"

"Don't you ever say that again," Cathy yelled. She was tired of this. Tired of bullies like Stuart—like Scott—shooting off their mouths as if their mean-spirited opinions meant anything. If she didn't stand up for what she believed in and protect her daughter, she might as well go home. "Anna is off limits to you and all your ugly friends, do you understand?"

Stuart took a step back, his eyebrows shooting up his forehead. "Chill out, will you?"

This kid, standing there with a cocky look on his face, needed to be stopped. "You get in your car and you drive away from here now."

"Or what? You've already got us called into a meeting over bullying Anna, but I'm not putting up with it. I've now got proof that they're bullying me. So good luck getting anyone to believe them. Go ahead and try to get me and my friends suspended from school."

"That's a very good idea." Her calm words momentarily wiped the smug smile off his face.

"Just try it," he warned, his lips curled in a sneer.

"You stay away from my daughter and Kyle," she said with a power and authority she didn't feel.

"This isn't the end of it. Those two punks—" he nodded at Kyle and Anna "—assaulted me and they're going to pay."

Cathy was flushed with the same emotions she'd felt all those times she endured Scott's putdowns and nastiness. She wanted to strike out at something, anything that would make her feel as if she'd avenged herself and her child.

Stuart, with his snide, cocky attitude, would grow up to be a bully, just like Scott. Until someone stronger shut him up.

The truth was she'd never really confronted Scott. It was time she showed her daughter and Kyle that being bullied didn't have to be tolerated, that standing up for yourself was better than allowing someone to hurt you. "You just try doing anything to either of these two, and I will go to the police. That's a promise."

"Like hell you will," Stuart shot back as he moved toward his car, his feet almost dancing on the pavement. "I'll get you for this." With that he climbed in his car then drove off with a scream of tires on pavement.

"Mom, you were amazing." Anna cocked her head and

watched the retreating car, a triumphant smile on her face. "Totally amazing. I've never seen you like that before."

"And I've never seen you threaten to hit anyone before. What's that all about?" Cathy asked.

"Something snapped when Stuart threatened us. Kyle and I were minding our own business. Even though Stuart and his gang had been warned about bullying us, he acted as if no one could touch him. That's not right."

"Well, we have no choice but to go to the police and tell them what happened. But first, we're calling your parents, Kyle."

"Ah, please, don't. I'm supposed to be at home doing some yard work for Dad. I'll tell them what happened. I promise."

Cathy understood where he was coming from. She was so desperately tired of all this upset and uncertainty. But she was determined to defend her daughter properly, and that meant going to the police and having Kyle corroborate her story. "Okay. Anna, you come with me. Kyle, after you talk to your parents, ask them to call me. I'll call the police and set up an appointment. I'll try for early tomorrow morning."

"But we have school," Anna complained.

"You can be late for once."

"Okay, if you say so." Anna hugged Kyle, grabbed her things, then trudged off to Cathy's SUV.

At home, Anna made for the kitchen. "I'm starving."

"As a matter of fact, so am I," Cathy said, amazed that she could be hungry after what had gone on in the school parking lot.

"Okay. You talk, and I'll make grilled cheese sandwiches with dill pickles."

"Yuck!" Cathy teased. "Hold the dill pickles. And thank you for offering to make dinner."

"I'd hardly call this dinner," Anna said, pulling the frying pan from the drawer next to the stove, and getting the ingredients from the fridge.

"Mom, this probably isn't the greatest time to tell you this, but I really need to get it off my chest," Anna said as she placed the sandwiches carefully in the pan.

Cathy's heart beat harder. "Go ahead," she said warily, fearing that Anna had more bad news for her.

"I didn't mean to make you worry the way I did. Every time I had the chance to say what was going on, I didn't, and I'm sorry."

Cathy breathed a sigh of relief. "That's okay. I didn't do a very good job of listening, and we kind of got stuck not saying what we really believed. But it won't happen again, will it?"

Anna flipped the sandwiches from one side to the other before turning to face her mother. "I don't know, Mom. But I know one thing for sure—you are a good mom, and I'm so lucky."

Her eyes filling with tears, Cathy went to her daughter and wrapped her arms around her. "I'm the lucky one."

"Mom, I've been thinking about things. As much as I want to see Dad, I don't want to babysit for him. It isn't fair to me. If I go there, I want to visit with him, not look after his kids. I guess I'll have to find a way to tell him."

Cathy smoothed the hair off Anna's forehead the way she'd done so many times when she was a child. "I'm so glad you told me this. I've worried that your dad was trying to take advantage of you, but I didn't do a very good job explaining that, either."

Anna eased out of her mother's arms before answering. "For a long time, I thought you and Dad broke up over me, that I did something."

"Oh, no. Never." She hugged her daughter close again. "You had nothing whatsoever to do with us splitting up. We were simply not compatible on so many fronts. When you find someone to love and who loves you, I want you to be sure that you are with her for the right reasons."

The sizzling sound emanating from the pan reminded them that dinner was about to burn. Anna pulled the frying pan off the burner. "If I had a dollar for every time Chloe and I made grilled cheese sandwiches—"

"Speaking of Chloe, what's going on with her? Why is she involved with Stuart?"

Anna loaded two plates, grabbed the pickles from the fridge then went to the table. "Chloe and I had an argument. She believes she loves Stuart, of all people. How dumb is that?"

"I think Chloe has to work out her own problems, but maybe one day she'll come to you for help or advice, and you can be there for her."

"After today Stuart won't let Chloe speak to me again. Anyone that's part of his group at school has to be totally loyal to him."

"You must feel awful to think that Chloe and you aren't friends the way you used to be."

"I do. That's been part of the reason I didn't know what to do. I didn't want to hurt Chloe, but the day Stuart and Eric knocked me down and I ended up in the emergency room, Kyle and I knew we couldn't rely on Chloe to help us."

"You and Kyle have had a lot to deal with."

As Cathy got a couple of napkins from the drawer she remembered... "Guess what? I met my sales goal. What would you say to Disney for New Year's?"

"Mom! That's awesome!"

"I thought so, too. I've booked a week for us. We leave the day after Christmas." She smiled at her daughter, making a silent vow to settle the bullying issue before they left for Florida. Nothing would be allowed to stand in the way of their first real vacation in years. She was still smiling when the phone rang. The caller ID showed Mark Wilson. Thrilled to be hearing from him, she answered.

Mark heard Cathy's voice on the other end of the line, her soft tone taking the edge off his worry, making him feel better about the past few hours. He'd had another appointment with a young teenager today, a child so withdrawn Mark had referred him to a psychiatrist, thinking the child needed medication to help manage his anxiety.

Then his sister Amelia had called to say her husband, Greg, a fighter pilot, was being posted to Hawaii. Mark was closest to Amelia, and he would miss her a lot. They'd agreed to meet during Thanksgiving for a family reunion that Amelia was happy to organize.

"How's your day going?" he asked.

She gave a long, contented sigh. "So much better than I expected."

"That's great." He leaned against the counter in his kitchen, contented that he was getting a chance to talk to Cathy, to share his day. He loved feeling connected to her.

This morning as he was feeding his cats, he'd missed having someone in the house, someone to wake up to, to share something as silly as feline antics. It was the first time in such a long time he'd felt his solitude. But deep inside he was acutely aware that since he'd gotten to know Cathy a little better, he wanted to have someone in his life, someone to care about.

"Can you hold on for a minute? I need to get out of my suit. I've been in a meeting all day," Cathy said.

Waiting for her to come back on the line, he imagined her removing her suit, her body arching as she pulled her top off over her head... His body hardened at the image.

"Okay. I'm back. Sorry, it's been a long day and I need a chance to relax."

Her voice was warm and melodious, if a little breathless. "Let's see. I imagine you in yoga pants and a top, settling into a chair in front of the TV. You've probably got a health drink and a nutrition bar for your snack."

"Nope. Sweatpants, stretched out on my bed. And there's a bag of potato chips in the kitchen calling my name. I don't know why I buy them. I'm doing my best to fight off temptation, but I might be ready to give in and let the pounds climb on board."

"Hey. Me, too. My weakness is chocolate. Never met a chocolate bar I didn't like."

She laughed that laugh of hers that made him unreasonably happy.

"Speaking of chocolate, I make a really gooey chocolate dessert. It's a recipe I got on the internet. It's so delicious that Anna and I eat it straight out of the baking dish until there's nothing left."

"How would you like to make that gooey chocolate dish and bring it over here? Tomorrow night, maybe? I could make dinner while you get to know my cats."

There was a short pause. Did she already have a date?

"I would love to make my dessert and come to your house for dinner tomorrow night," she said, and he wanted to whoop with glee.

"Then it's a date. Come over around six thirty."

"I'll be there. And, Mark... I'm so glad you called. I haven't said this to you before, but I really appreciate that you're...that you've been around recently. I don't know what I would have done without you." She gave a nervous laugh. "And to think how much I once disliked you."

He was so happy to hear her say those words. "You had reason to feel that way. And I have a small confession of my own. I called because I wanted to hear your voice, to know how you're doing," he said, feeling the sincerity of his words deep in his heart.

Another pause filled the air. "I'm really looking forward to tomorrow night."

"I am, too. Not to mention Lazarus and Jericho. Just remember—don't wear anything that shows cat fur."

"I'll bring my own lint roller," she said, her laughter filling his heart.

"I promise you the best Italian meal you've ever had," he said, wishing that she was with him now.

CHAPTER FIFTEEN

*T*he next evening, Cathy arrived at Mark's condo, eager to see him. They'd talked earlier in the day after she'd had a call from Officer Winters setting up an appointment about the incident with Stuart in the school parking lot. Mark had agreed to go to the meeting, and they'd both decided that for this evening they would not discuss anything going on in Anna's life.

When he opened the door, she couldn't help but chuckle as she held out a bottle of red wine and the gooey dessert she'd promised. "An apron?"

He took her gift, kissing her quickly as he closed the door behind her. "Yeah, I'm housebroken. Actually, I started wearing an apron when my mother taught me to cook—kept the spills from staining my clothes so my friends didn't find out I spent time in the kitchen."

Two cats appeared and started snaking around Mark's legs. "Are you going to introduce me?" she asked.

"Lazarus and Jericho, meet Cathy. Lazarus is the black-and-white one, Jericho is the orange one," he said, leading the way into the kitchen. One of the cats made an indignant sound as they left, their tails high, as they went down the hall toward what Cathy assumed was the bedroom area.

"This is lovely,' she said, her gaze moving around the room, past the gas fireplace to the large mural painting in bold slashes of orange, yellow and black hanging on the wall near windows that framed doors leading to the patio.

"I change things around on a whim. This week I sent two artist sketches out for reframing to change the color of the matting." His gaze swept the room. "I guess you could say it's a work in progress," he said simply. "Would you like a glass of red wine? Or a cocktail?"

"Wine would be fine."

She approached the raised counter dividing the kitchen from the living area, pulling out an art deco stool. He passed her a glass. "To a great evening," he said.

She tapped her glass on his. "To good food."

They sipped, their eyes meeting over the edge of the wine-glasses. She'd been so excited about tonight, and now that it was actually happening, she was thrilled to be in his home. "What are we having?" she asked, never taking her eyes from his.

"My very own homemade pasta and a Sicilian sauce my mother often made."

"Is there nothing for me to do?" She focused on the table, which was set with candles in tall glass containers, bright blue napkins and white dishes.

He came around the counter and led her to the table, holding out a chair. "Sit and let me wait on you." In the kitchen he filled two plates and took a salad bowl from the fridge.

He was so...so aware of her. And the way he wanted to please her... "No man has ever made a meal for me—ever."

He kissed her, his mouth warm and demanding. "There are a lot of things I want to do for you. Dinner is only the beginning."

"You're flirting with me."

"You're right. I am. Do you mind?"

"Not at all." Feeling pampered and special, she relaxed and enjoyed the food. Each bite seemed better than the last. They talked about so many things; his fishing, her mother's life as an artist.

As she ate the very last morsel, she said, "This was delicious! You're a really good cook. I have a confession to make."

"What's that?" he asked.

"I can't cook. Not really. Lasagna, maybe, but nothing as good as this."

"Would you like to learn?" he asked, his hand moving to cover hers.

Images of standing in his kitchen while he taught her to make pasta, his kisses driving her crazy... "Yeah, I think I would."

"Here's what we'll do. I'll put together a menu. You'll come over here and we'll spend hours..."

"Cooking?"

He laughed. "Some of the time."

She watched as he took the plates to the kitchen, then returned. He took her hands in his then led her to the sofa with the view of the patio. "I have plans for you, for us," he said as he kissed her slowly, his mouth covering hers. Easing her onto the sofa, he pulled her close, his fingers moving her hair off her face, his touch delighting her. All she wanted was for him to make love to her, to feel his hands on her body, to wake up beside him, knowing that she'd found someone she could really care for.

"Why don't we postpone dessert?" he asked as he nibbled her ear, his lips playing along her throat.

Her body trembled with desire. She pulled his face to hers, her mouth seeking his. "You're reading my mind," she whispered into the tiny wedge of space between them.

He leaned in, his fingers snagging her chin, tilting her head back, her throat fully exposed to his gaze. His lips touched her cheek, trailing down, gentle as a breeze, light and promising.

She breathed deep, her hands moving over the open neck of his shirt.

The pressure from his kiss changed as his lips sought hers. She gave a short gasp, clinging to him, feeling his body against hers, responding to his kiss with a ferocity she didn't know she possessed.

His groan of pleasure thrilled her. He eased her on top of him as he stretched out on the sofa, his erection pressing against her soft flesh, his body moving against hers.

She wanted him with every fiber of her being.

The kiss broke off, and his eyes met hers. His fingers slid beneath the hem of her top. She shivered in anticipation. "This time you're all mine," he whispered against her throat, sending a rush of tremors down her body.

Craving his touch, she lifted her top, yanking it over her head and tossing it on the floor. "Now," she pleaded.

Within seconds they were naked, hands reaching for each other. One minute their movements were sublime and controlled, the next minute they were tearing at each other to quench the fiery heat rising between them.

Cathy felt that if the world were to end now she would have missed nothing, would have wanted nothing more than what she had experienced here tonight. With him.

Much later, as her heart rate returned to normal, she felt a light thud. She shifted her gaze to the back of the sofa. A large black-and-white cat peered down at her.

"Ah, Lazarus. Get lost," Mark said, the look of annoyance on his face making it impossible for her not to laugh.

She smiled at him. "It would seem you have your very own sex police."

He groaned, kissed her, then tucked her against him. He

pressed his finger to her swollen lips. "Wait for it," he whispered, pointing to where Lazarus sat. "There!" he said as Jericho jumped up, landed expertly beside Lazarus and proceeded to join in staring at them. "Jericho is always late to investigate any infringement of the cat rules in this house."

She snuggled against him, her body languid as she let her gaze travel over Mark's face.

"You like what you see?" he asked.

"A little more than like," she said, smiling at him, wishing she could stay right where she was for the rest of the night and wake up in his arms. Pulling his wrist toward her, she checked his watch. "Whoops. I'd better get home. Anna has an early day tomorrow, and I have a meeting I cannot miss."

"Want me to drive you?"

"Mr. Wilson, is there such a thing as driving while sexually impaired?"

"Not that I'm aware of."

"Then I'm safe to drive." She kissed him, climbed over his naked body and picked up her clothes. "The bathroom would be..."

"First door on the left."

The next morning, Cathy couldn't get her evening with Mark out of her mind. The meal had been fantastic, but it was what happened after that was so exciting and so frightening it kept her awake the rest of the night. If she hadn't had an early morning meeting with the police today, and Anna alone in the house, she might have considered staying all night with Mark.

Yet, as much as Cathy had wanted to stay with Mark last night—to make love and wake up in his arms—she was equally overwhelmed by her feelings. She was so close to falling for him.

Her feelings frightened her, made her vulnerable, in need of his caring and attention, infatuated with how good he made her feel. She'd been here before, letting her feelings rule her life. That had led her to make a commitment to a man who had never had her best interests in mind. He'd been so smooth, so easy to be with that she'd succumbed to his charms without counting the personal cost to her.

She couldn't do it again. She couldn't go into a relationship feeling pressured to behave a certain way. Of course, she was a different person now. But she also had Anna to consider. Being in a relationship would work only if Mark was willing to take it slow, to give Cathy time to adjust.

She shook off her thoughts of the future. She had today to deal with first. Officer Winters had arranged an interview for nine o'clock at the house. She was very happy and relieved that Mark had agreed to join them.

She'd tidied a little, waiting for Anna to get up. When she entered the kitchen, she looked as if she hadn't slept. "Are you okay?" Cathy asked.

"I got an English essay back and I didn't do well," Anna said listlessly.

"Can I help?"

"No. I just need to talk to the teacher about it. See what I can do differently for next essay."

While she hated to see Anna do poorly, Cathy was pleased that Anna was taking an interest in school again. And it was reassuring she'd opened up about her essay—so different from the past weeks when Cathy had learned things about her daughter from the counselor.

They were just finishing breakfast when Kyle arrived. "I'm ready," he said, a determined smile on his face.

"You'd better be," Anna said, flopping down next to him on the sofa.

Mark was the next to arrive. When she answered the door, his smile surrounded her, his gorgeous body only inches away. "I'm so glad you're here," she said, wishing they were alone.

"I wouldn't miss it," he said, reaching for her hand, holding it in his warm fingers. "How are you doing?"

"I—I don't know."

At a loss for words, she leaned close to him, looking into his gorgeous dark eyes. They stood that way as the moments stretched on. Ever so gently he tilted her chin and kissed her, a slow kiss that reached into her soul. She wrapped her arms around him as his mouth moved over hers.

"Hey, you two," Anna said, coming toward the front door. "Enough of this. I knew I shouldn't have let you go out with Mark last night. But that's all in the past. For now we have business to do," she said, a huge grin on her face, a wry tone in her voice.

Laughing, they stepped apart. "Your daughter has spoken," Mark said, his tone light.

"Just when I thought I'd raised her to respect her elders," Cathy said.

"I do respect you, Mom. But making out in the hall is so '80s," Anna said. "Come on, we need to get organized for the interview. Mark, can you give Kyle and me some advice on how to do this?"

"Just tell him the truth," Mark said as he followed her to the family room. He listened, supportive and thoughtful, as Kyle and Anna talked about their worries.

A few minutes later, Officer Winters arrived. "So, if I understand correctly, you are reporting that Stuart Jameson threatened both of you," he said, watching Kyle and Anna.

"Yes, he did."

"Can you tell me what happened?"

Kyle and Anna told him about Stuart approaching the car. "He said that he'd been called into the principal's office over what we'd told Mrs. Chapman, our guidance counselor. He was really angry. We're both sorry we hit him, and it was wrong, but he threatened us," Kyle said.

"In what way?"

Kyle and Anna told him about Stuart knocking Anna down on the sidewalk several weeks earlier.

"And you didn't report that incident?"

"Because we didn't want to involve anyone else. We really believed we could reason with him."

"Any other incidents?" the officer asked.

Kyle sighed. "We met him two weeks ago on Lower Water Street and asked him to stop bullying Anna."

"Then Stuart showed up in the school parking lot making threats, correct?"

"Yes. He threatened both of them," Cathy interjected, anxious to have the officer understand why Kyle and Anna had done what they'd done.

Kyle scrubbed his hand over his face. "He called Anna names and threatened her."

"And what did you do?"

"I wanted to slap him. And if Mom hadn't shown up I would have," Anna said. "It was wrong, and I'm sorry."

"He's lodged a complaint that both of you came after him and assaulted him, and that your mother is a witness to the assault. Is that true?" He turned to Cathy.

"No! I witnessed threatening behavior from Stuart and because of all that's been going on, the incident when Anna was knocked to the sidewalk, I decided to call the police."

"Stuart says he didn't threaten anyone."

"That's not true!" Kyle and Anna said in unison.

"Officer, this has been going on for a while. The school is involved, trying to resolve these issues," Cathy offered by way of explanation.

Turning to Mark, the officer asked, "What is your involvement, Mr. Wilson?"

"I was called in to replace the school psychologist. I sat in on the first meeting concerning Anna's issues, which we now know relate to Stuart's bullying."

The officer nodded. "I've open a file on the assault. But with accusations coming from both sides, the situation is complicated."

"We're working with the school to find a solution," Cathy said, glancing quickly at Mark, relieved to see his eyes on her.

The room fell silent as the officer wrote down the information before he rose and tucked his notebook away.

"What do we do now?" Mark asked.

"Were there any other witnesses?" the officer said.

"Not as far as I know," Cathy said.

"If I were you, Anna and Kyle, I'd hire a lawyer. Stuart has the right to file a complaint, as do you. If he decides to pursue it, you should be prepared. As to what the school does will depend on their policies, and how they plan to proceed."

"Oh..." Cathy said, her head reeling from the implications.

After the officer left, Kyle and Anna remained on the sofa together looking despondent.

Mark began to pace. "So, I think you need to hire a lawyer. Then wait to see what Stuart does next."

"And if we end up in court?" Kyle asked. "What then? My mom and dad can't afford a big legal bill."

"We have the bullying incidents that Kyle and Anna reported to the school, and the fact that the school is addressing the issues. Mrs. Chapman told Anna she was going to meet with the principal," Cathy said. "I wonder if other witnesses would help. It could end up being Kyle's and Anna's word against Stuart's and Eric's."

"I've already talked to Chloe, and she doesn't want to be involved," Anna said.

"Sweetie, I'm sorry that Chloe isn't supporting you and Kyle in this," Cathy said.

"Me, too," Anna said, her face pale.

"I'll bet Stuart has already been in the principal's office with his version of what happened in the parking lot," Kyle muttered.

"Stuart seems to be the ringleader. Maybe we could arrange to talk with Eric. If he sees how Stuart behaved, he might be willing to admit to what they were doing," Mark offered.

"Was he anywhere in sight on that Wednesday night?" Cathy asked.

"I didn't see him," Anna said. "And Eric never comes near me at school."

"So, it's possible we can get him to testify for us, should it come to that?" Mark asked.

Cathy turned to say something to Anna, but the look on her daughter's face stopped her. "Anna what is it?"

Anna closed her eyes, her jaw set. "Nothing."

"That wasn't a 'nothing' look."

"Mom, leave it. I have something I need to do." With that, Anna left.

"What was that all about?" Cathy asked no one in particular.

"I should get to school," Kyle said. "Thanks for helping us with this," he offered half-heartedly as he headed for the door.

"I guess I need to find a lawyer," Cathy said. Where did she begin? Maybe she could find one through her real estate lawyer contacts.

"Maybe... Let me work on this."

"Meaning?"

"Meaning, if there's any chance that we can get Eric to talk to us, we might be able to stop Stuart."

"How do we do that?"

"I've joined the local chamber of commerce to make our practice more visible in the community. Eric Sanford's father was the one who approached me with the idea." Mark rubbed his jaw again. "I wonder if Michael knows that his son is involved in bullying."

Cathy didn't respond. She was simply too tired to think about it any longer.

Mark glanced at his watch. "I have to get back to the office. I have an appointment at one."

"I'm letting Anna stay home for the rest of the day. We're going to visit my mother," Cathy said.

"Nothing serious, I hope," Mark offered.

"Just family stuff."

"I'll talk to Michael Sanford," Mark said. "The school has probably contacted him by now." Mark's gaze met hers, soothing her anxiety. "Call me later."

"I will." She watched him drive away. He'd left without hugging her, or kissing her. She felt the pang of longing, the need for his touch in that tiny, guarded place near her heart.

Later, after lunch, Cathy drove over to her mother's with Anna. It would seem that Stuart and Eric had gotten away with what they'd done as far as the police were concerned. The school hadn't called to update Cathy on what steps they'd taken to reprimand Stuart and Eric.

"I'm going to visit with Butch, take him for a walk," Anna said when they arrived at Margaret's. "This will give you some time with Gram." She jumped out of the car and headed for the back door, her long blond hair flowing around her shoulders.

Cathy took her time going in.

"There you are. Come in," her mother said, meeting Cathy at the door.

"Mom, what's going on? Why did you need to talk to me so urgently?"

"I had a doctor's appointment a few weeks ago."

"But you said the tests were okay."

"Yes, I did, but they found something that I've never heard of before."

Cathy stared at her mother. "What do you mean? Do you have cancer?" Panic stopped her breath. Her mother couldn't be ill. Not now when they could spend more time together. There were so many things she wanted to do with her mother—Anna's volleyball games, school plays, shopping trips to Chicago.

"I don't have cancer. I have an aortic aneurysm."

"A what? I've never heard of it. What does it mean?" Cathy asked, her mind whirling over the implication of her mother's words.

"It means that there is a weak spot in the big blood vessel leading from the heart to the rest of my body. They told me it's like a tiny ballooned area along the blood vessel. I will have to go to a specialist regularly to determine if the area is getting bigger. If it does enlarge, I will have to have surgery."

"Have you had symptoms?"

"No. I've been tired, and sometimes have a little ache around my neck and back, but I put it down to how busy I've been. I'm fine, honey, really." Her mother took her hand in hers. "I don't want you to worry about this. I have good doctors to care for me. And I won't be traveling the way I was, so I'll be able to rest and pay more attention to my health."

Cathy stared at her mother, trying to understand what she'd just heard. "Is that why you decided to stop traveling?"

"Partly." Margaret sighed. "But it's more like I said—I'd like to concentrate on you and Anna and me for now. I'd like you to come to my next appointment so that you can understand what is going on. To be honest, I was so shocked that I'm not sure I understood everything the doctor said." She squeezed Cathy's fingers. "I need you, darling, to help me get through this. And I want to help you and Anna. It's a lot to take in."

Cathy felt numb. Her mother's illness combined with Anna's problems was almost more than she could handle. She couldn't take it all in right now. She needed a little time. "Mom,

I'm sorry. I know I should stay longer, but I need time to think about this. I wish I could stay with you, I really do."

"I understand. Truly. Do you want me to tell Anna?"

"No, Mom, I can do that." Cathy hugged her mother close. "I need to go home. I'll come back as soon as I can."

Margaret held Cathy at arm's length and looked into her eyes. "I know how you feel. I could barely get out of the doctor's office the day she told me. So don't worry that you've hurt my feelings."

Hurriedly Cathy explained to Anna that they had to go home. "Butch is coming with us, right?" Anna asked, a worried frown on her forehead.

"Yes."

Anna got the dog into the back of the vehicle before kissing her grandmother's cheek and climbing into the front seat. "What's going on, Mom?" she asked as she fastened her seat belt.

"Anna, I need to get home safely and then I will tell you." She put the car in gear and drove slowly down the narrow driveway, wishing with all her heart that Mark was with her.

She needed him in a way she'd never needed anyone. She needed his calmness, his solid, reasonable response to problems. And this was a problem so unexpected that Cathy could hardly get her head around it. She had never imagined anything being wrong with her mother, the woman whose strength and determination had been her guide all her life.

Cathy would be at the next appointment to find out everything she could. In the meantime, she needed to talk to Anna, a thought that saddened her. Anna had enough to deal with at the moment.

When they arrived home, she told Anna everything, the words spilling out so fast that several times Anna asked her to repeat what she'd said. Butch never left Anna's side, pushing his snout under her hand, whining plaintively whenever Anna reached for a tissue to wipe her tears.

Anna scooted across the sofa and cuddled next to Cathy. "We'll be there for Gram no matter what, won't we?"

Cathy pulled her daughter into her arms. "We will be there for her no matter what," she repeated.

"Is there anything I can do for you? I've given you so much to worry about, and I'm truly sorry."

She held her daughter tight, feeling such an overwhelming love for her that the air seemed trapped in her lungs. "That's all in the past or will be very soon." Cathy wondered if her words would prove to be true, but she knew Anna needed reassurance. "Maybe it's time you took Butch for his evening walk." She kissed Anna on the forehead. "Everything will work out. You'll see."

Cathy watched Anna walk down the street with Butch straining against his leash. She'd waited so long to have her mother in her life, there when she needed her. And now...

Feeling lost and alone, she began to cry so hard that she didn't hear the phone ringing at first. When she made it to the kitchen and picked up, Mark's voice filled her head. "Cathy, I called to see if you'd heard anything more from the police."

At the sound of his voice, she began to sob.

"Cathy, what's wrong?" Mark asked.

"It's my mother. She's ill."

"I'll be right there," he said.

Anna wasn't back from walking Butch when Mark pulled into the driveway. Needing to feel Mark's arms around her, Cathy ran from the house straight into his embrace. He kissed her and stroked her face. "Let's go into the house and you can tell me all about it," he said, pulling her close to his side as he walked with her to the door.

Inside she explained what had happened. Mark's eyes never left her face. He kept his arm around her as they sat on the sofa talking, their heads together. With each word she spoke, she felt closer to Mark.

Anna and Butch burst through the door and stopped so suddenly the dog gave a yelp. "Mom, did something else happen? Did the police—" Anna sat down across from them, a knowing look on her face. "You called Mark."

"No," Mark said. "I called your mother. I was worried about her."

"I'm glad you're here. Mom's had a rough day," Anna said, simply. "Butch and I are headed to my room. I have homework to do, and then I'm going to bed." She smiled as she kissed her mother's cheek. "You and Mark have a good evening."

"Do you want something to eat? You haven't eaten since lunchtime."

"I'll make a sandwich and take it with me. Butch can have one, too—he loves cheese." From the kitchen came sounds of the fridge opening, the utensil drawer opening and closing, all blended with the sound of Anna talking to Butch and the enthusiastic slap of the dog's tail on the cupboard doors.

After Anna went to her room, Mark asked, "Why don't I make you dinner? An omelet, maybe?"

She looked into his eyes, her heart pounding at the expression on his face. His attention was completely on her, warm and caring, creating an intimate space between them. It felt so good. So natural. So much like how it should be. "I would love that."

"Then come talk to me while I make you dinner."

She watched him gather the ingredients, not quite believing that her life was going in a new direction. She settled in at the table, her chin resting on her hand, and smiled to herself. Life was full of possibilities.

CHAPTER SIXTEEN

When Cathy awoke the next morning, her first thought was of Mark. As she watched the light peek through the slatted blinds, she realized that she'd let all the loneliness of the past hold her back. Yet in the end everything was perfect. Wrapped in the cozy memory of their dinner last evening, she put on the coffee, then went out to bring in the newspapers, being careful not to wake Anna.

The air was fresh and clean, boding well for another beautiful day. Across the street a mourning dove sang its plaintive song, and farther down the block a dog barked. She gazed around, taking in the tranquil street scene. Everything seemed so perfect this morning, so in sync with the universe. When was the last time she'd settled in the wicker chair on her front porch and simply listened to the sounds of the morning?

She decided this morning was the ideal time to do it. Perhaps she should take today off work, as well. Indulgent, yes, but she hardly ever took vacation days and she didn't have any bookings today. Plus, this would give her the chance to spend some time with her mom.

A little later, Anna arrived on the porch, Butch's leash

clasped securely in her hand. "Mom, what are you doing out here?"

"I'm enjoying the morning."

"I'm going to walk Butch and then get ready for school. Will you take Butch to Gram's for me? I have volleyball practice tonight."

"Not a problem. I'm going there anyway," she said.

Mark should be calling soon, but first, she had to let Gina know her plans. She dialed Gina's cell phone.

"How are you?" Gina's cheerful voice answered.

"I'm okay, but I'm not coming in to work today."

"That's two days in a row. Are you ill?"

Cathy explained what had happened yesterday concerning her mother.

"I'm here whenever you need me," Gina offered.

"I'll go see Mom after lunch, but right now I need a little time to myself."

"Listen, Cathy, I've known you for a long time, and I've watched you go through a divorce, put your life back together, all these issues with Anna and now your mother's health. Taking a day or two off is the least you can do for yourself."

"You wouldn't mind?"

"Of course not. We'll catch up this evening. Maybe I'll drop over on my way home from work," Gina said.

"You do that," Cathy said, smiling to herself.

When Anna came up the driveway, Cathy got out of the rocking chair. "Why don't I make you breakfast?"

"I got a better idea. I can skip my first class this morning. Why don't I go to Gram's with you? I want to see her, and she needs us. Both of us."

"Absolutely." Cathy followed Anna and Butch into the house. "I feel so much better about everything today."

"Would Mark have anything to do with that?" Anna asked, giving her mother a knowing look.

Her first impulse was to deny it. But she had asked Anna to be honest with her about what was going on in her life. She owed Anna the same. "I really like Mark. I enjoy his company. He's fun. He's caring. More than that...I don't know."

"That's good enough for me," Anna said, heading to her room, the dog trailing behind her. "I'll get my knapsack and you can drop me at school after we go to Gram's."

They phoned on the way over to tell Margaret that they were bringing breakfast. When they pulled into the driveway, she was waiting on the back step. Cathy climbed out of the car. Wordlessly, she reached for her mother, holding her gently, feeling the tremors ripple through her mother's body as she cried. "I'm sorry for leaving the way I did yesterday," Cathy said. "I should have stayed longer with you."

Her mother patted her arm. "I've had a little more time to get used to the whole idea than you have, and still it was hard," she said. She turned to Anna, then pulled her into an embrace. "Where's breakfast?"

"Right here, Gram." Anna eased away to hold up a bag from the coffee shop. "We brought croissants."

"Then let's go eat."

"Let me take Butch for a quick walk while you old folks organize breakfast," Anna said.

"We're not old!" Cathy and Margaret said.

Cathy and her mother walked arm in arm to the house. Cathy settled on a kitchen stool while Margaret pulled out a frying pan, eggs and butter. "We need more than croissants. I'm going to make your favorite breakfast—French toast with maple syrup and scrambled eggs."

As Cathy watched her mother, she thought about how lucky she and Anna were to have her. They were a family—maybe not the typical mom, dad and child, but a family all the same. What the future held, no one could predict. But she couldn't help but hope that Mark would be a part of it. He hadn't called her yet and she needed to hear his voice.

After breakfast, Cathy and her mother sat on the deck while Anna played with Butch nearby. "You must be tired, Mom."

"It's been a difficult time." Margaret lifted a strand of hair off her face.

"Gram, you do that just like Mom does," Anna said as she came up onto the deck.

"Do what?" Margaret asked.

"That thing where you tuck your hair behind your ears and smooth your neck with your fingers,' Anna said. "Mom has always done this strange thing with her hair...and now you do, too, Gram. This is so weird."

Cathy had never noticed the common gesture but loved that she shared something so unique with her mom. She glanced at her watch. "Anna, you're going to be late for school."

"Then let's get going," Anna said. "Let's cook a nice meal for Gram tonight. We could do roast chicken with potatoes and peas. And strawberry shortcake for dessert. What do you say?"

They exchanged hugs and agreed to dinner at six thirty. On the way to school, Anna chatted about Butch and his antics, but mostly about the dinner they'd prepare this evening. "Do you have a pen in your purse, Mom? I want to start a grocery list."

"In the outside pocket," she said, taking the street leading to the high school.

Anna got the pen and a notepad then wrote the list. "This is going to be so great."

Once she'd dropped Anna off at school, Cathy went home and decided she didn't want to sit around with nothing to do. If she did, she'd obsess and worry about why Mark hadn't called. Should she call him? She glanced at her phone lying on the kitchen counter.

It rang.

"Cathy, I'm sorry I didn't call this morning," Mark said

when she answered. "I had a child in crisis and couldn't get away. How are you?"

Relief was followed quickly by delight. "I'm fine. Anna and I visited with my mom this morning."

"I'm sure she appreciated it."

They chatted a bit about their mornings and Cathy's decision to take the day off.

"I think you deserve the break. I also think you deserve dinner. How would you and Anna like to go out with me?"

"That's really sweet, but my mom is coming here for dinner." Yet she didn't want the day to go by without seeing him.

"No problem. We can spend time together tomorrow. You look after your family tonight."

"Thank you for understanding. I really would like to see you, but..."

"Cathy, I want you to know how much I enjoyed last night. I haven't felt this way in a long time. I want to be part of your life," he said softly, filling her heart with unexpected joy.

"Me, too," she said, clutching the phone, clinging to the moment between them.

As he listened to her words, Mark wished he could be alone with Cathy. He wanted to share his past with her, to have her understand what he'd done and why. For the first time since Maria's passing, he wanted to share his guilt with someone. Yet his guilt was not Cathy's problem. It was his.

He needed to face the fact that he didn't trust his feelings for Cathy because he doubted his ability to feel deep and abiding love for another person. He was definitely attracted to her and he definitely wanted more. But he was worried.

He'd had to live with the guilt that he'd left his wife to die alone because of his selfish need to protect himself. His love for his wife had been shattered beyond repair when he'd learned that she was still abusing painkillers. The day his wife and daughter died, he'd been slow getting to the hospital, not because of the teenager he was helping, but because he couldn't face his feelings. Hadn't faced his feelings where his wife was concerned for a very long time.

That hesitation, that apathy he'd felt toward Maria was proof that he wasn't really capable of loving someone completely.

As he stared across his empty office, he knew he needed to find a way to prove to himself he could care for Cathy. And in that quiet moment of reflection he realized why he was there alone. He didn't have the kind of courage it took to face his past.

CHAPTER SEVENTEEN

*T*wo nights later, Cathy dialed Anna's cell phone and waited for her to pick up. She was running late after deciding to treat herself to a manicure following her hair appointment. Mark had invited her out to dinner tomorrow, and Cathy wanted to look really good.

Her SUV was still at the dealership for repairs, and she was finding the loaner car awkward to drive, especially in traffic. Finally, Anna answered.

"Hi, Anna, where are you?"

"I'm home...alone. Butch misses me, and Gram wants to see my new science project. "Where are you?"

"I'm running late. I'll be there in about half an hour. The traffic's bad, so I'm going to take another route along Maine Street. I'll see you as soon as I can get there."

"What's for supper?"

"I left a chicken casserole thawing in the fridge."

"Great. I'll put the oven on and get supper started."

How nice it was to have Anna back to her old self. They'd met with a lawyer and talked to the school principal about Anna being bullied. The issue still wasn't completely resolved, but Cathy trusted the school to do the right thing. And since there had been no word from the Jameson family about a lawsuit, Cathy felt reasonably confident nothing would come of his threat.

Cathy turned right at the stoplight and drove toward the waterfront. She loved the view of the pier jutting out along the water's edge. The sky was a swollen mass of dark blue clouds, spiked by shafts of light from a setting sun. The weather report had predicted late-afternoon showers, and Cathy remembered she'd left clothes on the line—among the items were a pair of Anna's favorite jeans that she wanted to wear tomorrow.

Driving slowly, she changed lanes, ready to take the road leading past a line of warehouses as she dialed the house. Just as she heard Anna's voice, a car pulled up beside her in the left lane...so close...dangerously so. She eased her car toward the curb.

"It's me, again."

"I just talked to Gram and she says she wants me to come over this evening and walk Butch. I was thinking that maybe Gram and I should have a sleepover."

"That sounds wonderful. Can you bring the clothes in off the—"

A sudden jolt rocked the car. The wheel jumped out of her hands. The screech of metal pierced her ears as the car swerved into a power pole. "Anna!" she screamed as her head smacked into the rear-view mirror. Pain jackknifed through her. Everything went black.

Mark had just finished with a client and was about to lock his office when his cell phone rang. Caller ID showed Cathy's home number. What a coincidence—Cathy had been on his mind every spare moment he'd had today. He couldn't wait to have dinner with her. He'd been working a lot of evenings recently.

"Hi, how are you?" he asked.

"Mark?" There was a pause during which all he could hear was someone sobbing.

"Is that you, Anna?"

"Mom's been hurt. I tried Gina's number, but she didn't pick up. I didn't want to worry Gram. Can you drive me to the hospital?"

Fear stopped his breath. "I'll be right there."

He drove quickly to the Cathy's house. Anxiety made his eyes burn and his hands grip the wheel tighter. What could have happened? He should have asked Anna. Skidding to a halt at the end of her driveway, he waited as Anna ran toward him.

"Hurry!" she said, sliding into the front seat.

"Anna, what's going on?"

Her hands shook as she fastened her seat belt. "Mom was on her way home when she had an accident. I was on the phone with her." She clamped her fist against her mouth as tears flowed down her cheeks. "I heard the accident."

Mark's stomach rose in his throat, heartsick at what Anna had heard and what condition Cathy might be in. "We'll look after your mom." He steered carefully out of the driveway, around a slow-moving vehicle, then hit the gas, eliciting a snarl from his tires as he roared down the street.

"I'm so afraid. I couldn't get her to talk to me. Her phone was still on, but she wasn't answering."

How badly had Cathy been hurt? Critically? Would they get to the hospital in time? He couldn't lose her. He had so many plans for their life together, plans he hadn't known about until this moment. "I'm sure your mom is okay, and we'll be there soon," he said to console her...and himself. He needed to believe that this time he'd make it. This time the woman he loved would be alive when he got there.

He had to reach Cathy before it was too late to say how much he cared. After the past few days, he knew beyond a doubt that he loved her. She made his life complete.

He turned into the emergency entrance of the hospital, swerved into a parking spot and slammed on the brakes. Anna was out of the passenger door before he had a chance to speak. He got out, locked the vehicle and raced through the sliding doors behind her.

"I'm afraid you'll have to wait. The doctors are still with Ms. Collins,' the nurse told them. "There's a waiting room—"

"I know where it is," Mark said, having been here with a client's family a few months before. "Just down this corridor," he said to Anna, taking her arm and leading her to the room.

Anna glanced around, blinking back tears. "This is where my mom waited for me, isn't it?"

"Probably." He watched Anna, her obvious distress, the way she circled the room as if searching for something.

"I've been so mean with Mom. The night I was here, I was really angry and scared, and I took it out on her. And now—"

Mark held her while she cried, huge gulping sobs that echoed around the room. "Your mom's going to be all right," he said, hearing the tremor in his voice. How he hoped his words were true. They had to be...

The minutes dragged by, and gradually Anna stopped sniffing. "Feeling better?" he asked as she straightened and pulled away from him.

"Yeah." She moved to the sofa and sat with her legs tucked up under her. "They'll be here soon to tell us about Mom, won't they?" She swiped at the residue of tears on her cheeks.

"They will." Seeing her need to gain control, and admiring her for it, he sat in the chair next to the sofa.

Anna's smile was faint as she looked over at him. "Kyle and I are really good friends."

"Yeah, you are."

"Is that how it is with you and Mom?"

Was it? Not really. As far as he was concerned, they were a whole lot more than friends. "I care for your mother very much."

"I thought so. And the other night when you made supper for Mom... Just how much do you care?" Anna asked, a glint of humor shining in her eyes.

He looked at Anna, at her tearstained face, and realized that he wanted to tell her the truth. He couldn't help but admire this teenager. And after seeing the way Scott had reacted to Anna and Cathy's calls, he regretted what he'd done when he suggested that she would be better off living with her father.

"Your mother means everything to me. I admire her strength, her resilience, her determination to give you the best life possible."

"You really mean that?"

"I do. Your mother had a huge role to play in how you turned out. Trust me, I know. It's my job to help troubled teens."

Anna watched him, her assessing gaze making him feel like he was under a microscope. "If you love my mother, you'd better say so pretty quick."

"Love?" he asked, the word circling his heart.

"Yes. My mom isn't getting any younger, and she deserves to be happy. I've seen the way she looks at you, the way she blushes when I mention your name. This is serious stuff."

He couldn't help but smile. "I hear ya."

"You'd better," Anna said, fixing him with a stare. They said nothing for several minutes before she started to fidget. "Where's the doctor?

"We should be hearing something pretty soon," he offered.

"You don't have to stay with me."

"I won't leave you by yourself."

"I can call Gina. Or Gram." She played with her hair.

A nurse appeared at the door. Anna leaped up and went to her. "Is my mom okay?"

"She's asking for you."

Anna hugged herself. "My mom's—" She glanced at Mark. "My mom's boyfriend is here with me."

"It's supposed to be immediate family only."

"He's immediate family," Anna said firmly.

The nurse glanced from Anna to Mark, her expression kind. "Follow me."

"So, I'm immediate family now, am I?" he whispered as he walked beside her.

"Yeah, so don't blow it," Anna said, smiling at him.

"I won't."

She gave him a look that made his heart twist in his chest. "I mean it," he said.

She sighed. "I know you do."

The nurse led them into a curtained-off cubicle at the far corner of an open area surrounding a nurses' station, where phones rang and people moved purposefully from one urgent task to another.

The nurse reached over and pulled back the curtain, then Anna rushed to take her mother's hand. "Mom, I've been so worried. How are you doing? Are you hurt?"

"Just a bump on my head. The doctor is keeping me overnight as a precaution. It all happened so fast."

"Do you have pain anywhere?" Anna asked.

"Not really. I'm fine now that you're here," she said, love for her daughter shining in her eyes so intensely it took Mark's breath away.

"I brought someone to see you," Anna said. "He gave me a ride here."

"I see." Cathy said, directing her gaze to Mark, her pupils widening into dark pools.

"There are a lot of inattentive drivers on the road," Mark offered, as a flood of emotions overtook him.

"Thank you," Cathy said.

He moved closer to the stretcher. "No thanks needed," he replied as he struggled to keep a professional tone in his voice. "She's a very strong woman, like her mother."

"Do you have to stay in this area tonight?" Anna asked, her eyes searching the room as if she were looking for something.

"They're just waiting for a room to be ready before they transfer me."

Anna tucked a strand of her mother's hair off the bandage hiding her forehead. "You look like someone from outer space with that huge wad of stuff on your head."

Cathy laughed, a clear ringing sound that overflowed the tiny space and bubbled around him. Seeing her now, her laughter, her courage, he wanted to hold her in his arms and reassure her that everything would be all right. He'd made it here on time, and he would continue to be here for her.

As his eyes met hers, he knew there was something he could do to make Cathy's life easier. He would talk to Melody to find out how they planned to address the bullying issue. "If you want, I can pick you up tomorrow after you're discharged."

"I'd like that." Her smile was everything he could have asked for in this world.

But he knew Anna needed time with her mother. "I'll leave you two, for now. Call me when you need a ride home?"

"I got this, Mark," Anna said. "Gina will want to see Mom. And after she has, I'll get her to drive me home," Anna said, her voice as cheerful as her smile.

"Then, I'll see you tomorrow," he said to Cathy, taking her hand.

"I'll be waiting," she smiled at him, filling his heart with joy. "I'm so glad you're here."

"Me too," he said.

. . .

The phone was ringing when Cathy arrived home from the hospital the next afternoon.

"I'm sorry I didn't call you, Mom, but the accident happened so fast. By the time Anna arrived and they got me to my room, it was too late to call. I didn't want to upset you."

"That's okay, dear. Anna told me about it when she came over to walk Butch this morning. She came with a very nice young man. I think his name is Kyle Donahue."

"He's a friend of hers from school," Cathy said, watching Mark move around her kitchen, making tea, getting milk out of the fridge.

"He's the one who was with her when she fell that day, isn't he?" her mother asked.

"Yes, he is."

"Is he her boyfriend?" her mother asked.

"No. Nothing like that," Cathy said, wondering how best to tell her mother about Anna being gay. Was it even her place to tell her? Maybe Anna wanted to be the one to share that. Funny, only a few weeks ago, she would have made the decision about something like this on her own. But seeing how capable Anna was in handling her life, she wanted Anna to decide.

They talked a little longer, Cathy reassuring her mom that she was doing well. Margaret offered to come over, but Cathy explained that she was waiting for the police to arrive to interview her. She promised to call back later.

"They're here," Anna said from the living room window.

"It'll be okay," Mark whispered, hugging her as he followed her to the door.

"So glad you're here," she murmured, opening the door.

"Hi, Officer Winters. We've got to stop meeting like this," Mark said in an attempt at humor.

The officer gave a half-smile then took a seat at the kitchen table while he opened his notebook. "We have a witness to your accident, Mrs. Collins. He was at the light a few feet from where your car was rammed. He said there were three people in the car—two males and a female. He saw the driver quite clearly and has given us a good description. He also remembers the last three numbers on the license plate. We have paint that was left on the door of your vehicle."

"So the paint chips on Cathy's vehicle, the partial plate and a good description of the driver means you should be able to find who did this," Mark said.

"Yes, we believe so. On a hunch I checked the plates on Stuart Jameson's car and they match the partial. The driver description matches him, as well." The officer turned to Anna. "If this was Stuart, do you have any idea who the woman in the car might be?"

Anna looked away, but not before Cathy saw the fury in her eyes. Did Anna know who might have been in the car?

"Do you have any enemies, anyone you can think of who would try to run you off the road?" the officer asked.

"No." The very idea shocked her—she usually tried so hard to please everyone.

"Was there anything you can remember about the car or the occupants? Anything at all?"

"The whole incident is pretty much a blur."

Officer Winters continued to make notes.

This all seemed surreal to Cathy. "What do we do now?" she asked.

"I've been in touch with the school. Stuart and Eric both deny participating in any bullying, claiming that it was a misunderstanding. But if they are involved in this incident, and if the eyewitness can identify the driver, we might be closer to the answer. The witness insisted that there were three in the car. If we could get the woman to come forward..." He flipped his notebook closed. "I'll be in touch when we find out more." He stood and looked at each of them. "If you have any more information about the accident, please call me." He placed his business card on the table.

With that he walked to the front door and Mark followed him. "We will see what we can find out about the woman in the car."

"That would help," the officer said as he left.

"I've got to get to the library for a couple of hours before tomorrow morning's class," Anna said. "You're not going to work, are you, Mom?"

"Not a chance. My head still hurts. I may just lie around and be lazy."

"I'm ordering bed rest," Anna said, winking at Mark.

Once they were alone, Mark and Cathy sat across from each other at the table. "You're sure you're okay?" he asked.

"Physically, I'm fine. Emotionally, I'm a wreck." She touched the bruise on her forehead to steady the trembling of her hands. "What if it was Stuart who hit me? And what if Chloe was in the car?"

"It would explain the expression on Anna's face," Mark mused.

"Were you able to contact Eric's father?" she asked.

"He and his wife are on vacation in China."

"Leaving Eric free to do as he pleases. Not a good sign." Cathy shifted in her chair, trying to ease the ache in her shoulder. "Anna has been very happy at Cambridge High School, but I can't let her stay there if she's going to be continually bullied. And if they caused my accident, that's a scary escalation. Maybe I should look into a private school. What do you think?"

Mark gave her a smile that warmed her heart, made her feel safe and cared for. "Let's let the police do their job. Meanwhile we'll keep in touch with the school about their progress. I expect the next action will be to expel the two boys or at least to suspend them."

"Do you think this will stop them from bullying Anna and Kyle?"

"I hope so," he said.

"What would I have done these past few weeks if you hadn't been here?"

He pulled both of her hands into his as he leaned across the table and kissed her. "I am here as long as you need me," he whispered against her lips.

She clung to him, not wanting him to stop. "Thank you," she replied.

"You're welcome." He stood and moved toward her, his smile warm and intimate as he put his arms around her. "You are a beautiful woman. You know that, don't you?" His dark eyes searched her face.

"I need to hear those words, especially with my bandaged head." She wound her hands around his neck and pressed her body to his.

"I haven't said those words to a woman for a very long time." He gently caressed her face, her lips, the skin of her throat, driving her crazy with need.

He eased away, looked in her eyes. "You're a very sexy woman."

"You obviously don't get out much," she kidded him, suddenly anxious to pull away. She'd wanted him all this time, but now she was afraid...of how easily she could be hurt by him.

"And you're not good at taking a compliment." He smoothed away the hair clinging to her cheeks. She rested her hands on his shirt-front, the warmth of his skin radiating through her fingers. She wanted him, ached for him...

His arms slid around her; his mouth sought hers. She wanted so much, yet she held back. Was this how real attraction was supposed to feel? The eagerness? This sense of losing it all in the moment?

The pressure of his body eased, his hands sliding up to her shoulders, holding them. "Maybe we should save this for later," he whispered. "I don't want you to think I'd take advantage of you under the circumstances." His dark eyes showed a depth of vulnerability she hadn't seen before.

"No, of course not," she managed to say as she pushed back her need. Whatever might have been between them wouldn't happen now. Her pride forced her to step out of his arms. "Why don't I make you something to eat?"

"Not for me, thank you." He hesitated. "I want to talk to you about something."

"Sure," she said, feeling as if she'd let a special opportunity slip through her fingers.

"I've let this go too long."

"Let what go too long?" she parroted, afraid of what he might say—almost certain his words would hurt her.

"I care deeply for you," he said gently and with feeling.

The words flowed around her in a soft wave. She cared about him, and caring was such a nice place to start. "Those are the best words I've heard in a long time," she said, trying to sound anything but vulnerable. Never vulnerable.

"I don't know how to say this, but I've never met anyone quite like you in my life," he said.

Everything hung suspended between them.

She was afraid to ask what he really meant, afraid that she'd make the wrong assumption. She was crazy about him, but she didn't trust her judgment where men were concerned. She didn't want to risk being hurt.

"I want to get to know you better. I want to be part of your life."

"What do you want to know about me?" she asked, the air between them charged with feelings she'd long kept buried.

"What about your hopes and dreams?"

His attention and support these past weeks had been so much more than she could have imagined when they'd met that day in Melody Chapman's office. His interest in her life, his caring, opened a part of her heart she'd thought would never respond to another man again. "I want Anna to be happy."

"And what about you? What about your happiness?"

She saw how serious he was. "I want to meet someone, someone like you," she said feeling exposed as his eyes swept her face.

"Cathy, I think it's time we faced our feelings," he said gently.

Her breath caught in her throat as he continued to focus solely on her. "This is so new to me, so much more...than I expected. You've changed everything in my life, and I've never cared for anyone like I do for you," she said, suddenly aware how much those words expressed her true feelings.

He touched her cheek, a caress that left her craving more. "I will never hurt you Cathy. Do you believe that?"

"I do," she said, touching his throat with her fingers, feeling his skin warm and inviting beneath her fingers.

It was as if they had known each other forever. She wanted him to stay with her, give her a little time to let his caring words sink in. "Why don't we have dinner together?" she said, then remembered he'd already refused her offer of food. Recklessly, she pressed on. "I could make dinner. You could help me," she said, feeling a little foolish.

"I'd like that, as long as you'll let me be your sous chef."

"You sure?"

"I remember a lasagna you made. It was delicious."

She glowed at the compliment. "Okay, let's see. I think we can start with my breakfast and go from there. I'm considered to be the best waffle maker in Anna's world."

"I'll get out the bacon. That's my specialty." He opened her fridge. "Where would I find a frying pan?"

"Here." She opened a drawer and pulled out the cast-iron skillet.

Their hands brushed as he took the pan, creating a tingling along her arm. His eyes locked on hers as he put the skillet on the stove and pulled her closer to him, his hard body aligned against hers. "Are we sure we want to eat?" he whispered against her ear, making her breath come in small snatches.

"Yes," she breathed, feeling her body melding to his.

"How are we going to make a meal if we don't take our hands off each other?"

She turned her face up to his. When she did, he lowered his head and kissed her, his tongue circling hers, heating that place deep in her belly. She clung to him, her lips begging him not to stop. She slid her arms around his shoulders, lacing her fingers behind his head.

"To new beginnings," he whispered close to her mouth as his hands slid up her body.

CHAPTER EIGHTEEN

Fueled by his demanding touch, she sank into his embrace. "This would be a lot easier on the sofa." He nibbled gently on her earlobe. "What do you say?"

"Are you planning to carry me? My legs don't seem to be responding."

"I've got you," he said, picking her up and holding her close as he entered the living room. He'd waited a long time to have this woman to himself. He planned to make every minute count.

"I've never been carried anywhere in my entire life," she murmured, kissing his jawline, his throat, while her hands eased beneath his shirt.

His blood ran hot, his body tightening. "Careful, or we'll both end up on the floor," he said.

She trailed kisses over his neck and undid one button. "Would that be so bad?" She grinned at him, reaching for another button.

He deepened the kiss, his hand pressing her body to his. "I want you," he whispered urgently.

She clung to him, her hands working inside his shirt, hr body moving against his.

Somewhere a phone rang.

She gasped, a startled look in her eyes.

"Let it ring," he whispered, kissing her.

She looked into his eyes. "That might be Anna."

He pulled away. "You'd better answer it."

She answered, listened for a minute, then said, "Anna's at the library with Kyle. Did you try her cell?" Cathy asked, her eyes connecting with his, worry evident on her face. "Chloe, is there something I can help you with? You want to talk to her...Oh, I see. Then maybe you could call tomorrow morning."

She hung up the phone, looking pensive.

"What is it?" he asked, feeling the moment slip away.

"Chloe sounded as if she'd been crying. Maybe I should have asked to speak to her mother." Cathy glanced at him, her thoughts clearly on the conversation she'd had with Anna's friend.

"Or you could let Anna handle it when she gets home," his tone one of exasperation.

Cathy didn't understand the change in Mark. "You're upset with me," she said.

"A little. Call me selfish, but you could have let the phone go to voicemail."

"Yes, I could have. And you could be a little more understanding, given what has been going on in Anna's and my life."

"Yes, and I apologize for that. But you aren't comfortable with me being here, about where things stand with us. Otherwise you wouldn't have answered the phone."

"That's not true! You know what's going on in my life right now."

"But that's not all that's going on in your life. I'm here. You're here. We have something going on between us."

"I'm aware of that. I... I'm sorry that taking that call..." She didn't know what to say.

He took her shoulders in his powerful hands. "Here's what I think. You have a lot on your mind right now, and you don't want to date someone, especially someone who could remind you of your problems."

"You're not being fair. You know how important it is to me to take care of Anna, to look after my mom. Surely you can be a little more considerate."

"I have been. I will be. It's just that we can't put our lives on the back burner all the time. Anna is your daughter. But you're far too protective of her." His voice softened, his eyes held hers. "You and I have a chance at something special. Let's not lose out on that."

How had they gone from almost making love to this?

"Cathy, life happens to all of us, and it can be especially hard on teenagers—"

"Don't give me your esteemed words on teenagers and how they deal with problems." She seethed at the idea that she was the one in the wrong. Yes, she was scared about entering into a relationship, but he had no right to hold her very real life against her.

"I didn't intend to," he said, his tone cool, withdrawn, his arms crossed over his chest.

"And don't pull your King Kong routine on me."

He slumped. Dropped his arms to his sides. A smile twitched at the corners of his mouth. "I wasn't." He gave a low chuckle. "What are we doing, you and me?"

"Pardon?" She wasn't willing to let him off the hook yet, despite how charming he might be.

"I'm attracted to you. You're attracted to me. Why can't we simply enjoy each other?"

The phone rang again. "Oh, for heaven's sake, what next?" Cathy went for the phone. "It's Anna."

"Mom, Kyle and I may be out past our curfews tonight."

"What's going on?" She glanced over at Mark.

He was at her side instantly.

"Because Kyle and I are going out for coffee, if that's okay."

"I—I don't know. When will you be home?"

"We won't be late."

Mark gave her a questioning glance.

"Anna and Kyle want to go out for coffee," she whispered. "I don't know what to say."

"She's asking. That's a good sign. Give her a chance to show you she can be trusted to make her own decisions," he whispered.

She drew confidence from the look in his eyes. "Anna, I need to know what time you'll be home."

A silence ensued in which Cathy could hear Anna's muffled voice. "Kyle says we'll be in by midnight."

"That seems late."

"Mom!"

"Where are you going?" she asked, stalling for time.

"We're just going out for coffee. I need to have time with Kyle away from school."

With his head close to hers so he could listen in, Mark put his arm around her shoulders and hugged her. "Let her go," he whispered.

She met his glance, aware of what it meant to have his advice despite their earlier argument. "Honey, I'll see you no later than midnight. Agreed?"

"Agreed."

"And, by the way, Chloe called."

"She did?"

"Yes."

"I'll talk to her tomorrow, maybe. I just want to go out with Kyle for a little while," Anna said.

"Have a good time, and say hi to Kyle for me."

"Say hi to Mark for me." There were animated giggles on the other end of the line. "Kyle and I compared notes tonight. Have a good evening, Mom. I love you."

"I love you, too."

"You were great," Mark said, as she got off the phone. "And you did the right thing. Anna needs a chance to prove herself to you, and she will."

"I hope you're right." She glanced at him. "Why is there always something to worry about? Why couldn't they come back here?"

"They're young. They're barely aware of how their behavior affects us, and there's nothing malicious in it. You must remember that need to be cool, to be with your friends?"

"I do." She put her hands in his, his touch soothing her.

"But what if they meet up with Stuart and his buddies?"

"You have to trust your daughter."

"And if he—"

"Cathy, don't do this."

"That's easy for you to say, you're not a parent, you don't have a meddling ex waiting to accuse you of being a poor mother—"

He took his hands away, and the loneliness created by his action wrapped her in misery and self-doubt. "Oh, Mark, I'm so sorry. What a stupid thing for me to say. I didn't mean it. I wasn't thinking."

He didn't answer.

Was the intimacy between them so fragile, so easily broken? Did he know so little about her, was his trust so shallow that he didn't believe her when she said she was sorry? Or was what she believed they had going between them a figment of her imagination?

"Cathy, you've had a rough few weeks with all that's going on with Anna. But she has to take responsibility for her actions, whatever they are."

His words sounded so familiar, so condescending, so much an indictment of her shortcomings as a mother and a woman. They were words plucked from her past. A past she'd vowed to overcome, whatever it took, but she clearly had a way to go before that happened.

She wrapped her arms around herself, seeking the only comfort truly available to her. Regardless of what Mark believed about her, she would never relinquish her promise to Anna and herself—that they would be there for each other. She didn't need Mark. She didn't need anyone. She'd proven that over the past four years, and she'd prove it again.

She would never allow anyone to make her feel inadequate. Not ever again. From now on, it would be her life that mattered—and Anna's, of course. "It's time for you to go."

Whatever he'd expected her to say, that was not it. He almost didn't believe she'd said those words. He started to reach for her but stopped at her cool expression. "Cathy, please don't worry about Kyle and Anna. They're good kids. They won't let you down."

For one exhilarating moment he'd truly believed that he'd found someone special, someone who understood him, who could appreciate him and how much he needed her. Admittedly, he hadn't been able to put into words the caring and connection he felt. So that responsibility was on him. Still, given Cathy's distancing behavior, perhaps it was just as well he hadn't bared his soul. For the life of him, he couldn't figure out what in hell was going on with her—one minute she was warm and alluring, the next she was ready to pick a fight.

He struggled with what he could say that would ease the

impasse between them. He didn't want the evening to end this way. He wanted to stay with her, to wait for Anna to come home so they could be convinced giving her space was the right decision. He wanted to reassure Cathy that he cared a great deal for her.

At the hospital after her accident, when he'd seen her and the reality of what might have happened to her hit home for him, he'd faced the fact that he loved her. So why couldn't he say it to her now, or at least find some words to reach her?

Did he need her to be the one to say it first? Was he that insecure? If he said those three words, there would be no backing out for him.

Yet given how this evening had started, he sure as hell hadn't expected to find himself sitting on the outside looking in where Cathy was concerned. "You want me to leave?"

"I'm not sure what I want. Time, maybe, to get my head straight..."

"And you want to do it alone."

"I've been… It's always been just me." She rubbed her eyes.

"Cathy, you don't have to go it alone."

"It's how I do things," she said, exhaustion lacing her words.

He could see the struggle in her eyes, the uncertainty she was coping with. "I want to be here for you—"

"Please don't. It's better this way." She turned away.

"Why?" he asked, searching for the old control that had shielded him from his emotions for so long.

"Because this way no one gets hurt."

He almost reached for her but thought better of it. "Gets hurt? I'm not going to hurt you."

"You might not mean to."

"How can you possibly know anything about me when you keep pushing me away?" he asked.

"Please. I don't need any more pressure. I'm not ready for this...for us."

"Will you ever be?"

Her eyes widened. She hugged herself as she stood there staring at him.

He saw his words had hurt her. He hadn't meant to. His words came from his frustration and need. But it was too late to take them back.

So maybe she was right. He might not mean to, but he could still hurt her.

CHAPTER NINETEEN

*M*ark had been right. Kyle had dropped Anna off a few minutes before twelve, and Anna breezed in and kissed Cathy as if she didn't have a care in the world. The next day Anna came home from school excited by the news that the police had interviewed Stuart and Eric.

Over the next few days, life returned to what passed for normal. Normal except where Mark was concerned. Cathy hadn't heard a word from him—not a phone call or an email. It was as if he had disappeared. Of course, after the way their last evening had ended, there was really no reason for Mark to call. She'd blown him off, and he'd taken her at her word.

She missed Mark so much more than she'd ever imagined possible. He'd gotten into her life and under her skin. Even while she waited for him to call, she consoled herself with the idea that her attraction to him probably had more to do with the highly emotional time they'd shared than anything else. She'd even tried to convince herself that wanting to see him was her loneliness talking rather than any genuine feelings for Mark.

The longer she waited for him, the more she recognized

how wrong she'd been about everything. Missing Mark was about how he made her feel and the bond that had formed between them.

As the days dragged on, she couldn't get thoughts of him out of her mind. She'd thought about calling him several times, but she didn't want him to feel he owed her something—she hated the idea that he'd take her call out of pity. And she felt that letting her guard down, accepting her feelings where he was concerned, would only lead to disappointment. She'd convinced herself that she didn't have the energy to be involved with someone. If Mark really wanted a relationship with her, he'd have to figure it out. And if he wanted to see her, he could call.

Thankfully, it was Friday. She wasn't on call this weekend, had come home early and she planned to go out with Gina for a well-deserved drink and dinner tonight. Gina had vowed there would be no work or family talk. Cathy wasn't sure if they'd be able to meet that goal, but she sure wanted to give it a try. She rinsed her cup in the sink and was about to put it in the dishwasher when the doorbell rang.

"I'll get it," she called to Anna as she went to the door.

When she opened it, Chloe stood there, clearly distraught. "Chloe, honey, what's wrong?"

"I need to talk to you and Anna."

"Sure, come in. I'll get her, and you two can talk."

"No, please. I need to speak to both of you."

"Anna's in her bedroom. I'll get her."

She hurried to Anna's room. "Chloe's here."

"I don't want to talk to her." Anna's stubborn pout told Cathy she was determined.

"Look, Anna. I'm aware Chloe hasn't helped you and hasn't been a great friend, but I think you need to hear what she has to say. It took a lot of courage for her to show up here."

Anna didn't say anything for a long time. "Fine. If you insist, I'll listen to her."

They returned to the kitchen. Chloe hadn't moved from the spot where Cathy had left her.

"What are you doing here?" Anna demanded.

"Let's hear what she has to say," Cathy said quietly.

Chloe looked at Anna then Cathy, tears hovering on her lashes. "I made a bad mistake. I was with Stuart the day he knocked Anna down on the sidewalk."

Cathy gasped. "Anna! Why didn't you tell me this?"

"I wanted to give Chloe the chance to do the right thing. I thought we were friends, that she would come forward and tell the police what had happened. I was wrong."

"I couldn't! Stuart wouldn't let me."

"You mean you really didn't want to. You do have a mind of your own, don't you?" Anna's tone was harsh, judgmental.

"I don't understand. Why would you go out with someone like Stuart, Chloe? You know his reputation. Everybody does," Cathy said.

"At first I hung around with him a bit. This sounds really stupid now, but I kinda liked being with him. He made me feel special, and when he asked me out on a real date I was thrilled. No one I liked had ever asked me out before."

"What did your mother say?"

"Mom warned me away from him. So I didn't tell her."

"You didn't tell me, either, and we were supposed to be best friends," Anna said, hurt evident in her tone.

"But, Anna, you would have told me to drop the deadbeat. That's what you called him."

"Chloe, all the kids at school know what he's like. Why didn't you?"

"I guess because I wanted to believe what he said, that I was special, that I meant something to him. Then he told me he loved me."

"And you believed him." Cathy smothered a sigh when she saw the pained expression on Chloe's face. Chloe was a sweet, gullible teenager who'd been taken advantage of by someone with no scruples.

"My mom says I owe an explanation to you about what happened."

"You were with Stuart that night downtown as well, but you didn't go to the police," Cathy said.

"No. Stuart would have been so angry. Anna tried to talk to me, but I wouldn't listen. Even when she and Kyle went to Mrs. Chapman, I wouldn't go with them. Anna, you're my friend and I hurt you. I let you down." More tears coursed over her cheeks. "I'm sorry. I want to make it up to you."

"You can make it up to me by telling my mother the whole story."

"The whole story?" Chloe winced.

"Did Stuart cause my mother's accident?" Anna demanded.

"Yes." Chloe's whisper was barely audible. "We were driving around when he saw your mother in the lane beside us. I said something about it being your mother." She turned to Cathy. "When Stuart saw you, he laughed and said something about getting you. I thought he was kidding, but then he swerved and hit you. I yelled, but he and Eric just laughed at me."

Chloe studied her trembling hands. "I never felt so bad in all my life." She began to sob. "I'm so, so sorry. I never meant for any of this to happen." She took a shuddery breath. "I told him I couldn't go out with him anymore after he hit your mom's car. Then he got real angry and said that if I told anyone about what he and Eric had done, he'd get me. He's a bully. He bragged about bullying you. Now I'm afraid of what he'll do to me."

Cathy hugged Chloe, wishing with all her heart that none of this had ever happened. "Chloe, thank you for telling us. This was the right thing to do."

"I feel so awful. I hurt so many people. Anna begged me to tell, but I couldn't. When you got hurt, I just knew I had to do something." Chloe pulled away, wiping the tears from her eyes as she did so. "You've always been so good to me. I never meant any harm to either of you. When he hit your car, I knew you were hurt, but he wouldn't stop. I'm going to the police and telling them everything."

"You mean it?" Anna asked.

"I do. My stepdad overheard my mom and me talking about you. He said I shouldn't snitch on Stuart and Eric."

"Your stepdad is wrong," Cathy said.

"Yeah, but it doesn't matter. I don't care what he thinks. He and Mom are fighting all the time anyway."

Anna put her arms around Chloe and they stayed that way for a few minutes. Cathy couldn't help but smile. 'Her girls', she'd called them years ago, and it was still true.

"Will you both go with me to the police?" Chloe asked.

"What about your mother?" Cathy asked, wondering at the same time whether she should ask Mark to go with them.

Face it. You want an excuse to call him.

Chloe chewed her lip. "Mom would like to come, but she's... She doesn't want to upset my stepdad."

As much as Cathy wanted a night out, getting this mess straightened out mattered more. "I'll call Officer Winters and ask to meet him."

The officer was available and said he'd be waiting for them. She called Gina. "I'm not going to be able to make it tonight. Something's come up."

"What?" Her friend's voice held concern.

"I'm going to the police station with Chloe and Anna. I'll explain later. Can we do this tomorrow night?"

"Sure. I'm coming over to go with you. Wait for me."

"You don't have to do this," Cathy protested.

"No, I don't, but I'm going to. See you in a few minutes."

When they arrived at the police station, Officer Winters was waiting for them and got right down to business. Gina sat in one of the chairs at the back of the office.

As Chloe talked, crying at times, and the officer took notes, nodding occasionally and asking questions for clarification. Chloe told him what she'd told Cathy and Anna, including the fact that Anna tried to get her to come forward.

"Chloe, I'm glad you've come here to speak up on your friends' behalf," the officer said.

"But I made it worse by not coming forward sooner, didn't I?"

He nodded.

"What happens now?" Chloe asked.

"With your testimony, Stuart will be charged with leaving the scene of an accident under the Maine Motor Vehicle Code. Given the circumstances there will be other charges. You will have to testify."

Shock darkened her eyes. She bit her lip. "I will."

Office Winters closed his notebook. "In any bullying situation, people like you, bystanders, have a huge responsibility. If you're willing to come forward and talk about what you witnessed, there is a better chance to get the bullies to stop because they are exposed for what they've done."

"But I was afraid...and what if I am bullied for coming here?" Chloe asked, trembling.

"Chloe, what matters is that you've done the right thing now," Anna said, hugging her.

Cathy was so proud of her daughter for being willing to forgive her friend. "Officer Winters, the girls have been through a lot. Can I take them home now?"

For the first time since they'd arrived, the officer smiled. "Of course. I'll be in touch."

"Thank you," she said, turning to the two teenagers.

"We're ready, Mom," Anna said.

"Can I dare hope that this is finally over?" Cathy asked Gina as they made their way out of the police station.

"Works for me."

"Anything more positive?"

Gina laughed. "Yeah, it's probably over."

When they arrived at the house, the phone was ringing. "I'll get it' Anna called, heading for the kitchen.

"Probably a telemarketer," Gina said.

"Want coffee?" Cathy asked, following her daughter.

"That would be great."

"Mom, the phone's for you," Anna said, a strange smile on her face.

"Who is it?"

"You'll see," she said, passing the phone to her mother before whispering loudly to Gina. "It's Mom's boyfriend, Mark."

"I don't have a boyfriend," she whispered back as she took the phone. Thrilled that Mark had called, but aware that Gina and her daughter were listening intently, she tried for a cool tone. "Hello."

"It's Mark," he said, his voice gentle, filling her with anticipation.

"How are you?" she asked, taking the phone into the family room, her spirits lifting.

"I'm fine. I'm concerned about you."

Cathy steadied the phone against her shoulder as she settled onto the sofa. "I'm doing much better. Chloe finally confessed that she was with Stuart and Eric. Between the paint chips and Chloe's testimony, Stuart will face criminal charges."

"That's a relief."

"It is," she said, waiting for Mark to make some sort of personal comment, something that would restart their last conversation that had ended so badly. "Kyle and Anna can now get their lives back."

"I'm so glad to hear that," he said.

"Anna and Chloe are finally on speaking terms, which is good," she said.

"Did you get the notification the principal sent home to the parents? I guess he also sent an email to the students," Mark said.

"What about?"

"Mr. Hanson wants to hold an assembly in the school auditorium to talk about bullying. I called him to see if I could be of any help in organizing it."

"Hold on for a minute," Cathy said, placing her hand over the receiver as she went back into the kitchen. "Does anyone here know about an email sent around to the students about an assembly on bullying?"

Anna looked surprised for a minute but recovered quickly. "Yes. I wanted to talk about that. I've been asked to speak at the assembly. I meant to tell you, but so much has been happening..."

"I know. It's been busy," Cathy said.

"If Anna is going to participate, the whole student body should be there," Mark said, hesitating. "Look, this is a little out of the blue, but can I come over for a few minutes?"

Caught between her excitement at the prospect of seeing Mark and her concern over Anna's role in the assembly, she thought for a moment. Her desire to see Mark made the decision for her. "That would be great."

She and Gina settled in with a cup of coffee while Chloe and Anna waited in the family room, huddled together and talking in low tones. They had just finished their coffee when Mark arrived.

"I've been wanting to see you all week," he said, his eyes alight as he kissed Cathy's cheek.

Her body tingling with pleasure, she whispered, "'There's a conspiracy going on. Anna is matchmaking, so behave yourself."

"Do I have to?" he asked, his tone teasing and familiar.

"For now, at least," she said, leading the way to the kitchen, so happy she wanted to dance all the way down the hall.

"The cavalry has arrived," Gina chirped.

"Don't know about that." Mark waved to Anna and Chloe, who rushed into the kitchen.

"I'm so glad you're here,' Anna said, coming to stand next to him. "You've got to talk to my mom. She's got that look on, the one that says she's about to nix my plan to speak at the school assembly."

"I'm not going to nix it. I want to talk it over so we know what you're getting yourself into," Cathy said.

Mark settled in at the table, waving off an offer of coffee from Gina. "This is a huge step, Anna. You'll have to tell them why you were being bullied. And you're coming out might elicit different reactions from your classmates, some good, some not so good. Do you feel you can face that?" he asked.

There was a short silence as the four of them exchanged glances.

Anna spoke first. "I know it will be hard, but Kyle and I talked it over. If I don't speak out about what happened, it will mean that other people like me will feel they can't either."

"Do you really believe that will stop the bullies, Mark?" Cathy asked, fearful at the thought that speaking out might escalate the violence.

He met her questioning gaze head-on. "No one can say for sure, but Anna's actions may offer the opportunity for other students to speak out."

"I'm afraid for my daughter," Cathy said.

"A natural feeling," he said hurriedly, covering her hand with his.

His touch felt so right, so needed. Her eyes met his. It was as if the room was empty except for his smile. "I'm so glad you're here," she said, her heart awash in need for this man.

"I am, too."

"Mom, can we get back to the subject at hand?" Anna asked. "Am I going to speak at the assembly?"

"Are you sure you want to?" Cathy asked, pulling her gaze from Mark's.

"Yes. I can make a difference. I'm tired of feeling like I don't have a voice."

Cathy's anxious feelings tugged at her. She wanted to caution her daughter, to encourage her to think long and hard about the possible repercussions of speaking out. But Anna's expression made her realize that her only choice was to support her brave, caring daughter. "You do what you need to do. I'll be there for you."

Anna threw her arms around Cathy's shoulders and hugged her tight. "You're the best mom in the world," Anna gushed.

"Glad that's settled," Gina said. "Is this where I say 'I told you so'?"

"That things would work out, you mean?"

"Exactly." Gina's smug smile said it all.

Mark went over the details of the assembly. As he spoke, Cathy watched his face and wished that they were alone. She wanted him in her life. He made her feel that she was finally home, somehow at ease with who she was.

When Mark was finished, he rose. "I have to get back to the office and finish up some paperwork."

"I'll walk you to the door," Cathy said, hoping he'd kiss her again—this time on the lips.

As he opened the front door, he turned and pulled her into his arms. "I've missed you, us, being close to each other."

"Me, too," was all she could manage before he kissed her. A kiss that left her pressed to him, her body eager for his touch.

He smiled into her eyes. "I really have to go, but if I didn't..."

"I get it. We'll find time for the two of us." Giddy with excitement, she gave him a gentle push. "Now off you go."

"Count on it," he said, kissing her quickly one more time before heading out the door. She watched him leave, her heart brimming with anticipation.

"So, you got a hot date?" Gina inquired, smiling mischievously when Cathy came back into the kitchen.

"Maybe..." She crossed her fingers.

"Mom, you gotta start getting a life."

"This from the daughter who not so long ago was upset about me going fishing with Mark?" Cathy asked.

Anna shrugged and gave her mother a jaunty grin. "So I made a mistake."

Hugging her daughter close, Cathy knew that whatever happened in the coming days, she was ready for it. She had Gina and Mark in her life and a brave daughter, who just might make a difference to a group of students trying to figure out what being teenager was all about. "Why don't I make us something to eat?"

"I'm with you," Gina said.

"Well, I don't want to be left out, so count me in." Anna held the fridge door open. "We could always have scrambled eggs, leftovers, spaghetti sauce on something." She opened the freezer. "Or what about we microwave the hamburger casserole and make a salad?"

Cathy felt a rush of love for her daughter so powerful she clutched the edge of the counter. The past few weeks had shown her so much about her daughter she hadn't known, and all of it renewed her belief that Anna was a wonderful, caring human being. "Let's have the casserole."

"I wonder if many people will show up at the assembly," Chloe said.

"The email said the entire school—teachers and students—

is invited to attend," Anna said, digging rolls out of the freezer and popping them into the convection oven.

"I hope the parents come to hear what the school has to say. It would do everyone good to be more aware."

"It's Monday afternoon, right?" Chloe asked.

"Yeah," Anna said. "I'm going to focus more on the bullying part rather than the reason. Sure, I'll tell them about me and who I am, but the most important part is that people recognize when they're being bullied, or that their friend is being bullied, and do something about it."

As Cathy cut up tomatoes, radishes and green peppers, she wondered what it would have been like for her if she'd been well-informed on bullying when she was Anna's age. Would she have seen Scott's behavior differently, rather than blaming herself for the problems in her marriage?

"Kyle's going to help me prepare what I'm going to say," Anna said, setting the table.

"What would you and Kyle do without cell phones?" Cathy asked.

"Move in together? You could adopt him or his mother could adopt me," she said, giving her mother a cheeky grin. "I'm going to call Gram. She'll want to know what going on around here. Maybe she'd like to come."

"Maybe she'd like to hear her granddaughter tell her story. Have you come out to her?" Cathy asked, not wanting her mother to be blindsided by such a personal revelation from anyone other than Anna or her.

Anna nodded as she crunched on a celery stick. "One day when I went over to walk Butch, we had a chat."

Cathy had talked to her mother yesterday, and Margaret hadn't mentioned anything about Anna. "How did she take it?"

"She seemed okay. She wanted to know if I had someone special in my life."

"And do you?" Cathy asked.

"No. No time for that at the moment."

"I'm going to call her in a little while to arrange to take her to her next doctor's appointment. Do you want to talk to her after I do?"

"Sure. I'm going to invite Butch over for the weekend. Poor dog misses me," Anna said, a twinkle in her eye.

CHAPTER TWENTY

*M*ark planned to attend this afternoon's assembly at the high school mostly to be there for Cathy and Anna. He also wanted to support the school's initiative in talking to students and parents about bullying.

He admired Anna for being willing to speak out, to share what she went through with her classmates. But what had taken him so completely by surprise was Cathy's willingness to support her daughter in all this. A few weeks ago, he would have expected her to encourage Anna not speak out. The Cathy Collins he'd known had changed her approach to her daughter, and for that he was immensely pleased. It must have been very difficult for her to relinquish control, to let her daughter do what she felt was right.

One of the best things about going this afternoon, besides supporting Anna and her classmates, was that he would see Cathy. He parked the car and climbed out, hoping that he might see Cathy. She was probably inside with Anna. Entering the auditorium, he made his way up the center aisle to a seat on the end of a row about halfway to the stage. He glanced around, but the only person he recognized was a high school student who was a client of his. While he waited for the assembly to begin, he scanned the crowd, searching for Cathy.

A little later, he saw Cathy, Gina and Anna enter. The principal approached the three of them, shaking hands with Cathy and Gina while smiling encouragingly at Anna. Mark wanted to approach them, but he was suddenly not sure if he should.

His strong feelings for Cathy had taken him by surprise. His need to accept how he felt about her forced him to face his own insecurities. He was still trying to figure out how to deal with his guilt, his deep-seated fear that, underneath everything, he hadn't really loved his wife. Just the memory of that time in his life made his stomach churn. During those long months of grieving, he'd been plagued by the knowledge that Maria's addiction had driven them apart, that her behavior made it harder and harder to feel any emotion other than despair and disgust. After she passed away, he'd denied those feelings. He'd been more comfortable believing he'd had a good marriage, despite their problems. But it wasn't really true, and he was at least partly to blame.

For so long he'd struggled with the belief that he wasn't capable of building a relationship, that keeping it superficial was the only way he could cope. When faced with the anxiety of making a commitment to Cathy, he'd let his fear of making another mistake hold him back.

Even now, as much as he wanted to be with her, he hung back, afraid that going to her would mean some sort of declaration of his feelings. He knew how stupid that sounded, how awful it made him feel, but he couldn't seem to help it. The agony of trying to figure out his feelings—to accept that he needed someone, someone like Cathy—was intimidating.

Cathy stood on the other side of the auditorium. She met his gaze and smiled at him, a smile that filled him with joy, and suddenly he knew…he was certain.

He'd been wrong. So wrong. He wanted Cathy regardless of anything else. He needed her. His life would be empty without her.

It was as if they were suspended together alone. He walked toward her, the most natural action in the world, his eyes never leaving hers. This was right for him.

Cathy's stomach ached with apprehension as the principal spoke to Anna, offering his encouragement. She and Anna had talked late last night about what Anna would say today, whether she'd take questions from the audience. Through their entire conversation, Cathy had not been able to get past her fear for her only child. She didn't want Anna hurt by what others might say to her once this assembly was over. Feeling shaky and anxious, she understood why Gina had offered to drive them to the school.

She had seen Mark out of the corner of her eye when she came in, but she didn't acknowledge him. She couldn't. She debated whether she should offer to say something in support of her daughter at this assembly. She'd gone back and forth with the idea the entire trip here.

As she stood there, trying to decide what to do, the principal said, "Well, Anna, I think it's time we made our way to the backstage area. Are you ready?"

Anna took Cathy's hand. "Are you okay, Mom?"

Her daughter was asking about how she felt when she had to be very anxious about the next hour, about how her speech would be received. Despite Cathy's doubts, her lack of sleep and her fear that this could backfire on Anna, she said the only words she could. "I'm fine, sweetie. Just go up there and tell the truth about how you feel, what you've been through, how you'd like things to change."

Anna's gaze met hers. "I know you can do it, Anna."

She watched her daughter walk toward the stage with the principal before searching the room for Mark. When she found him, he was looking straight at her, a look that held her. Her heart filled with happiness. She watched as he started toward her, his eyes never leaving hers.

Mark nodded at Gina, then turned to Cathy. "How are you doing?"

"Worried. Scared for her and anxious about how people will react."

He moved closer, sheltering her from the crowd milling around them. "I'm here for you."

His words were just what she needed to hear. "I wonder if I should volunteer to speak today, to let these young people know that bullying can happen in any relationship, not just in friendships and in school situations."

His arm went around her shoulders. "You mean you and Scott?"

She leaned into him, seeking his support and solace. "Yeah."

"But how will that make you feel?" he asked, his arm creating a protective circle. "Are you ready to talk about this to strangers? You've only begun to see how it affected your own life."

"But it's important to speak up, to say that bullying can happen anytime at any age, in any relationship. Did you know she's been getting ugly text messages from several of her so-called friends?"

"No, I didn't. Can she block the number that's sending the texts?"

"She blocked them, but they just find someone else's number to use. But she's doing better since Stuart was charged."

"Would it change Stuart's or his friends' behavior to hear your story?"

"Probably not."

Leaning closer, Mark murmured close to her ear. "I don't want to see you go through something like this in such a public forum. But if you feel you need to, I'll support you."

Who was she doing this for? And what impact would it have? The students and parents had been invited here to learn what had been going on in the school, not to hear about her personal issues. "This isn't the time, is it?"

Mark surprised her with a fierce hug. "You made the right decision. This is about Anna and what is going on in her life." He kissed her, a fleeting kiss that made her want more. "Let's find a seat."

"Right in the front row so Anna can see me, if you don't mind."

"Can we sit with you?" Mark asked as Kyle approached from the front of the auditorium.

"Awesome. How many are you?" Kyle asked. "Just the two of us and Gina," said Cathy. "Cool," Kyle said, waving to more of his friends, who were seated at the front.

Settling into the front row with Gina, Kyle and Mark, Cathy waited anxiously for the principal to begin, crossing her fingers that Anna would be okay once she started to speak.

She watched Mark surreptitiously, remembering how good his arms felt. She hoped that they would spend time together later this evening. She didn't care where they were or what they did, only that they were with each other.

She watched him talking to Kyle, leaning across her to joke with Gina, and all she really wanted was to be there beside him. She was suddenly aware that Mark was looking at her, his warm smile capturing her as his body leaned closer to hers. She imagined him kissing her...

"How's it going?" he asked.

"Okay, I guess."

"Ladies and gentlemen, welcome. My name is Mike Hanson, and I'm the principal of Cambridge High School." He gazed around at the crowd of people. "We've invited you here to talk about one of the major issues in our school today. Bullying has caused many students, boys and girls, so much heartache and unhappiness, has damaged self-esteem and, in some cases, caused physical harm. Unfortunately, we've had a very serious incident of bullying that has finally been resolved with the expulsion of one student and the suspension of another."

Sounds of surprise reverberated around the auditorium.

"This afternoon we have with us one of our guidance counselors, who was instrumental in beginning the process of intervention, Mrs. Chapman, along with our school psychologist, Ed Jenkins, our vice principal, Carmen Banks, and Anna Collins, a student at Cambridge High School who is willing to speak up about being bullied." The principal indicated those who were seated on the stage.

"I've asked Mrs. Chapman to lead off with how an incident of bullying is being handled by the school. Mr. Jenkins and Mrs. Banks will offer their insights into how bullying damages not only the students being bullied, but also the student population in general. Anna will be the final speaker, and she will talk about her personal experience with being bullied. Without further comment, I'd like to introduce Mrs. Chapman."

Each member of the school faculty spoke, to the undivided attention of the audience, about their role in addressing the issues around bullying.

Cathy held her breath in a state of fearful anticipation as Anna approached the podium. Cathy wanted to rescue her child from this situation, and take her home where she would be safe and loved.

"Are you okay?" Mark whispered, his hand sliding into hers.

Cathy nodded, taking comfort from his touch.

On stage, Anna looked so much more relaxed than she had weeks ago. Before she began, she smiled at her mother and winked at Kyle.

Cathy relaxed a little, her pride in her daughter filling her heart.

"My name is Anna Collins. I am a junior at Cambridge High School." She glanced at Cathy and smiled again. "I have the best mom in the world. She has always done everything a mom could do, including listening to me when I needed her to listen, and being there for me when I need her advice. That doesn't mean I always took her advice, but I knew her heart was in the right place and that she loved me." Anna turned a page and looked out over the audience. "The truth is I'm gay, and because I am gay, I was bullied."

The audience hushed. How would these people take Anna's declaration? Cathy resisted the urge to glance around, choosing instead to focus on her daughter's face.

"The bullying started when I was leaving the locker room after volleyball practice a few weeks ago. When it started I couldn't believe it was happening, that two of my classmates were determined to hurt me because I'm gay. I don't know how they found out, but I couldn't deny the truth. They said other things, other words that were nasty and hurtful. I felt afraid and somehow ashamed that I'd been found out. And most of all, I was afraid of what they'd do next."

Cathy glanced at Kyle, who was leaning forward, smiling his encouragement. She loved that young man for his support of her daughter.

"Then a couple of the boys in my class knocked me off the sidewalk near the school, and I had to go to the hospital."

A few quiet gasps of surprise could be heard around the room.

"If it hadn't been for my friend and his support, I don't know what I would have done. My mom was so worried, and I worried her more by not telling her what was going on. I was afraid to tell her, and a little ashamed, that my classmates, kids I'd grown up with, were so mean about something I had no control over. I can't change who I am no matter how much I'm bullied. I wish that everyone here could understand what it is like to be gay in our world. I didn't choose to be gay. Being gay is not a temporary state of mind, or an affectation, it's a fact of life. A fact of *my* life."

Cathy listened intently, aware that Anna was saying publicly what so many people struggled with privately. Yet she felt anxious over her daughter's words.

Mark squeezed her hand. "She's doing great, don't you think?"

She nodded, her anxiety for her daughter growing. Now that everyone knew, what would Anna's life be like? Would people accept her? Or would they avoid her? And would the bullying continue? Anna had so much to look forward to as she continued with her education. But would people like Stuart Jameson continue to harass her, make her life difficult?

"When three members of my class nearly drove my mother off the road, I was terrified. Even though I'd finally confessed to my mom that I was being bullied, I had no idea the bullies would attack my mom.

"This was serious stuff, and I had to do something to stop them. I was ashamed, convinced that I was to blame for these people wanting to hurt me, and now my mother. That I'd done something wrong. I didn't want to involve my mom, because I thought I could fix this on my own. I'm here to tell you that no one person can stop a bully. It takes a lot of people willing to stand up and say enough. When I told my mother what was going on, she was shocked and worried, and I felt terrible that I'd kept it from her. But she was awesome. With her encouragement, I decided to speak to Mrs. Chapman. I was really afraid that no one would believe me because the people involved in the bullying were from good families and popular in the school."

Anna cleared her throat and continued. "But Mrs. Chapman took action immediately, and I can honestly say that Cambridge High School and its staff supported me in every way they could. I'm glad that it's all out in the open now."

There was a smattering of applause.

"The point I want to make here is that although I was being bullied because I'm gay, you can be bullied about anything, and in any relationship, not just in school. The only one who can stop the bullying is you. You stop it by seeking help and support from your friends and family. And if you're a bystander in a bullying situation, you have to speak out. To not speak out is to condone bullying."

Anna glanced at Cathy, holding her gaze. "Before I finish, I'd like to thank my mom and those who stood by me during all this. My courage to speak out came from you, Mom," Anna said.

Cathy fought back tears at her daughter's words. Anna had done something today that many students could not or would not do. She was so proud of her daughter.

"That's all I have to say. Thank you for listening." Anna stepped away from the podium. The room was strangely quiet. Someone coughed, another sniffled.

What now? Cathy worried. She couldn't leave her daughter waiting there for a response, for some kind of acceptance or validation. She loved Anna more than life itself. Her daughter had decided to take a stand, and she deserved the support of everyone in this auditorium.

Cathy rose and began to clap. Mark stood with her, followed quickly by Kyle and Gina. From behind her she heard sporadic clapping from other rows in the auditorium. A deep voice from somewhere behind her yelled, "Bravo!"

Suddenly the entire audience was on its feet, clapping and

whistling. Two of the students seated in the row across from her ran onto the stage—Kyle joined them—and surrounded Anna in a group hug.

Bursting with pride for her daughter, Cathy followed them.

Anna stepped away from the students and came toward her. "Mom, how did I do?"

"You were great." She hugged Anna tight, vowing to never lose faith in her daughter again. "You set a great example."

Tears shone in Anna's eyes. "Do you suppose Gram would have liked it?"

"I know she would. She would be proud of who you are and what you did this afternoon."

"I asked Gram to come but she said that it was my day to shine, that she'd wait to hear all about it when I came over to walk Butch this evening."

Kyle rejoined them. "Wow! Anna, I thought you'd never shut up," he teased, giving her another hug.

"You're the one who helped me write the words. If I talked too long, you have to share the blame," she countered, giving him a high five.

"We're all getting together at Martin's house," Kyle said.

"Who's Martin?" Mark asked, exchanging glances with Cathy.

"He's the head of the student council and he wants Anna to run. We've decided that Anna's got a brilliant political future ahead of her," Kyle said smugly.

Suddenly students wanting to speak to Anna surrounded them, and Cathy could see she wanted to be with her friends. "I'll see you at home," Cathy said, giving her daughter one last hug.

"You bet," Anna said hugging her back.

Kyle reached for Mark, wrapping him in a bear hug. "Anna and I want to know that you two won't stay out too late this evening."

"That's my line. You have a good time, and enjoy your friends," Cathy said as memories flashed and spiraled through her mind—of trips to the library, days spent making cookies, evenings in front of the TV watching movies. All good memories.

Cathy followed Mark off the stage to where Gina was waiting. "Anna was fantastic," Gina said.

"She was." Cathy hugged Gina, all the while acutely aware that Mark hadn't left her side. She turned to him. "Since Anna wants to be with her friends, would you like to go out and celebrate with Gina and me?"

He looked at her, a smile teasing his lips, his eyes alight with awareness. "Sounds good."

"Thanks for being here." She clasped his hand as she fought the urge to pull him close, to feel his body next to hers. That would come later when they were alone. "And thanks for getting me to see what was right in front of me."

He raised his eyebrows in question.

"Remember you're the one who got me to see Scott was bullying me. And remember how I didn't want to believe you, because that would make me one of the dumbest women on the planet?"

"You just freed yourself from a bully—don't start bullying yourself."

Her brow furrowed. "Is that how you see it?"

"Sorry. Didn't mean to lecture you."

"Apology accepted."

"So, where would you like to go?" he asked, tucking his hand beneath her elbow as they followed Gina toward the rear of the auditorium.

"Let's see," she said, hugging his arm as they walked, feeling a wave of pleasure at being with him. "Anywhere we can talk."

"What about Bogart's?" he asked.

"Should we ask Gina?" Cathy said.

"Where is Gina?" Mark asked, his eyes searching the corridor outside the auditorium.

Surprised, Cathy glanced around. "I don't know. She was here a second ago, walking ahead of us."

Mark scanned the milling crowd. "Try her cell phone."

Cathy called, and Gina answered on the first ring. "I hope you're with Mark."

"You know I am. Is that why you disappeared?"

Gina gave a low laugh. "Anna and I decided we had to take action or the two of you would never get together. Have fun, and I'll talk to you tomorrow."

Cathy put her phone away. "Gina has decided to go home."

"She wouldn't be playing matchmaker, would she?"

"It seems she would. Along with Anna." Seeing the smile in his eyes, her body warmed and her cheeks grew hot. If everything went the way she hoped, she would be in for a wonderful evening with the man who made her happier than she'd ever been in her whole life.

"I have a confession to make." He stopped to kiss her. "I'm pleased that I'll have you to myself tonight."

Her head whirling, her heart beating hard and fast, she asked, "Is this an official date, a follow-up to dinner at your house?"

"It most certainly is."

Walking with the crowd making their way out to the school parking lot, he asked, "Your car or mine?"

Cathy looked startled and then gave a triumphant smile. "That sneaky woman."

"What?"

"Anna and I came here in Gina's car. She knew that without a car, I would ask you to drive me home."

"Do you mind?" he asked, opening the car door for her.

"Mind? I have no intention of letting you out of my sight

this evening, regardless of how Jericho and Lazarus behave," he said.

She waited while he got into the driver's seat and closed the door. "What are you grinning about?" she asked, turning her face to his.

"I'm happy. For the first time in years, I'm really, really happy."

His words chased away all her doubts. "Me, too," she murmured around a throat suddenly tight with emotion.

He placed his hands on her cheeks then kissed her gently. "To new beginnings."

"To new beginnings, and to a little celebration—dinner— just the two of us."

"We are entitled to more than dinner. A lot more," he said, his mouth covering hers. It was the best feeling in the world.

His hand shifted to the back of her head, holding her lips on his. She felt the heat of his touch as overwhelming feelings of love settled close to her heart. Eager for more, yet content to remain here, she poured her emotions into the kiss, hoping he'd feel what she hadn't yet said. "I think I love you," he whispered.

She focused all her attention on him, treasuring this moment. "You think you love me?"

He shook his head as he took her hand in his. "No. Not think." He looked into her eyes. "I *know* I love you."

"Is love that easy?" she asked, searching his face for an explanation, hoping that he had spoken the truth to her.

"My love is," he whispered.

All the days and months alone without someone who loved her. All the times she wished she had someone to love. Every moment leading up to now. She was grateful for all of it. But especially for the man sitting across the console from her, a man who had the courage to say the words she most wanted to hear.

"I never imagined that you'd be the one. When you came into Melody's office that day, all I could think of was how much I disliked you."

She saw the shocked look on his face. "You had to know that. I was angry, but you taught me to let go of my anger, to see life differently. You showed me how much you'd been hurt by things in your past. We have a lot in common, things that drew us together. And through this all, I've come to realize that I can't live without you. I don't want to live without you ever again. I love you."

His arms went around her, his kisses raining down on her. "You will never, ever regret saying those words. I promise you."

She clung to him, to his strength and his love. There would never be another moment like this one. "I am so glad you came back into my life."

His smile embraced her. "We are really going to have a celebration this evening. There is so much I want to tell you. We'll start with dinner at my place."

"We will," she said, overcome with all her feelings of love and caring for this man.

"Let's get to the market before it closes. I've got a recipe in mind that I know you'll really enjoy," he said enthusiastically. "We can share a bottle of champagne."

"Do your cats drink champagne?" she asked, the happiness he'd brought her bubbling over.

His laughter filled the car. "They'd better not. I'll lock them in the laundry room tonight. Should stop them from messing with us," he said, taking her hand and kissing each finger slowly and deliberately, driving her crazy with desire.

"We'd better get a move on," she said, her voice low and husky in her ears.

"I've got something else I want to ask you, but it can wait for the right moment," he said as he started the car.

"What? Tell me."

"You'll know soon enough," he said.

They left the school parking lot and drove through the tree-lined streets, kissing at every stoplight like a pair of teenagers.

THE END

~

Dear Reader,

I hope you enjoyed **Anything for Anna**. And thank you so much for being there, for reading the story I've created. It is such a blessing to have you in my life. I write my stories for you and no one else. Simple as that. The Spencer Island series is filled with characters I love, and hope you do too.

If you could, I would really appreciate you posting a review on your favorite review site.

My next book in the Spencer Island series, **One and Only Love**, is the story of one woman's profound love for her husband, tested by events beyond her control.

Being a mother means everything to Carolyn Turner. She's married to her childhood sweet-heart, Lucas Turner, and they both want children. But after years of trying for a family, they decide to adopt. And as fate would have it, the moment they make the decision to adopt Lucas discovers he's already a dad. A terrible accident has left five-year-old Summer without a mother and Carolyn with the devasting realization that the man she's loved all her life had an affair.

Smart, loving and full of life, redheaded Summer is charming and everything any mother could wish for in a little girl. She's everything Carolyn has ever wanted; and a clear reminder of Lucas's infidelity. Most of all, Summer needs a family who love her, and Lucas can't deny his need to have her in his life. Summer could be the best thing that ever happened to Carolyn, the one thing that strengthens her marriage: If Carolyn can forgive Lucas.

One and Only Love is going to be released later this fall. Subscribe to Stella's newsletter to receive updates as they become available.

https://stellamaclean.com/newsletter/

ABOUT THE AUTHOR

Stella MacLean is a story teller. Simple as that.

An author of books, both fiction and nonfiction, she has served as Writer in Residence at Vancouver Public Library in Vancouver, British Columbia. She loves to travel, spend time with family, along with her husband and her fur babies in her home near the Bay of Fundy in Atlantic Canada.

Stella relishes the hours she spends hiding out in her office making up stories about the lives of imaginary people. Having found love again in the third act of her life, Stella enjoys telling stories about people who find love elusive and complicated, but still try with all their hearts.

Stella's past includes being a registered nurse, from which she has drawn story ideas for several of her books. She went back to university when her children were older and was granted a Commerce Degree, majoring in Accounting, from Mount Allison University in Sackville, New Brunswick, Canada.

Visit Stella's website; www.stellamaclean.com

Subscribe to Stella's newsletter for all the latest news and quick previews of upcoming books and events.
https://stellamaclean.com/newsletter/

Follow Stella on Bookbub for special offers and new releases:
https://www.bookbub.com/profile/stella-maclean

Follow Stella on Amazon for up-to-date information on all her Kindle books:
https://www.amazon.com/~/e/B0796MD3B8

Connect with Stella on:

Facebook: https://www.facebook.com/StellaMaclean RomanceAuthor

Twitter: https://twitter.com/Stella__MacLean

OTHER BOOKS BY STELLA MACLEAN